Death at Tammany Hall

Books by Charles O'Brien

DEATH OF A ROBBER BARON

DEATH IN SARATOGA SPRINGS

DEATH AT TAMMANY HALL

Published by Kensington Publishing Corporation

Death at Tammany Hall

A GILDED AGE MYSTERY

CHARLES O'BRIEN

KENSINGTON BOOKS
www.kensingtonbooks.com

KENSINGTON BOOKS are published by

Kensington Publishing Corp.
119 West 40th Street
New York, NY 10018

All Kensington titles, imprints, and distributed lines are available at special quantity discounts for bulk purchases for sales promotion, premiums, fund-raising, educational, or institutional use.

Special book excerpts or customized printings can also be created to fit specific needs. For details, write or phone the office of the Kensington Sales Manager: Kensington Publishing Corp., 119 West 40th Street, New York, NY 10018. Attn. Sales Department. Phone: 1-800-221-2647.

eISBN-13: 978-0-7582-8647-5
eISBN-10: 0-7582-8647-3
First Kensington Electronic Edition: July 2015

ISBN-13: 978-0-7582-8646-8
ISBN-10: 0-7582-8646-5
First Kensington Trade Paperback Printing: July 2015

10 9 8 7 6 5 4 3 2 1

Printed in the United States of America

For Elvy

Acknowledgments

Thanks are due to the helpful editors and other professionals at Kensington Publishing who produced this book. I'm especially grateful to the staff of the Sawyer Library at Williams College for making my research in their special collections both pleasant and profitable. The book also benefited from the valuable suggestions of my colleague, Walter Gibson. Finally, I am especially grateful to my wife, Elvy, art historian, for services well beyond the call of duty.

Chapter 1

Heartbreak

New York City
Thursday, November 8, 1894

Pamela Thompson closed a case file and glanced up at the clock. Noon. Her stomach grumbled—time for lunch. At that moment Harry Miller, fellow investigator in the Prescott law firm, appeared at the open door, glum-faced.

"Pamela, may I take you to the coffee shop on Irving Place for a bite to eat? I need to talk to a friendly ear."

"In a minute, Harry." She wondered, something serious? Harry rarely brought up personal problems or complained.

The coffee shop was crowded, but they found a quiet corner, shielded by a tall potted plant. They each ordered a cup of clam chowder and a cheese sandwich. When the waiter left, Harry leaned forward, arms resting on the table, and said softly, "Last night, as I walked Theresa home from the music hall, she was strangely quiet. At the door she suddenly said she didn't want to see me anymore. I asked her why. She just shook her head and ran into the house." His lips quivered, and his eyes began to tear.

Pamela gasped, astonished. Harry was a hard-bitten, scarred, veteran detective. He had tender feelings but almost never showed them. Pamela pushed her food aside and listened carefully. She knew his friend, Theresa Sullivan Blake, a young widow, about thirty, with a nine-year-old son, James. Late in August, Harry had met her while on vacation with his friend, Larry White, a New York Police Department detective, and his family. Theresa was White's sister-in-law.

"I can't figure it out," Harry continued. "We became good friends in the summer and have been dating for a couple of months. She's the finest woman I've ever met, present company excluded. I'm sure she likes me, and so does her son. Recently, we had talked about getting married."

"I'm sorry for you, Harry. How well do you know her family?"

"I've been introduced, but I've had little contact with them. I sense they may not like me. Since her husband died, a few years ago, Theresa has lived with her parents and an older, unmarried brother, Michael, who works in the trust department of the Union Square Bank and Trust Company. Her father, Patrick Sullivan, is a retired bank clerk in poor health."

"I have to ask, Harry, do they know that you were once an NYPD detective, wrongly convicted of a felony and put in prison?"

While investigating a murder case, he had suspected that someone at Tammany Hall, the headquarters of the Democratic Party in Manhattan, might have contracted the killing. The police authorities had taken Harry off the case and suppressed the evidence. When Harry protested, he was wrongly convicted of extortion and spent four years in Sing Sing, the notorious prison thirty miles north of New York City. His wife divorced him, taking their two children.

Harry reflected for a moment before replying, "Once I started dating Theresa, her brother must have become curious and learned my story, then passed it on to their parents. After leaving her last night, I called on Larry White and his wife.

They seemed embarrassed and couldn't explain Theresa's behavior, or why her family would object to me. Of course, I can guess."

Pamela finished her sandwich and rose from the table. "I'll ask my friend Peter Yates about Theresa's brother. I'm sure Theresa loves you, Harry. Someone is intimidating her."

An elderly, scholarly man, Yates worked part-time as Prescott's law librarian and research clerk and knew Harry's criminal background. He was at his desk that afternoon when Pamela knocked on his door. She explained Harry's apparent problem with Michael Sullivan and asked about his job at the bank.

Yates replied, "Union Square Bank and Trust is a large, important bank in Lower Manhattan with close ties to Tammany Hall. I haven't heard of Theresa Blake's brother. He could be a simple clerk. I'll enquire."

Later that afternoon, Yates came to Pamela's office. "I can report that Michael Sullivan holds a responsible position in the bank's trust department and manages a trust belonging to Noah Fawcett."

"Fawcett!" exclaimed Pamela. "There's the problem. He's the judge who convicted Harry in a mockery of a trial."

Yates nodded. "To avoid conflicts of interest Fawcett, like other respectable judges, placed his financial assets—and they are large—in a trust that he couldn't control while in office. Since he left his judicial post in 1890, his trust is no longer blind, but Michael Sullivan still manages it."

"I can imagine," remarked Pamela, "that the judge gave Theresa's brother a highly biased account of Harry's case. The brother would put his job in jeopardy if he were to befriend Harry or become his brother-in-law."

Yates added, "And Theresa's parents would likely share her brother's concern."

"Then they probably wouldn't welcome me, either," she

mused. "I'd better talk to her sister, Patricia, Larry White's wife. I believe the sisters are close."

The White family lived in an apartment on Fourteenth Street near Union Square. This evening, Larry was away from home on duty at police headquarters. His wife, Trish, met Pamela with a generous smile, drew her into the tiny hallway, and took her coat. Pamela felt at home here and occasionally looked after the children when the stresses of a policeman's life overwhelmed her friend.

"I know why you've come, Pamela," said Trish. "It's about my sister. When Harry stopped by last night, asking why she broke off their relationship, Larry and I were caught off guard and didn't know what to say. Later, we figured out that my father and my brother had forced her to give up Harry."

"How could they *force* her? She's a grown woman and a widow."

Trish nodded. "Misfortune has badly bruised my sister. She lacks confidence in her own judgment. This evening, our brother, Michael, is away. I've lured Theresa out of our parents' house. She's in the kitchen now—I've told her you're coming. We'll have tea together."

As Pamela entered the kitchen, she was momentarily at a loss for words. Theresa looked so desperate standing by the table. Her eyes were red from crying; her shoulders sagged under the weight of her problems. Nonetheless, she forced a smile to greet Pamela.

Trish poured the tea.

"Thank you for coming," Theresa said to Pamela. "I suppose you've heard from Harry." Tears welled up in her eyes. "Why should I go on living?" she asked. "All my hopes for a little happiness are gone."

"Tell me what happened."

"They made me send Harry away."

"Who are *they?*"

"Michael and my father, but mainly Michael." Her reply had a bitter edge. "Yesterday morning, they confronted me about Harry. Michael had suspected we were thinking of marriage. I told them that we loved each other. If he were to propose, I would accept. Michael exploded. 'How dare you think of marrying a divorced man? Your church won't allow it. Miller is also a jailbird and bad from the start. Prison life only made him worse.' My father chimed in, like Michael's echo."

She had argued that they had scarcely met Harry and didn't know him.

Michael had quoted Inspector Williams of the NYPD that Harry was a bad apple and untrustworthy. She had retorted that Williams was a brutal cop—they called him "Clubber." She didn't believe him.

"You have pluck!" said Pamela.

Theresa smiled wanly. "Then Michael insisted that I listen to Judge Noah Fawcett, a respectable gentleman, twice elected a judge. I said that I didn't trust him. Michael sneered at me and claimed that many prominent men highly regard Fawcett's grasp of the law and his insight into the criminal mind. He would give me a carefully reasoned opinion."

Pamela added, "The judge's critics say that he knows the letter of the law but not its spirit. His decisions are sometimes unfair."

"So I've heard," said Theresa. "Nonetheless, for peace in the family, I agreed reluctantly to listen to the judge. Yesterday afternoon, Michael brought me to the courthouse. Fawcett has retired but still has an office there."

"I've never met him," said Pamela. "Describe him for me."

"He's a stout, good-looking man with thick, wavy silver hair. His voice is deep and loud, and he uses words I don't understand. At my arrival, his welcome was gracious. As I spoke about my relationship with Harry, he smiled politely and listened without interrupting. I had the feeling that Michael must have already fixed Fawcett's mind about me.

"When I finished, he joined his hands, as if in prayer, and appeared to reflect on what I had said. Then he began slowly and distinctly, like speaking to a child.

" 'Theresa,' he said with lines of concern on his brow, 'I studied Harry Miller's case very carefully before convicting him. He is a man of flawed character and certainly guilty of the crime as charged. In violation of an order from his superior, Inspector Williams, he made public, unsubstantiated accusations of murder against Mr. Kelly, and secretly demanded $2,000 to cease the investigation. Miller's bad behavior came from too much confidence in his own untutored judgment and disrespect for the wise rules of duly constituted authority.' The judge went on about Harry's faults for a couple of minutes and concluded, 'Theresa, you should keep Mr. Miller at a distance.' I thanked the judge and left the room. Michael stayed behind for a few minutes to talk with him and then joined me."

"What happened when you returned home?"

"Michael and I met Father in the parlor, and they asked what I thought of the judge's remarks. In fact, I thought he had carried on like a pompous ass, but I kept that opinion to myself. I said politely that my mind hadn't changed. I knew Harry better than they or the judge. Harry has an upright character and a kindly nature. He loves me and I love him. That's all that matters."

She dabbed a tear from her eye and drew a deep breath.

"Unfortunately, they grew angry. Michael shouted at me, 'You would ruin your boy James and yourself and shame our family.' Prompted by Michael, my father insisted, 'You must break with Harry immediately. Otherwise the family will disown you, take your son away, and commit you to a lunatic asylum.' Michael added, 'I asked Judge Fawcett for his assessment of you. He said that you appeared unstable and advised placing your son in my care. So there's your choice: You can have your son or Harry, not both of them.' "

Theresa now appeared drained of energy. "At that point, I gave up fighting." She fell silent, sipping tea, staring into the cup. Finally, she rose from the table. "Tell Harry not to think badly of me. I love him dearly."

Pamela nodded and remarked softly, "Your situation is difficult, Theresa. Let me think about it for a few days. Don't be discouraged. I see grounds for hope. We'll talk again soon."

When Theresa left, Pamela turned to Trish. "The threat to her son, together with Judge Fawcett's negative opinion of her character, temporarily broke her resistance. She has spirit and should recover her nerve."

"There's more, unfortunately," said Trish hesitantly, as if approaching a dark secret. Pamela prodded her on with a gentle "Yes?"

Trish sighed. "Michael has tormented Theresa since childhood with all kinds of teasing, bullying, criticizing, and . . ." Trish averted her eyes.

"And, assault?"

"Yes, several times, beginning when Theresa was twelve and unusually pretty. I didn't learn about it until much later. He silenced her by threatening to tell the world that she had a dirty mind. She married the first man who would have her, just to get away from the family."

"How has Michael managed to deceive your parents all these years?"

"He has always been a sly, talented liar, but also good-looking, smart, and personable, a darling boy to my father. He would never believe anything Theresa or I said against him. It's worse now that my parents are financially dependent on Michael. My mother is a kind woman, but weak-willed. She defers to her husband and fears Michael."

"How did you escape becoming trapped like your sister?"

"Michael tried once to assault me but I kicked his private parts until he screamed for mercy. He has never bothered me again. He's basically a coward and a bully and afraid of my husband, Larry. Nonetheless, I keep Michael at a safe distance, for he would harm me if he could."

"And Theresa?"

"Despite her troubles she still has her sweet disposition and good looks. But she's much less sure of herself than I—and more easily intimidated." Trish paused, cocked her head in a skeptical gesture. "Why are you hopeful of a solution?"

"Michael is bluffing. As of now, he doesn't have solid grounds for taking the boy away from Theresa. In the eyes of the law she's a grown woman and a suitable mother with no history of abusing or neglecting her child. Harry would be a suitable stepfather, notwithstanding the social stigma of having been convicted of a crime. He is presently employed and could support Theresa and the boy."

Pamela paused for a sip of the tea, reflecting. "In his twisted mind Michael probably hopes to drive Theresa into helpless dependence on him. Her son would become his ward. Key to his plan must be Judge Fawcett's support."

Trish frowned. "Why would the judge help Michael in this personal or family matter? It would appear to have little to do with their mutual financial interests."

Pamela shook her head. "The judge's reputation for integrity and competence is at stake. To support his wrongful verdict in Harry's case the judge painted a false picture of Harry's character. Therefore, the judge must guard that picture and seize every opportunity to cast Harry in a bad light and block his path to respectability. We must proceed carefully. Though retired from the bench, the judge remains influential in the inner circles of Tammany Hall and could put Harry and Theresa under great stress."

"True," granted Trish. "And that could jeopardize their young and fragile relationship."

Pamela finished her tea and got up to go. "Theresa must soon leave her parents' house and escape from Michael's clutches. Mr. Prescott could perhaps arrange temporary accommodations and defend her from any charges that Michael or his mentors, Inspector Williams and Judge Fawcett, might invent. I'll talk to Prescott tomorrow. In the meantime, you can assure Theresa that Harry still loves her and we shall help her."

Chapter 2

The Plan

Friday, November 9

"We have to do something for Harry and his friend," Pamela exclaimed. She was with Prescott in his office, explaining Theresa's situation. "Harry is made once again unfairly a victim. That could lead to depression and affect his work as an investigator."

Prescott had listened intently and now appeared exasperated. "It's true that Harry suffers grievously from the injustice that the city's corrupt judicial system has done to him. In 1887, I suspected that the police had fabricated the evidence against him. Investigating his case convinced me of his innocence, and I arranged his parole from prison. But the police and the court have blocked his exoneration. This is very frustrating to me."

"Are the authorities always so reluctant to correct an injustice?"

"Judging from my experience I'd have to say yes. Four years after Harry was arrested, the NYPD framed a poor, illiterate Algerian sailor, Ameer Ben Ali, for the gruesome murder of an aging prostitute in the East River Hotel. Though the evidence was circumstantial, the prosecutor wanted to hang him. Still, a jury quickly convicted Ben Ali of second-degree murder, and he was sentenced to life in Sing Sing. He's still there."

"So where had justice gone wrong?"

"The killer had mutilated the prostitute's body after the manner of Jack the Ripper in London. Our gutter press claimed that an American ripper was on the loose, and whipped up the public's fears. Chief of Detectives Mr. Byrnes declared he'd do better than Scotland Yard and find the culprit in less than two weeks. Under pressure from Byrnes, the New York detectives quickly arrested the Algerian sailor, most likely because he *looked* suspicious—dark-skinned, foreign, and indigent. He had chanced to lodge in the room across the hall from the prostitute on the night of the murder. At the trial the detectives claimed to have followed a trail of blood between the rooms."

"How did you become involved?"

"My friend, the journalist Jacob Riis, believed that the Algerian was wrongly convicted and asked me for help. Riis had gone to the murder scene with the detectives immediately after the body was discovered and hadn't seen a trail of blood. The detectives had most likely planted it a day later. Furthermore, Mr. George Damon in Crawford, New Jersey, reported that his former Danish servant resembled the light-haired young man who had checked into the hotel with the prostitute and had vanished shortly after the crime. He left behind in Crawford the key to the victim's hotel room, number thirty-one, as well as blood-stained clothing."

Pamela remarked, "A few years earlier, police detectives might have forged an extortion letter and framed Harry in the same way as the Algerian. What did you do for the poor suspect?"

"I prepared two affidavits based on statements from Riis and Damon and submitted them to Governor Roswell P. Flower with a request for a pardon. He refused, saying merely that justice had been served."

"Why do you suppose he ignored the affidavits?"

Prescott replied, his jaw tightening with anger, "The cynical—and perhaps most likely—reason is that Governor Flower, a Tammany Democrat, didn't wish to embarrass his ally, Mr. Byrnes, or his detectives. Governor Flower might also have passed the petition to a busy assistant who decided that the Algerian was a man of no importance—social, political, or otherwise—and could be conveniently ignored. Governors do not give out pardons wholesale, but ration them only to the most worthy."

Pamela took his point: He and she had a steep hill to climb to clear Harry. "The Algerian's fate is distressing and could discourage me. But circumstances today might be more favorable to Harry. Thanks to civic-minded men like Reverend Charles Parkhurst, there's a movement in the city for judicial and police reform."

"Right," Prescott conceded, still struggling to control his feelings. "We must seize this opportunity to clear Harry's name."

Pamela added, "Meanwhile, we should figure out a way to free Theresa and her son from her parents' home and put her into safe lodgings."

"I agree," said Prescott. "Then we'll need to restrain her brother, Michael, and perhaps her father in case they try to commit Theresa to an institution or take her boy away. Where should we look?"

"Beneath Michael's polished surface," Pamela replied, "he probably has a deeply flawed character that should disqualify him from becoming the boy's guardian—which is what I think he's after."

"Then you should investigate him for a few days. He might steal from his law firm or frequent brothels or both. Yates will help you."

"Shouldn't we include Judge Fawcett in our investigation? He may be our biggest and most dangerous obstacle."

Prescott appeared skeptical.

"I'm serious," insisted Pamela. "In his verdict the judge went out of his way to blacken Harry's character. If we are to restore his reputation, we must expose the judge's possibly criminal behavior in the bench trial." She paused. "By the way, why wasn't Harry tried before a jury?"

"His lawyer feared that a jury would assume that Harry was corrupt, like much of the NYPD. Harry's alleged attempt at extortion wouldn't seem to differ from common police protection rackets, except that Harry was said to put his threats in writing. Neither Harry nor his lawyer suspected that Fawcett had been bribed. In the community he was reputed to be upright and philanthropic."

"Nonetheless," Pamela countered, "Harry's lawyer must have known that Fawcett was elected to his judgeship, thanks to Tammany Hall, and could be expected to do Tammany's bidding. Harry should have gambled with a jury. I would like to see Fawcett and form my own impression of his character."

"Then join me for lunch at Delmonico's. The judge is usually there at noon."

They arrived at the restaurant shortly before the noonday crowd. A waiter greeted Prescott in a politely familiar manner. He asked for a table at the far end of the dining room, near a middle-aged man with thick, wavy silver hair.

Prescott murmured to Pamela, "That's him, Noah Fawcett." As the waiter handed them a menu, Prescott whispered, "Tell me what the judge is up to." The waiter flashed a thin smile and left.

Intrigued, Pamela asked, "What's going on?"

"Our waiter spies for me. His wife is deaf, so he has learned to read lips. He'll serve the judge's table, take note of anything of interest, and report back to me."

"Have you defended clients in Fawcett's court?"

"Occasionally. He's a demanding magistrate—intelligent but narrow-minded. When the law isn't clear or the evidence is sparse or ambiguous, he usually rules in favor of the prosecution. And if the convicted man or woman also has a criminal record or looks shabby, Fawcett imposes the maximum sentence."

"That's too bad for your pro bono clients, isn't it?"

Prescott nodded grimly. "I've questioned his judgments, especially in Harry's case. Fawcett took the prosecution's trumped-up charges against Harry at face value and sentenced him to five years in prison. Adding insult to injury, he accused Harry of betraying a sacred trust and undermining the public's respect for the police. When I secured Harry's release on probation a year early and hired him, Fawcett objected. I'm sure he was personally offended."

After Pamela had studied the judge, she agreed with Theresa's verdict: "a pompous ass." A well-dressed man soon joined the judge. The waiter handed him a menu and hovered near the table, offering advice about the food.

"The judge's acquaintance is John C. Sheehan, Tammany Hall's temporary boss," Prescott remarked. "The former boss, Richard Croker, figured out that the current wave of reform would sink him. So he has prudently retired to an estate in England with wealth looted from New York City. They say he lives like a duke, indulging his love of racehorses and bulldogs."

"Mr. Sheehan looks unhappy. Why should he?" Pamela asked.

"I'll soon find out. Here comes our waiter."

He arrived with vegetable omelets and white wine. While serving the food, he murmured, "Mr. Sheehan has received a telegram from Mr. Croker and is relating its contents to Judge

Fawcett. Tammany Hall's heavy losses in Tuesday's election have displeased Croker, and he orders Sheehan to shake up the organization."

For years, Pamela hadn't paid attention to city politics and usually discounted the misleading or inflated rhetoric coming from Republican and Democratic politicians. Their political organizations appeared equally bent on power and patronage to the detriment of both state and municipal government. If she had to choose, she'd favor Tammany, because its neighborhood clubs often helped the needy people she worked with—in return for their votes, of course.

"What's your opinion of Tammany Hall?" Pamela asked Prescott.

He studied his wine thoughtfully. "It's an ingenious political machine for winning elections and distributing patronage. Tammany's leaders come from the people and know their strengths and weaknesses. Richard Croker, the boss at the time of Harry's arrest, was a poor Irish immigrant boy who clawed his way to the top of the organization. Though he became rich, he didn't lose the common touch."

With a side-glance toward Fawcett and Sheehan, Pamela asked Prescott, "Since Tammany lost the election, will it lose control of the city's police and judicial system?"

He shook his head. "This election will have only a temporary effect. Still, Mr. William Strong, the incoming mayor, may appoint progressive reformers like young Theodore Roosevelt to the commission overseeing the police. That could give us a window of opportunity to vindicate Harry. But Tammany Hall will surely survive because of its deep roots in almost every neighborhood of the city. Even while wealthy, educated folks complain that Tammany corrupts civic life, they make cozy business deals with Tammany's politicians and solicit Tammany's help in breaking strikes and protecting property."

The judge was now smiling and nodding at something the Tammany boss had said. Pamela asked Prescott, "Do you think Fawcett is corrupt? Did Tammany pay him off in Harry's case?"

"I don't know yet. Unlike some of his Tammany colleagues, Fawcett was rich before he became a judge, so he might have been less tempted to take bribes. His admirers claim he's a strict Christian, leads a blameless private life, and gives generously to worthy causes."

"Is he married?" she asked. Pamela's mind was uneasy about the judge. He was obviously intelligent, and he seemed to be an island of integrity in a sea of corruption. Still, there must be something wrong with the man if he couldn't acknowledge Harry's innocence and dismiss the charges against him.

Prescott shrugged. "He's a bachelor and claims he's married to Lady Justice. A few skeptics insinuate that he satisfies his carnal desires on his housekeeper, a distant female cousin."

Over coffee at the end of the meal, Pamela said that she needed a better understanding of Harry's story if she was to carry out a serious investigation.

Prescott hesitated a moment. "Let's return to the office. I'll send Harry to you."

Back at the office, Pamela browsed in her notes on Harry and recalled the hardships of his early life. He was born into a poor family in upstate New York, and his mentally ill mother died in an asylum in 1863 when he was eight. His father placed him in an orphanage, joined the Union army for the enlistment bonus, and was killed in battle shortly afterward.

Adversity seemed to spur Harry on. In the orphanage, he proved to be a good student and a resourceful worker. At eighteen, he joined the NYPD as a patrolman in the Five Points, the most crime-ridden and dangerous district in the city. Bright, inquisitive, and fearless, he showed a talent for investigation and worked his way up to police detective.

As Harry walked into the office, Pamela put aside the notes and asked, "When did your problem with the law begin?"

"Early in January 1887," he replied, sitting across from her at the desk. "Inspector 'Clubber' Williams assigned me to check the police report of a cabdriver's death in the late afternoon outside a saloon in Chelsea. Eyewitnesses told Michael Malone, the investigating officer at the scene, that the cabdriver, Tony Palermo, had pulled out a knife and threatened Dan Kelly, a patron at the saloon, who then had drawn his own knife and killed Palermo. The officer accepted Kelly's claim of self-defense and concluded that the killing was justifiable homicide."

"What kind of man was Tony Palermo?"

"That's what I asked his aunt. He had boarded with her for two years and sometimes confided in her. She told me that he came from the Italian slum on Mulberry Bend but had learned to read and write and to seize an opportunity when it came his way. A big, rough man, he let everyone know that he carried a knife and knew how to use it."

"Why did you suspect that Officer Malone's report was wrong?"

"The cabdriver's aunt planted a seed of doubt in my mind. She mentioned that, one morning, a gentleman from Tammany Hall had left a portfolio in her nephew's cab. Palermo had come home afterward, hugging the shiny black portfolio as if it were precious. Its owner's initials, H. C., were printed in gold in the leather. Palermo had said he would receive a large reward when he returned the portfolio."

"How did he know it belonged to Tammany Hall?"

"She said he had looked inside, but he didn't tell her what he found."

"Did the references to Tammany Hall and the reward make you feel uneasy?" Pamela understood that Tammany had a notorious reputation for cheating where money was involved.

Harry nodded. "My suspicion grew when I learned that the killer, Dan Kelly, worked as a guard at Tammany Hall and had spent a few years in prison in his youth for manslaughter. Released, he was soon arrested again for assault with a knife. The charge was dismissed. The police had probably recruited Kelly to collect the proceeds in their protection rackets."

"Did you discover the gentleman H. C. and his lost portfolio?"

"I inquired at Tammany Hall and hit a stone wall of denial. Alarm bells went off in my head. I reported to Inspector Williams that Palermo's death looked suspiciously like a carefully planned killing involving Tammany Hall and deserved a thorough investigation. The inspector flatly refused and took me off the case."

"Did Williams give a reason for his decision?" Pamela asked.

Harry shook his head. "Williams said my suggestion was foolish. Tammany Hall was a legitimate political club and wouldn't countenance murder. I saw no point in arguing with him. Certain Tammany politicians had probably paid him to suppress the report."

"How did you react?"

"At the time, I was outraged. Unwisely, I went over Williams's head to Chief of Detectives Mr. Byrnes and complained of a cover-up. News of my protest leaked to the press. Shortly afterward, I was arrested and charged with secretly demanding a bribe from Tim Smith of Tammany Hall in return for dropping the investigation."

Harry poured himself a glass of water. For a moment, the room fell silent while he seemed lost in the past. With a sigh he resumed his story. "Smith gave the police an extortion letter in my handwriting. Someone at Tammany Hall or in the NYPD must have fabricated the letter to Smith. Inspector Williams declared the letter to be authentic. At the bench trial, Judge Fawcett convicted me of extortion and sentenced me to five years in Sing Sing."

"What evidence did the judge have?" Pamela asked.

"Not much," Harry replied. "Chiefly the letter to Smith, but also testimony from Williams and several NYPD officers describing me as overly ambitious, reckless, and insubordinate. One of the officers claimed that I had said more than once I would make Smith pay."

"A remark obviously taken out of context," Pamela said, then asked Harry, "What happened in prison and afterward?"

"Tammany Hall's agents tried to silence me. I managed to defend myself, but I couldn't clear my name. After four years, Prescott got me out on probation, and I joined the firm."

"It's a distressing story," said Pamela. "We need to find out why the cabdriver was killed and who was responsible for the false extortion letter that framed you. Now is the time to begin."

Harry smiled. "For the first time in seven years I'm hopeful. What can be done for my friend, Theresa?"

Pamela reflected for a moment. "If she were to escape from the Sullivan house with her son, she could temporarily live in my empty room. She might prefer to stay with her sister, but the White family's apartment is crowded and would suit her only in an emergency. We must act soon before Michael's harassment causes Theresa's mental state to deteriorate."

"What can I do to help?"

"While I speak to Theresa's sister, Trish, you could investigate Michael Sullivan."

Harry rubbed his hands with relish. "I'll find someone in his office who sees through his respectability, and I'll check out his nightlife for a pattern of immorality and/or crime. A man who treats his younger sister so badly may also have injured other women."

"Yes, we'll prove that he's unfit to judge Theresa or to assume custody of her boy."

CHAPTER 3

Victim of Abuse

Saturday, November 10

"How shall we free Theresa and James from her family's grip?" Trish asked Pamela. It was midmorning, and they were at tea in the White family kitchen.

"I must gauge the level of her distress and her will to become her own master. When can I meet her again?"

"Let's go to her now," Trish replied. "Earlier this morning, I expected her here, but she didn't show up. I should enquire about her. She lives nearby."

They walked the short distance to the Sullivan home on a side street off Union Square. Though an older building, it still would have cost more than a retired bank clerk like Theresa's father could afford. His son, Michael, must be paying the mortgage and other bills, and thus controlling the family.

Pamela waited across the street behind a parked carriage where she could observe the front of the house. A sour-looking maid opened the door, spoke brusquely to Trish, and shut the door in her face.

Livid with anger, Trish rejoined Pamela. "That bitch of a maid said my sister was ill and would not receive any visitors. I asked if I could speak to my nephew. The maid said no, he was also ill."

"That was a lame excuse," said Pamela. "They've locked up Theresa and her boy in the house. Michael will provoke her to the point of despair where she would appear mad. Can you trust anyone in the house?"

Trish thought for a moment. "Mrs. Donovan, the cook, knows Theresa's story and hates Michael. But she's afraid of him and fears he would throw her out on the street without references if she displeased him in the slightest way. At this time of day, she's usually in the market on Union Square."

"We must go there immediately and find out what's happened to Theresa and her boy."

Even on a chilly late morning in November, the market was still busy. The short, stout, pink-cheeked older woman was studying a head of lettuce. As Trish and Pamela approached, Mrs. Donovan looked up and frowned, appearing to sense trouble.

Trish asked, "How is my sister, Theresa? She and I were supposed to take a walk."

"I wouldn't know, ma'am. She took breakfast in her room with her boy. Mrs. Sullivan's maid served her."

Mrs. Donovan had quickly grown agitated, her eyes darting left and right as if searching for Michael Sullivan's spies. Then her gaze fixed on Pamela. "You look familiar, ma'am. Haven't I seen you here in the market? Yes, you're Mrs. Thompson, the lady who helps children in trouble. One of yours, the young Italian singer, was kidnapped some months ago in broad daylight."

"That was Francesca." Pamela smiled. "She came back safe and sound. I live across the square on Fourteenth. You're right, I often shop here." Pamela looked the cook in the eye. "Would you like to join us in my apartment for tea? It's time we were better acquainted."

Mrs. Donovan hesitated. Pamela cajoled her. "You look chilled. I'll put a few drops of the good sauce in your cup."

"Well, your place is on my way home. I may as well go with you."

In Pamela's kitchen, the three women relaxed with chitchat and spiked tea. The cook turned to Trish and said, "You should look after your sister. She's very unhappy at home."

"What's wrong?" Trish asked.

"Michael picks on her and bosses her. She used to talk back to him; but lately he has threatened to take away her son, and she gives in to him more frequently. At dinner recently, they argued when she wanted to go out for some reason. 'Take care of young James,' he shouted at her. She told him to mind his own business."

"That's encouraging," Pamela said in an aside to Trish.

Mrs. Donovan shook her head. "Michael exploded with anger. I thought he would have a stroke. 'You listen to me,' he shouted again. 'My friend Judge Fawcett will declare you unfit to be a mother.' She turned white in the face and didn't say another word. Judge Fawcett is God in the Sullivan house."

"Is Michael always so mean to Theresa?"

"He brings her flowers on her birthday, compliments her appearance when she dresses up, and pets or embraces her in a familiar way. But he doesn't seem genuine. She stiffens when he touches her. Frankly, his behavior looks indecent and makes my skin prickle."

Pamela met the cook's eye. "Then would you agree that Theresa and her son ought to leave the Sullivan house?"

The cook's response was hesitant. "It's a bad place for her, certainly, but how can she leave? She has no money and no decent way to earn any. Michael would try to prevent her. With the judge behind him, and the child a hostage, he might succeed." She lifted her cup in a salute to the others and drank up her tea. "That was refreshing. I thank you for the hospitality." As she rose from the table, she said earnestly, "I trust you won't repeat what I've said."

When the cook left, Pamela turned to Trish. "To free Theresa we must take bold measures."

"Where shall we start?" Trish's tone was skeptical.

"We have to break Michael's hold on the Sullivan family and then get the judge out of the way. Even though he has retired from the bench, he has sufficient influence in New York's courts to threaten Theresa's hold on her child. As long as that's true, she will remain a prisoner in the Sullivan house." And, Pamela thought, the judge would also block any attempt to rehabilitate Harry's reputation.

Early in the afternoon, Pamela was back in her office, gazing out the window, reflecting on Theresa's predicament. Prescott appeared at the open door. "May I come in?"

"Yes, of course." She returned to her desk. His eyes were bright and eager.

"Do you have news?" she asked.

"I do." He pulled up a chair and sat leaning toward her. "I've just heard from my lawyer in Connecticut that my marriage to Gloria has finally been dissolved."

"I'm happy for you. This has been a difficult issue." Her heart beat faster.

He showed Pamela the court's decree. Gloria's alimony would continue until she married again. Prescott seemed pleased with the terms, probably assuming Gloria would soon marry her friend, the banker George Fisher, and the alimony would end. But if Fisher broke with her, then she would likely remain single and be a financial burden for a long time.

Pamela was puzzled. "Shouldn't Gloria have insisted on more money?"

"You would think so," Prescott replied. "Apparently, she's anxious that her friend, Fisher, might grow impatient with any delay and slip out of her hands. That prospect might have made her more willing to settle on reasonable terms. The process has often been a nightmare, but it's over and I'm free."

"Congratulations!" Pamela added in her own mind that now their relationship rested on a new and sounder footing. In the two and a half years they had known each other she had grown fond of Prescott, and the thought of marrying him had crossed her mind, but she hadn't allowed herself to pursue the idea or to raise hopes. Her failed marriage with Jack Thompson had left her scarred and wary. She was reluctant to commit herself legally or romantically to another man.

"Dinner and dancing tonight?" Prescott asked. There was a new lilt in his voice.

"Gladly," she replied, banishing for the moment any lingering anxieties.

At the Volksgarten Café, their favorite Austrian music hall, they chose a table in the mezzanine that offered a view of young couples waltzing to the music of Johann Strauss. After an aperitif, they joined the dancers for the popular "Blue Danube." Back at the table they ordered the traditional Austrian Wiener schnitzel with spaetzle and a light red wine.

During the meal Pamela asked Prescott about his son Edward, a junior at Williams College, whom she had never met. Through his father, however, she already knew the young man well and was fond of him.

"He's thriving. Next weekend, I'll visit him in Williamstown for the annual football game with Amherst College, Williams's chief rival. Edward has always been a good student, but he has also grown into an outstanding athlete in several sports and will play fullback on Saturday."

"Will the game be well attended?"

Prescott nodded. "It's the main event of the college's autumn social season and attracts many parents, friends, and alumni. Franklin Carter, the college president, invited me, so I feel obliged to go."

He gazed fondly at Pamela. "Would you care to join me? I'll leave Friday morning and return on Sunday evening."

Her mind immediately urged caution, but her heart leaped at the opportunity. The conflict lasted but a moment. "I'd be delighted to meet Edward and on such an auspicious occasion."

"Then I'll reserve rooms for us at the Greylock Hotel on Main Street in the village, a stone's throw from Edward's fraternity house." He raised his glass. "Shall we toast the weekend?"

Pamela lifted her glass and they clinked. She shivered with anticipated pleasure.

Their conversation shifted to Harry's problems with the Sullivan family. Pamela mentioned that she would closely observe the situation. "I'll start tomorrow at High Mass in their church."

"Do you mind if I join you?" he asked.

"Not at all. It might do you some good," she replied kindly.

Chapter 4

A Hidden Life

Sunday, November 11

From a cab across the street Pamela and Prescott watched the Sullivan family leave their home. A tall, heavy, vigorous man about thirty-five, Michael looked magisterial in a well-tailored dark gray suit and a matching silk top hat. As he emerged from the building, he glanced up at the sky's scattered clouds. Reassured that rain didn't threaten him or his flock, he brusquely beckoned them to a waiting cab in the street. The driver placed a stool at the cab door to assist them.

Michael stood by the cab, offering a helping arm to his feeble, crippled father, who had shuffled from the house with tiny steps. Michael then extended his arm to his frail mother and to her maid. When it was Theresa's turn, Michael seized her by the waist and lifted her up into the cab, as if she were a child.

Pamela turned to her companion and gasped, "How demeaning! Theresa is petite but perfectly capable of stepping into the cab on her own." Michael lifted the boy James in the same familiar way, climbed in after him, and ordered the driver to set off.

Prescott lifted a cautionary finger. "If we were outside observers of this scene, we'd think Michael Sullivan was a big brother stepping into his failing father's role, awkwardly to be sure. His true character is hidden."

The Sullivans drove up Lexington Avenue to St. Stephen's Roman Catholic Church on East Twenty-eighth Street. Pamela and Prescott followed at a distance. Mrs. Donovan had earlier informed Pamela that the family would attend the High Mass at eleven and sit in a reserved pew at a halfway point of the nave. For years that was their custom.

The family tarried at the entrance while Michael greeted acquaintances. Hidden in the crowd, Pamela and Prescott slipped into the church and hastened to a pew off to the side.

While the great organ was sending out dramatic flourishes, Michael led his family down the main aisle and showed them into their pew. He placed Theresa to his right and the boy to his left.

Pamela pulled an opera glass from her bag and focused the diagonal lens on Theresa. Her face was waxen and utterly devoid of expression. Then a bell rang, and the priest, clad in a glittering chasuble and accompanied by acolytes, entered the chancel. The congregation rose to their feet while Michael lifted Theresa by the elbow. She appeared to grimace.

"Is Michael going to harass her throughout the service?" Pamela whispered to Prescott, and handed him the opera glass.

Prescott nodded, then watched the Sullivans. "Michael also glances sidewise toward her and whispers. She doesn't appear to respond."

The Mass was conducted with great solemnity. As the choir sang the majestic hymn, "Gloria in Excelsis Deo," clouds of incense rose toward the chancel ceiling, and a sweet, pungent scent enveloped the congregation. Brilliantly tinted light poured through the tall stained glass windows. During the sermon, the preacher held the congregation spellbound, except for Michael and his family. Throughout the service he seemed to function mechanically, his mind somewhere else. The other adults of his family appeared equally self-absorbed. Only the boy seemed engaged in the liturgy, his eyes wide with wonder.

Prescott handed the opera glass back to Pamela. "Study Michael's face. He looks ill."

She focused on him again. His cheeks sagged and were slightly rouged in a vain attempt to conceal a sallow complexion; his eyes were heavy-lidded and half-closed. He frequently tried to suppress what appeared to be a chronic hacking cough. "Frankly," she whispered, "he appears debauched. What was he doing last night?"

Like many others, the Sullivans remained in their pew during Communion. When the Mass ended, they hurried out with half the congregation during an organ postlude. Pamela and Prescott followed at a discreet distance.

A few blocks north on Lexington Avenue, Michael guided his family into an elegant teashop to a table in the middle of the room. Pamela and Prescott had hurried through a back door and sat at a small, secluded table where they could observe the Sullivans. Michael again made the seating arrangements, placing Theresa between him and her father. After he eased her into a chair, he laid both hands on her shoulder in a firm, lengthy caress. She frowned and stiffened; he appeared not to notice. He smiled benevolently over the family, then took his seat.

When the waiter arrived with the menu, Michael led the discussion of choices—loudly enough that Pamela and Prescott could overhear. When the waiter came around to Theresa, she said she wasn't hungry and would only have tea.

Michael shook his head in an expression of deep concern. "No, Theresa," he insisted, again loudly. "You must eat or you will never be well." He turned to the waiter. "Madam will have a cup of chicken soup and a Swiss cheese sandwich."

He was about to order for himself when Theresa interrupted

him. "Thank you, Michael. I'm well enough to feed myself." She turned to the waiter and said distinctly, "Cancel that order. I only want tea." Her voice was strained, her jaw set in a defiant attitude.

Michael bristled and appeared about to shout at her, but he looked around and realized that other diners were taking notice. "As you wish," he muttered.

A heavy silence descended on the Sullivan table. Then Mrs. Sullivan tried to relieve the tension. "The choir was lovely this morning." She looked at the others hopefully. Her maid joined her. "I thought the preacher's message was inspiring."

Old Mr. Sullivan broke in. "What I could hear of it was sound." He turned to his grandson. "I suppose it was all Greek to you."

"I liked the organ," the boy said. "The sound tickled my skin. In my feet I could feel the floor throbbing. Maybe I'll be an organist when I grow up."

The conversation continued in this feeble way until food and drink arrived and dissipated the tension. A few minutes later, however, Theresa excused herself curtly and walked toward the women's restroom. Michael looked surprised and confused. Mrs. Sullivan's brow furrowed with concern. She started to rise, as if to follow Theresa, then wavered and sat down.

As Theresa came within sight of Pamela, she beckoned secretly.

Pamela glanced at Prescott. He silently mouthed, *Talk to her.*

She waited a few moments, then went to the women's room, knocked, and said softly, "It's Pamela Thompson. Let me in."

The door opened and Theresa stood there, anger in her eyes. "Come in, Pamela. I saw you in church and figured you would follow me here. I had to get away from Michael or I'd explode. He pretends to be kind and concerned, but he's really a loathsome monster, at least toward me. Trish told you what he did years ago and is trying to do again. I hate to think of being at home with him. He treats me as if I'm his loving wife and James is his darling son."

"I agree," said Pamela. "That's the impression he has created here and in the church." She added, "Let's move away from the door. Someone might try to listen in."

"That wouldn't surprise me," muttered Theresa.

"I noticed that Michael was paying unusual attention to your son, James. Is it genuine?"

Theresa shook her head. "Michael used to ignore the boy, but recently he started petting him and giving him presents. I think he's trying to win James away from me, or worse. Yesterday afternoon, he insisted that the three of us go for a carriage ride in Central Park. He turned on his charm, chattered about the sights, and bought sweets for the boy. Strangers looking on would say that he's being a kind, generous uncle. I think he's false to his core, an evil predator. I fear he will harm James. What shall I do?"

Pamela measured her words. "Assert yourself, as you did at the table. Michael is a bully, a coward in the face of firm resistance. Cultivate your mother's good will. She may be weak, but she's on your side. Confide in Mrs. Donovan. She'll keep me informed."

"How is Harry?" Theresa asked. "I often think of him."

"He's desperately fond of you. And, like me, he's confident that we'll soon free you and your son from this distressing situation." Pamela took Theresa's hands. "Now you'd better go back to the table. We'll keep in touch."

Pamela and Prescott left the teashop by the back door. Once in a cab, she reported what Theresa had told her.

He thoughtfully stroked his chin. When she finished, he said, "Michael's interest in James is disturbing. We must act quickly. You and Harry should investigate Michael full-time, starting tomorrow. Hire extra help if you need it. He may lead an expensive hidden life and probably skims money from accounts in his care."

"If that's a fact, Harry and I will expose him and break his hold on his sister."

Early next morning, Pamela called Harry to her office and shared what she had learned yesterday. "Theresa suffers under brother Michael's unrelenting pressure, but she's brave and misses you. He presents himself to the public as an upright gentleman and concerned head of his family. He's false, however, and we need to discover the chinks in his armor. What can you tell me about his habits?"

"Quite a bit," Harry replied. "When I first realized that he disliked me, I figured it was because of my felony conviction and the years in Sing Sing. I needed to know him better. But I couldn't investigate him entirely by myself, since he would recognize me and become alarmed. So I asked Barney Flynn, a fellow private investigator, to help me. We trade favors with each other."

"Could we talk to Flynn this afternoon?"

"I'll set up a meeting. Barney has followed Sullivan for several days and should have something to report."

Flynn's office was a small, sparsely furnished room in a decrepit building off West Twenty-third Street in Chelsea. A large map of New York City covered one wall. Cheap, signed prints of unsmiling, bearded men hung on another. Flynn followed her gaze. "My rogues' gallery," he said with a chuckle, and pointed to a big-boned man in the middle of the collection. "That's Richard Croker, Tammany's boss, together with his confederates in crime, the ward bosses."

Flynn was an older man, slightly built, with a self-effacing manner. He gave Pamela a quick, penetrating glance as he shook her hand, then smiled in a friendly way. Harry introduced her as Mrs. Thompson, his partner. They sat around a drink-stained table.

"What can you tell us about Michael Sullivan?" Harry began.

Flynn leaned back in his chair, hands clasped behind his head. "I tracked him for about a week. He's straight as an arrow in public, Monday through Friday."

"What's his routine?" Pamela asked.

"After breakfast at home, he walks briskly to his office at the Union Square Bank and Trust Company, the same route every day. At a shop on Broadway he buys a morning paper. The doorman at the bank lets him in. That's as far as I could follow him. After work, Sullivan simply retraces his steps, buying an evening paper on the way."

Flynn paused for a moment, evidently enjoying a look of disappointment growing on the faces of his visitors. Then he resumed. "Since I couldn't follow him inside, I made the acquaintance of Ambrose Norton, a young, ambitious clerk at the bank, who appears to detest Sullivan and covets his position as assistant to the head of the bank's trust department. According to the clerk, Sullivan settles down every morning in his small, plain office adjacent to the large, splendid one of his boss. A pot of tea soon arrives. Sullivan sips at his desk while glancing at the financial pages of the morning paper and clipping articles of special interest for later use. Routine meetings and appointments follow at regular intervals until noon."

"Nothing remarkable about him this far," Harry remarked. "But how did you get Norton to speak to you at all?"

"A friend of a friend of mine knows and respects him, and introduced us at a bar. He's a young lawyer with good credentials from the Columbia Law School. For three years, he has worked as a clerk in the trust department learning the business. He's very eager to get ahead but recently has become frustrated.

Sullivan overworks him, fails to give him credit, and has written an unfair review of his work."

"Is Norton angry?"

"Yes, I'd say he'd be willing to help ease Sullivan out of the way, but he'd be afraid of being regarded as an intriguer. He hinted that Sullivan is vulnerable but wouldn't tell me why—not yet."

Pamela remarked, "We clearly need to encourage Norton to take us deeper into Sullivan's secrets, but now lead us through the rest of his day."

Flynn nodded. "Norton has spoken to servants at the club where Sullivan lunches at noon. While others indulge in loose talk and large beefsteaks, washed down with beer and wine, he eats slowly and drinks little, attending instead to investment opportunities and pitfalls. He prides himself on the nuggets of useful information he gleans there. But Norton complains that he has to correct or discard most of it.

"At two o'clock, Sullivan walks back to his office for an afternoon of more meetings and appointments. After business hours, he lingers in his office writing memos to himself presumably for buying and selling stocks and bonds and real estate."

"What does Sullivan do on the weekend?" asked Harry, appearing a little impatient at Flynn's slow pace.

"Norton didn't know," replied Flynn.

"I can fill in a few details," said Pamela. "According to Mrs. Donovan and Trish White, Michael takes a long walk on Saturday morning, lunches alone, then retires to his study. He spends hours going over household and personal accounts and meeting with members of his family and the servants. Saturday evening, he dines with family and occasional guests from a narrow circle of relatives and business acquaintances."

"So far his behavior seems proper, if dull," remarked Harry. "Aren't there any traces of bad behavior?"

"There's still the night," said Pamela. "Mrs. Donovan's room is near the back door. She has noticed him slipping out of the house late on Saturday when everyone has gone to bed. He's at home other nights. Whenever he's in the house, however, he's a threat to Theresa. Mrs. Donovan has also instructed her to barricade the door when she's alone in her room or in bed."

"She shouldn't have to live in fear," Harry said. He looked grim, his jaw rigid. "If he harms her, I'll kill him," he muttered under his breath. "I'll follow him next Saturday night. In the meantime, we'll get better acquainted with Norton."

Monday evening, Flynn, Harry, and Pamela went by cab to the Cooper Union on Astor Place to meet the clerk. Flynn had arranged with Norton to set aside an hour before he went to his financial magazines and books. He regularly spent the evenings, Monday through Friday, in the institution's great reading room.

As they left the cab on Astor Place, Flynn said, "I'll introduce you and Mrs. Thompson, then I'll leave. I must meet a client in the office."

Norton was waiting for them in a coffee shop on the ground floor facing Astor Place. Flynn pointed him out at a remote, secluded table. About thirty years old, a trim, athletic man with a frank, open countenance, he sat relaxed at a table, a cup of coffee before him, reading a newspaper.

He looked up and smiled when Flynn approached him. "Mrs. Thompson and Mr. Miller would like to speak to you about a matter of mutual concern. Are you willing?"

"Yes, I have done my homework, so I know with whom I'm dealing." He gestured them to chairs facing him. "We can speak freely here."

"Then I'll leave you now," said Flynn. With a wave over his shoulder he hurried to his appointment.

Pamela met Norton's eye. "I'll go right to the point. Mr. Michael Sullivan has wrongly created serious problems for all of us. Shall we discuss how we can work together to resolve them?"

"I believe we can find a way," Norton replied. "As Mr. Flynn has told you, Mr. Sullivan has deliberately blocked my path to promotion. The senior members of the firm are impressed by his successful investments and support him. In fact, for the past two years, I've researched most of those investments and determined the most opportune moments to buy or sell. Sullivan has adopted my recommendations and taken the credit. I must either discredit him in the eyes of the firm—a daunting task—or find a trust department in another firm, a poor option since Sullivan would give me a bad reference."

He paused. "Now, would you explain how Mr. Sullivan causes you pain? Mr. Flynn mentioned a serious domestic issue."

Pamela described Sullivan's threat to Theresa and her son and his opposition to Harry's relationship to her. "Judge Fawcett aggravates the problem by supporting Sullivan's claim that Theresa is incompetent to raise her son."

Norton listened intently to Pamela, occasionally glancing at Harry. When she finished, the clerk folded his hands and raised them to his chin. For a long moment he gazed at his companions. "I probably have the information that you need to disarm or even ruin Sullivan, but if I were to give it to you, I would risk ruining myself. Tammany Hall has invested significantly in Sullivan and Fawcett and will protect them. Think of its long reach into city government, private businesses, and law firms."

"I fully agree with the need for caution," said Harry. "I once challenged Tammany Hall and paid dearly with four years of my life in Sing Sing on a false charge of extortion."

The clerk nodded. "At the time that Mr. Prescott was arranging your parole, I overheard Sullivan and Judge Fawcett in the office discussing your investigation of the cabdriver's death. They apparently were trying to prevent your release."

Anger flashed momentarily in Harry's eyes, but he continued. "The recent reform movement at the municipal and state level has weakened Tammany and made it more cautious. If we can convict Sullivan and Fawcett of major crimes, Tammany might abandon them."

Pamela added, "The risk to you, Mr. Norton, would be much less if you were to move to a trust department in an independent law firm beyond Tammany's reach. You should speak to Mr. Prescott. I'm sure he would give you a friendly hearing."

Norton smiled broadly. "That offer is an encouraging step toward solving our problems with Michael Sullivan. Would you please pursue it?"

At a nod from Harry, she replied, "Yes, with the utmost secrecy."

Chapter 5

Helpful Clerk

Tuesday, November 13–Thursday, November 15

The next morning, Pamela met Prescott in his office and asked, "Could your law firm use a new trust officer?" She reported that Ambrose Norton appeared to have access to valuable evidence of Harry Miller's wrongful conviction, but he wanted a safe, secure position before he would be helpful.

"I'm intrigued," Prescott replied. "I'll need a couple of days to study your question and to consult my associates. If we agree to hire a trust officer, then we can discuss Mr. Norton. In the meantime, investigate him further. He might be our kind of man, but let's be sure."

"What evidence would you like to see?"

"Bring me a sample of correspondence and documents showing that Sullivan and Fawcett took part in a criminal conspiracy against Harry. I would also like a better sense of the risks Norton is willing to take in dealing with us."

"That's helpful. I'll talk to him again."

Prescott met her eye. "Need I mention caution? If agents of Tammany Hall were to suspect him of betraying their secrets, they would quickly end his usefulness to us."

Pamela understood. Put in less circumspect terms, Mr. Norton would "accidentally" fall off a ferryboat, or down a flight of stairs, or out of a window. "I'll follow up on tips that Barney Flynn has given us."

To assess Norton's risks Pamela went immediately to Flynn's office for more information. Flynn offered her coffee. "I warn you, I made it myself, yesterday."

"No thanks, Barney. What can you tell me about Norton's family?"

"They live in a modest brownstone house on a side street north of Washington Square. His father owns a profitable freight company in Manhattan that Ambrose's older brother manages. His mother is the company's secretary. The family expects Ambrose to join the company as its unpaid legal clerk."

"Wouldn't Norton's testimony against Tammany Hall bring harm to his family?"

"As surely as night follows day," Flynn replied. "Tammany Hall would divert customers from the freight company to its competitors. Tammany's agents would vandalize the company's warehouses, carts, and horses and beat up the drivers. The Tammany-controlled city government would revoke the company's license to operate on the city's streets."

Flynn drank deeply from his cup, grimaced at the bitter taste, and added, "Ambrose must be keenly aware of those dangers. A Prescott offer would have to be very tempting to overcome his reluctance."

"The poor man's caught in a dilemma," Pamela remarked. "He could choose a safe, secure position either at the bank or with his family but with no prospect for a prosperous, happy life. Or, he could risk everything and cooperate with our investigation of Sullivan and Fawcett. In return, he could become a trust officer with excellent prospects for wealth."

As Pamela left Flynn's office, she wondered about Norton's personal character. How courageous was he? Even if Prescott's firm were to hire him, would he stand by his testimony in the face of Tammany's aggressive denial? And finally, how much evidence could a mere clerk like him produce? She would have to know him better, secretly.

That evening she returned to Cooper Union to meet him, this time without an appointment. Ambrose was sitting alone at a table in the main reading room; a newspaper, oddly printed on salmon-colored paper, lay open before him. Pencils and paper were off to one side. His eyes were fixed on an article, and he seemed oblivious to the low, soft rustle of paper, the shuffling of chairs, and the faint murmur of voices in the room. Pamela sat across the table from him and opened a magazine. He still didn't notice her.

She shoved a note across the table to him. He looked up, blinked, and frowned, then read the note. She had asked when could he meet her in the downstairs café.

He appeared to reflect for a moment and then wrote on her note, *I'll be there in ten minutes.*

As she sat by herself in the rear of the café, Pamela at first felt ill at ease, fearing that a Tammany spy might take note of her. But she soon relaxed. Other patrons were absorbed in reading or conversation and ignored her.

Since taking on this case, Pamela had grown increasingly aware of the wide reach of Tammany Hall's organization on Manhattan. Its eighty thousand members, together with its allies and clients, fed a huge, constant stream of information to the leadership about everything of interest to them. The cab-driver's murder and the framing of Harry Miller seven years ago would still be on their list of concerns.

When Ambrose failed to arrive on time, Pamela's heart sank. Had he changed his mind and would he refuse to cooperate? A minute later, as he hurried into the room, she breathed easier. He slowed down so as not to attract attention and sat across from her.

After a waiter had served them, Ambrose asked, "What do you want?"

"I've spoken to Prescott. He's interested in hiring a trust officer, but he's asking for evidence that you can deliver what you've promised."

"That's reasonable and what I've expected. I have something to give him. Ever since I began working for Sullivan, I've sensed he was false, so I've investigated him to protect myself. From his wastebasket I've gathered torn and crumbled messages that he exchanged with Judge Noah Fawcett and others. When put together, these messages indicate that Sullivan acts as a broker in Tammany's dubious, possibly illegal financial transactions."

"That sounds promising. Shall we meet tomorrow in the reading room? You could pass the memos to me in a plain folder." He agreed, then she asked, "Are you aware of other evidence of Sullivan's criminal behavior?"

Norton nodded. "Sullivan, like many financial tricksters, keeps two account books, one for the auditors and the other for himself. He locks his own book in his office desk drawer and takes it with him when he leaves for the day—I've seen him put it into his portfolio. I assume he keeps it in a secret place at home."

"Your assumption appears correct. We've followed him and are sure that he goes directly home rather than to a secret office. Can you describe his private book?"

"It has a dark green worn cover and is octavo in size and

about an inch thick. In black letters it says 'Miscellaneous Accounts.' He writes the entries in a clear, tiny script."

"How have you come to know so much about the book?"

"Once, when I was in the office with him, he hurried out—I think he was sick. Since this summer, he has appeared increasingly distracted and often looks like he hasn't slept. While he was away, I discovered that he didn't lock his desk drawer. I found his secret book and glanced at a few pages but didn't see enough to draw any conclusions."

Pamela surveyed the room. No one seemed to be spying on them. "I'll leave now. You've been helpful, Ambrose. I'll see you tomorrow."

While riding back to her apartment in a cab, Pamela wondered about Michael's secret book, hidden somewhere in the Sullivan home—like a needle in a haystack. To find it without alerting Sullivan to the investigation would be difficult. His entries might also be unintelligible to anyone but himself. Nonetheless, Pamela would speak with Mrs. Donovan and with Theresa, her only reliable contacts in the house.

The next morning, Pamela saw Mrs. Donovan again in the outdoor market in Union Square, studying a cabbage. This time, Theresa was with her. Pamela sidled up to them, also picked up a cabbage, and murmured, "Tea in my apartment?"

Mrs. Donovan glanced nervously left and right, then nodded. Pamela hurried home.

Ten minutes later, Mrs. Donovan and Theresa arrived, carrying sacks of produce. They relaxed at the kitchen table while Pamela poured their tea and offered cream and honey. Pamela and Mrs. Donovan each added a shot of brandy.

"What have you learned?" Mrs. Donovan asked Pamela.

"Michael secretly records suspicious financial transactions

in a small green book with the title 'Miscellaneous Accounts' on the cover. He carries it to and from the office in his portfolio." She gazed at Mrs. Donovan and Theresa. "Would either of you have seen it?"

The two women glanced at each other, brows furrowed in the effort to recall.

Mrs. Donovan was the first to reply. "I've seen it two or three times, closed, and on his desk in the study. That would be on Saturdays when he calls me in to give an account of kitchen expenses."

Theresa asked, "Does the fact that he hides the book at home really mean that he's stealing money from the law firm or from his clients?"

"Perhaps," replied Pamela. "Whatever he's writing in the secret account book concerns money and is important to him, and he doesn't want anyone to know about it. That makes me very curious. Where does he keep his valuables?"

Mrs. Donovan replied, "He has a safe in his study for money and jewelry. The family silver is in locked cabinets in the pantry."

Theresa added, "Family and household financial records are also locked in his study."

"Who cleans his study?"

"The maid. Don't count on her to help you. She's loyal to him and spies on us."

That evening, Pamela went again to the Cooper Union reading room. Ambrose was at his usual place, the salmon-colored newspaper spread out before him. She slipped a note to him, asking for a meeting. This time she added, *What are you reading? I like the color.*

He replied on the note, *The* Financial Times *from London, the investor's Holy Grail. I'll see you in five minutes. Same place.*

Pamela was waiting at the usual table. This time, he arrived promptly, carrying a portfolio. After their tea arrived, Ambrose slipped an envelope into Pamela's sack.

Sullivan's messages? she mouthed.

"As I promised."

"Thanks. While we finish our tea, tell me about your financial research here at Cooper Union."

"Gladly. I look for investment opportunities and pitfalls over the U.S. and the world. Early last year, I learned that American banks had overextended their lending; railroads like the Philadelphia and Reading had taken on too much debt. A few days before the market crashed, I persuaded Sullivan to sell off our most exposed stock. He made large profits for himself and for Judge Fawcett."

"Did they share their bounty with you?" Pamela let a hint of irony creep into her voice.

Ambrose shook his head, smiling wryly. "I hadn't expected anything from them, so I wasn't disappointed."

The following morning, Pamela brought Ambrose's envelope with her to the office. She had browsed in the messages last night, but couldn't easily make sense of them. They resembled a puzzle with too many pieces missing. Harry would have to help her determine their value, if any.

He soon came to her office, and they studied the messages. Harry said, "Ambrose has given us an intriguing sample of useful evidence. Late in 1890 Fawcett seems to have ordered Sullivan to find ways to prevent my parole. In the end, he offered bribes to members of the parole board. I recognize the names. Fortunately, the bribes were unsuccessful, though they weren't exposed."

Pamela asked Harry, "Are you ready to recommend that Prescott and his associates hire Norton as a trust officer?"

He patted the pile of memos. "Over the weekend, I'll speak to my friend Barney Flynn—while you and Prescott are enjoying a football game in Williamstown."

CHAPTER 6

A Dark and Thorny Place

Williamstown
Friday, November 16

"Are you well, Jeremiah?" Pamela gazed at her companion with sympathetic concern. He had just moaned as the train bounced over a rough patch of track.

With a grimace Jeremiah Prescott stretched out his ailing legs. Even in a spacious parlor car, the train ride from New York to Williamstown was uncomfortable for a wounded veteran of the Civil War. Pamela patted his arm and then rose to her feet to stretch. With a firm grip on the overhead luggage rack, she swayed gently with the car's rocking motion.

Prescott nodded toward a middle-aged man at the far end of the car and remarked softly, "Noah Fawcett is our traveling companion. You saw him a week ago at Delmonico's." The judge was reading a New York newspaper through thick spectacles. At his side was a bulging legal portfolio.

"Is Fawcett really corrupt?" Pamela asked. Yesterday afternoon, she had shown Prescott the incriminating messages that Norton had pieced together.

"The messages raise suspicions," Prescott replied, "but they are too fragmentary to convict Fawcett in a court of law or in public opinion."

The train rattled on through the countryside. The view out the window was bleak November. Trees in the distance had shed their leaves. Stubble covered the fields. The sky was gray, and low clouds shrouded the Berkshire Hills.

Pamela asked Prescott, "Why would Fawcett be traveling north in November? This isn't the season for a vacation. The colorful foliage of autumn is gone."

"He might have personal business in North Adams. He was raised in the area and still has a home there. His family's woolen factory is in nearby Williamstown. Since his father died a few years ago, the judge owns the business and has hired a manager to run it."

Intrigued, Pamela studied Fawcett more closely. He had laid down the newspaper, leaned back, and closed his eyes, but not to rest. His lips were pressed tightly together, his brow creased.

"He looks troubled," she remarked. "Perhaps his workers have upset him. They might be on strike. In today's depressed economy I can imagine the factory's management has cut their wages or laid them off."

"You could be right, Pamela. On the other hand, he might simply be suffering from indigestion." He smiled in a teasing way.

"You lack imagination, Jeremiah." She frowned in mock reproach, and then whispered, "Don't look now. I believe the judge is beginning to show interest in us." Fawcett had opened his eyes and glanced in their direction.

"He probably has recognized me and wonders who my lovely companion is."

"Tush!" she murmured.

* * *

As the train pulled into the North Adams railroad station, most passengers scrambled to their feet and rushed to the doors. Pamela and Prescott remained seated. Their connecting train to Williamstown wasn't due to arrive for a couple of hours, and their bags were checked through. They would walk the short distance to Main Street to see the town. It had a bustling, rapidly growing population and was seeking a municipal charter from the state government.

On the station platform they ran into Judge Fawcett as he descended from the car. "Prescott!" he said coolly. "What brings you here?" He glanced with interest at Pamela.

"We're on our way to Williamstown for an important football game. My son is playing for Williams College against Amherst tomorrow. May I introduce my assistant, Mrs. Pamela Thompson?"

The judge appeared to recognize her name and frowned slightly. Pamela suspected that he had heard of her husband Jack's embezzlement of bank funds and his subsequent suicide nearly three years ago. She was distressed when a stranger seemed to brand her with her husband's disgrace.

He politely tipped his hat and then remarked to Prescott, "I'm going to the game as well and will watch from the bleachers with my nephew Isaac, also a student, though he excels in Latin and Greek rather than football." The judge glanced at his watch. "Shall we have tea together at the Wilson Hotel? It's quite decent and close to the station."

Prescott glanced the question to Pamela.

"We'd be delighted, sir." There was calculation in her friendliness toward the judge. She was trying to figure him out. Thus far, she didn't like or trust him.

At tea, Fawcett proved to be a learned, well-mannered gentleman. Their conversation sought common ground and avoided courtroom disputes, politics, and other sources of contention. Pamela learned that the judge's nephew, Isaac, was a junior at the college and an industrious young man who had won awards for his essays on Latin literature.

The judge explained that Isaac's parents had passed away. "I am his legal guardian." The judge's tone of voice hinted at a disagreeable burden.

In turn, the judge asked about Edward Prescott. His father replied that the young man was a good student with wide-ranging interests. Most recently, he had enjoyed a summer of gardening at Mrs. Morgan's estate, Ventfort, in Lenox.

The judge seemed impressed. "Mrs. Morgan has spent millions on the mansion, and her husband has invested nearly as much in the gardens. Your lad is fortunate. He may later find the Morgans to be powerful patrons."

In the course of conversation Pamela realized that Fawcett had once attended Williams. "How was your experience at the college?" she asked.

"That was thirty years ago," he replied readily, apparently pleased by the question. "I was a classics and religion scholar, rather like my nephew. Nature hadn't designed me for the rough and tumble of college sports. In those days, I preferred to hike to the summit of Mount Greylock and enjoy the view. Professor Mark Hopkins had the greatest influence on my education. I was drawn especially to his lectures on the moral foundations of character." He glanced quizzically at Prescott. "How was it to study at Columbia College?"

"Our course of studies was like yours at Williams: Latin, English literature, mathematics, and philosophy. But, as you can imagine, we had many distractions in New York City."

Pamela detected a knowing smile on the judge's lips, as if he felt confirmed in his view of Prescott, a godless cynic with little respect for law and order.

* * *

After tea, they returned to the station and caught a late afternoon train. In a few minutes, they crossed the town line into Blackinton, a small village belonging to Williamstown.

"We are approaching my family's woolen factory," the judge announced, pointing with obvious pride to a long, three-and-a-half-story industrial building, built of fieldstones and mortar. "It's now fifty years old. We employ some two hundred and fifty men and women and provide them with houses, a school, a church, and a store. The blue military uniform you wore thirty years ago, Captain, might have been made here. We supplied the Union army with thousands of them."

At a large profit, Pamela remarked to herself. During the war, her mother used to complain of the poor quality of the uniforms worn by the wounded enlisted men she tended.

Pamela asked the judge, "Has your firm seen any labor unrest during the present economic depression?"

"No, madam. When we reduced production and therefore wages and employment, we made it clear to the workers that troublemakers would be the first to go, and they would leave with nothing but a bad reputation. We didn't tolerate any discussion of a union, not to mention a strike, and we fired a few complainers to show we meant business. Our firmness has cowed the workers. Snuff the first spark, I say."

Pamela was tempted to ask if docile workers were also fired. Were they and their families evicted from the company houses? But she wanted information from the judge rather than an argument. So she gave him a noncommittal nod.

"Is Blue Monday a problem here?" Prescott asked the judge.

"What's that?" Pamela asked.

Prescott explained, "Over the weekend, many workers indulge in heavy drinking. By Monday, they are so tired or ill that they slow down production in the factory and cause accidents."

The judge agreed that many of the larger mills had that problem. "But we simply don't allow production to slow down on Mondays. If a worker is unfit for the job, we fire him or her on the spot and require other workers to fill in for him. Half of our workers, by the way, are female, mostly young, and some of the males are children. They are less likely to drink than grown men. In any case, no liquor whatsoever is legally sold in the area. Because our workers don't waste their wages on drink, we can afford to pay them less. That helps to keep us competitive."

While he spoke, Pamela tried to imagine the lives of typical workers in Williamstown. Dawn to dusk for six days a week, they tended noisy, dangerous machines, repeating the same mechanical process remorselessly, and breathed air filled with dust. If distracted for a moment, a worker could easily lose a finger or an arm or life itself, with disastrous consequences especially for a family.

Pamela had recently witnessed a similar system in New York's meatpacking plants. She could understand why many workers would seek relief and drink themselves sick on Sunday, their only day off. The judge showed no sympathy or compassion for his workers, a fault that appeared to have carried over into his administration of justice to the poor and unfortunate in New York. She imagined that his heart was a dry and thorny place.

At the Williamstown railroad station they hired a cab for the one-mile ride into the village and waited on the platform for their luggage. A large brick factory stood across the Hoosac River.

"It makes coarse cotton cloth and is the main employer in Williamstown," the judge remarked, resuming his role as guide.

Pamela shook her head. "Williamstown appears to have greatly changed. When I vacationed here as a child, it was a small, charming New England rural village. Now it's beginning to look like an ugly factory town." In an aside to Prescott she asked, "Has the college suffered?"

"No, it has become a splendid little island of leisure and learning for young gentlemen."

Pamela silently resented the image: a splendid island indeed, now surrounded by regimented, soul-killing textile mills.

Their luggage arrived. They followed the judge into the cab and set off for the center of the village and the college campus.

On Main Street, Pamela recognized old, ivy-covered college buildings on spacious lawns: Griffin Hall, the Observatory, East Hall, and the Chapel.

Near the head of Spring Street, the village shopping center, the judge remarked: "President Carter has overseen a remarkable expansion of the college campus: Hopkins Hall on the right, Lasell Gymnasium and Morgan Hall on the left are among the most handsome academic buildings in New England. Set back from the road you'll see three new science buildings, outfitted to the highest modern standard. The enrollment has doubled during Carter's tenure to over three hundred students."

It was now late in the afternoon, the sun had set, and students were returning from the athletic fields to their fraternities and residence halls. Shouts and laughter filled the air. In the distance a band of musicians was practicing. Classes had ended for the week, and the young men were looking forward to tomorrow's game and to visits with family and female friends.

Pamela and her companions passed a large twin-towered Congregational church on the right, where college ceremonies and other events were held. Next door stood the college president's house, a white, well-proportioned building in the neoclassical style from the beginning of the century.

Farther up Main Street, the cab pulled into a drive and stopped at the door of the Greylock Hotel. It had closed a few weeks earlier after the summer season but opened again for this special weekend. The Greylock and its companion across Main Street, the Taconic Inn, offered modern conveniences, including hot and cold running water and electricity. The judge arranged for a room, then left in the cab to meet his nephew. Pamela and Prescott took adjoining rooms.

"I've invited Edward to join us here for supper this evening," Prescott remarked. "Shall we freshen up now?"

"Yes, I want to make a good impression." For a moment, a troubling apprehension gripped her. Would she and Edward like each other? Prescott would be watching, concerned.

An hour later, Pamela sat in the hotel lobby, Prescott at her side, waiting nervously for the young man's arrival. She had dressed to present herself as she was, not for fashion's sake. Her black hair was in a chignon; the streaks of gray served as accents. From her slim wardrobe she had chosen a blue silk gown with a high collar and added a pearl necklace.

"You look lovely," Prescott assured her, smiling fondly.

A few minutes late, Edward entered the lobby, his eyes searching the guests gathered there. Seeing his father, he brightened instantly then started toward him in an easy, loping gait. He was broad-shouldered like his father, but a little taller and more muscular. In his blue eyes there was keen intelligence, in his facial expression, candor and good humor.

A half smile came to his lips as he approached Pamela. "I'm pleased to meet you, Mrs. Thompson." He took her hand in a surprisingly gentle grip and bowed slightly, his eyes locking on to hers.

"Please call me Pamela, and you must be Edward." She noticed that he had his mother's manners and good looks, combined with his father's genuine character. She liked him instantly.

Prescott led them to the dining room and took a table off to a side at a good distance from louder, livelier diners. From a simple menu they agreed on broiled scrod from Boston, caught early that morning. Pamela and Prescott chose a white French wine from the Loire Valley. The waiter glanced at Edward.

"Cider for me. I'm in training for tomorrow's game."

The waiter smiled. "Good luck."

When the waiter left, Edward leaned toward Pamela and softly remarked, "Williamstown prohibits the sale and public consumption of intoxicating beverages. By custom the law isn't enforced in the hotels—summer guests would go elsewhere."

"If liquor can't be sold in local stores, where do people find it?"

"Vermont is only a mile north of us. A notorious store stands precisely on the state line. Special Officer Starkweather of the local constabulary has tried in vain to close it down."

"I've heard," continued Pamela, "that students at other colleges imbibe as much as they wish. What is the custom here?"

"A college statute forbids the consumption of intoxicating beverages. In practice the rule applies only to public drunkenness or other scandalous behavior. In my fraternity we police ourselves with reasonable discretion. I haven't observed any problems that would cause the college authorities to take action."

Shifting the topic, Pamela asked Edward about his favorite professors.

"Professor Arthur Perry comes to mind. He teaches political economy. In today's passionate controversy over tariffs on imported goods, especially British, Perry is on the free trade side. I believe tariffs are necessary, if New England's textile industry is to compete with Great Britain's. Without protection the mills in Williamstown and elsewhere in Massachusetts would close. Their workers would be laid off, and their families would become destitute. Perry might be wrong, but his arguments are vivid and lively and spiced with humor, and he encourages us to think for ourselves."

Prescott had listened attentively to his son. Now he asked, "Are you acquainted with a student at Williams named Isaac

Fawcett? On our way here, we met his uncle, a retired judge from New York."

"Indeed!" replied Edward, his eyes suddenly dark with anger. "Isaac unfortunately belongs to my fraternity and is a troublesome snitch. His uncle is a gilded tyrant—bright and shining on the surface but contemptible within."

"How do you know him?" Pamela probed, finding the young man's reaction to be harsher than she would have expected.

"Through the college YMCA a few of us in the fraternity try to do some good in the community. Judge Fawcett has replaced discontented workers with scabs and reduced the wages of others to the point that they can't support their families. Some have been evicted from company houses. For a while we brought food and clothing and some money to the worst cases of need. Then, suddenly, Fawcett ordered us off the company's property, claiming that we were causing unrest among his workers and undermining his authority."

"Why would he suspect you?" asked Prescott.

"Isaac overheard us speaking about the situation of the mill workers. Thinking we were alone, we had criticized the judge and his company's harsh treatment of the men and women we knew. His nephew carried our remarks back to the judge, provoking his anger and our banishment. In truth, we had been careful not to roil the workers."

"How have the fraternity brothers reacted to Isaac's disloyalty?"

"At first we confronted him. He denied our accusation and showed no regret. Since then we've shunned him."

"In a way, shouldn't he be pitied?" Pamela asked. "Someone has failed to teach him honor and self-respect."

"That's true," Edward replied. "His parents are dead. He has no brothers or sisters and no true friends. The judge pays his bills and demands that he excel in his studies. In fact, he earns good grades, but his uncle offers him little appreciation or encouragement. Frankly, I think he brought his tale to the judge to win a smile of approval. I doubt that he got it."

"Are you still in touch with any of Judge Fawcett's victims?" Pamela asked.

Edward hesitated a fraction. "Yes, I visit Mr. Clark, a skilled machinist and father of an eighteen-year-old daughter, Mary, and a fifteen-year-old son, Tom. Mrs. Clark, a schoolteacher, died a year ago of influenza. The children go to school and look after their father, as best they can. I try to cheer him up and also encourage the young people in their schoolwork."

"What's the machinist's problem?" Prescott seemed skeptical.

"Fawcett claimed he was a troublemaker and recently fired him and evicted the family from a company house."

"How have they managed?" asked Pamela, touched by the family's plight.

"A friend lent them a cabin near the railroad depot; other friends bring them food. Clark found part-time temporary work in the railroad yard nearby. But winter is coming, the cabin isn't heated, and he's growing desperate and angry. Unfortunately, he has turned to alcohol for relief. His daughter can't cope with him and calls on me for help. When he's tempted to drink, we talk, or I ask his friends to play cards with him."

Prescott looked askance. "Has Judge Fawcett noticed your kindness to his former troublemaker?"

"The judge's nephew has warned me to stay away from the machinist's family. I suppose he complains to his uncle."

The food arrived and the conversation switched to the vacation trip that Prescott and Edward had taken together in upstate New York's Adirondack Mountains. "The region is as different from Manhattan as the mind can imagine," said Prescott. "For several days, we traveled mostly alone by canoe through a chain of lakes, fishing and swimming in the clear, cold mountain waters and observing bear and moose, eagles and herons, and other wildlife up close. At night we pitched a tent and cooked a meal over an open fire."

"We got to know each other better," Edward added. "For the first time, Father talked about the war in the South—he had been in the thick of battle at Antietam and Gettysburg. His stories helped me understand him."

Pamela was surprised but pleased. Until recently, Prescott's memories of the carnage of the war pained, even at times crippled him. He had hidden his feelings for fear he'd be thought weak and cowardly.

"Edward has a sympathetic ear for my tales," Prescott remarked. "In turn he shared with me the trials of growing up in a boarding school with his quarreling parents in the distance."

The meal ended with apple pie. "We'll forgo drinks and smokes?" said Prescott. "I'll pay the bill. Then we'll walk Edward to his fraternity house. He must rest for the game tomorrow."

While waiting at the door, Edward leaned toward Pamela and said softly, "Father has talked so much about you that I feel we are already friends."

"He has likewise spoken fondly of you."

The young man hesitated, then said, "He has told me how you've helped him deal with the war's injury to his spirit. I now realize that his suffering accounts for the remote, detached attitude and erratic behavior that made it difficult for me and others to draw near him." Edward gazed at her tenderly. "He's always been a good man and a kind father, but he's much more at peace with himself since he met you. I'm very grateful."

Before preparing for bed, Pamela wrote in her journal her impressions of the judge, Edward, and Prescott. Keeping a journal had become a precious habit, a way to sharpen her powers of observation and to understand herself and others. The judge was her greatest challenge. He had been a courteous and helpful guide today. But what she had learned of his heart and mind was distressing.

Meeting Edward had touched her deeply. She was saddened that the war's lingering effects had repressed Prescott's feelings toward his son. How could she be sure of his feelings toward her? Still, tonight, through his son, he had professed something like true love for her. That was a hopeful step forward in their relationship.

CHAPTER 7

The Game

Williamstown
Saturday, November 17

Pamela and Prescott were midway through breakfast in the hotel dining room, when Judge Fawcett approached them. His demeanor appeared cooler than yesterday. "May I have a word with you, Prescott?"

"Of course, please join us." Prescott gestured to a chair.

Fawcett remained standing and stared at Pamela.

"She may hear whatever you have to say, sir." Prescott continued to smile but his tone had become brusque.

"All right then." Fawcett moistened his lips. "Last night I visited with my nephew Isaac and found him depressed. For the past few months, his fraternity brothers have been treating him like a pariah, barely speaking to him."

"That's unfortunate," said Prescott evenly. "What might be the reason?"

"When I pressed my nephew, he said he was being punished for reporting to me that Edward and the other brothers had criticized my management of the woolen mill and had agitated the workers. Isaac shouldn't be punished for doing the right thing. College students must stick to their studies and let me run the mill." Fawcett's voice was rising.

Prescott waved a calming hand. "Edward has mentioned this incident to me. He claims that Isaac is a snitch and has distorted the charitable help that Edward and other students were giving to needy workers. I agree with you, sir, that the present tension in the fraternity can't be healthy. I'll suggest to Edward that the brothers work on a plan to restore peace and harmony."

Fawcett's eyes narrowed. "This harassment is harming my nephew's health. It's got to stop. Edward and his gang must cease punishing Isaac and make amends. Otherwise, I'll complain to President Carter." Fawcett snapped a nod to Pamela, gave Prescott a curt "Good day, sir," and strode stiffly from the room.

"Well!" said Pamela. "He'll cause trouble for Edward."

"And for us," Prescott added. "I don't see an easy way out. But I'll begin with a visit to President Carter."

While Prescott was arranging a meeting with the president, Pamela went by cab with Edward to visit the unemployed machinist William Clark and his family. "Since I'm involved in helping people in difficult circumstances," she had said, "I'd like to see for myself the plight of your textile workers. I understand that several hundred of them live in the village."

As they were riding east on Main Street, Edward turned to Pamela and casually mentioned, "This morning at breakfast, someone tried to poison me, or at least make me too sick to play in this afternoon's game."

Pamela drew back in horror. "How is that possible here? It must have been accidental."

He shook his head. "I usually share my breakfast porridge with Socrates, the fraternity cat. I put it in his own dish, of course. This morning, he sniffed the porridge, shook his paw at it, and backed away. A brother who is a chemist determined that someone had laced the porridge with a small quantity of rat poison."

"Who could have done it?" Pamela asked, still shocked.

"Who else but Isaac Fawcett, or one of the few brothers who share his point of view on the textile worker controversy."

"Or who envy your accomplishments, Edward. I pity your fraternity, afflicted with such dangerous dissension. What can be done?"

His jaw tightened for a moment, then relaxed. "We'll have to sort out the bad apples. But here we are at Clark's cabin."

The cab pulled up to an unpainted, single-story wooden building on the hillside above the railroad yard. A bearded man splitting firewood looked up and greeted them. "Welcome, Mrs. Thompson. Edward has often spoken of you." He showed them inside, where a young woman was helping her younger brother with lessons at a wide plank table.

"My scholars, Mary and Tom," said Clark with pride in his voice. "They must finish homework before going to the football game this afternoon." Mary looked up and smiled a warm welcome. She was eighteen, shapely, black-haired, and blue-eyed. Her brother, Tom, was fifteen, tall for his age, slender, and fair-complexioned. Edward stood behind them like a schoolmaster, examining their work, and gave each of them a pat on the back. "Well done!" he said. "Stick to it."

Pamela also spoke to the children. "Since I don't want to distract you, this will be a brief visit. But Mr. Prescott and I invite you to lunch today at the hotel. We'll take a tour of the college before the game. Edward will join us when he's free." She turned to Mr. Clark. "And you are welcome as well, sir."

He shook his head slowly. "No lunch or game for me. The freight yard hired me for this afternoon. I must take work whenever it's offered." He turned to the children. "But you two are free to go after schoolwork. Put on your Sunday best."

Pamela gazed at the young people, their faces beaming with

anticipation. "Then I'll pick you up at noon." Their happiness touched her heart. For an instant, the memory of her daughter, Julia, lost to influenza four years ago, nearly brought her to tears.

Pamela left Edward off at his fraternity and returned to the hotel. Prescott had just come back from a long walk in the village and was about to go to a late-morning appointment with the president. "I want to fend off Fawcett's criticism of Edward."

"You might mention this morning's attempt to injure Edward." She described the incident with the rat poison. "Edward can't say yet with certainty that Isaac Fawcett is the culprit."

"This rivalry is much more serious than I first thought!" Prescott exclaimed. "President Carter will be deeply concerned."

Close to noon, Pamela went by coach to the Clark cabin and picked up the children. At the hotel they met Prescott, who appeared troubled. He spoke into Pamela's ear. "The attack on Edward has upset Carter. We'll talk about it after lunch."

Pamela nodded. "We can't disappoint the children." She put on a smile and led the children to the table. Their faces were brimming at the prospect of a treat, though they looked well fed. Their father had seen to that, most likely denying himself. Their usual diet probably consisted of fruit in season, boiled root vegetables from a friend's garden, stale leftover bread from a bakery on Spring Street, and porridge. They probably had felt little pleasure at the table.

Prescott ordered veal cutlets and scalloped potatoes for the main course and strawberry ice cream for dessert. In the table conversation Mary spoke enthusiastically of her studies at the high school on Spring Street. If she could earn enough money working part-time in a dry-goods store nearby, she would study next year at the new state normal school being built in North Adams and become a teacher like her late mother.

Her brother, Tom, used to struggle in school. He was intelligent but easily bored or distracted. However, he had the athletic physique for baseball. With Edward coaching him, he became an outstanding player for his age and his grades improved.

After lunch, Edward showed the campus to the children. Pamela drew Prescott into a parlor and inquired about his conversation with President Carter.

"When I mentioned Judge Fawcett's threats at breakfast, Carter frowned and said he'd have to hear him out, since Fawcett was a Williams alumnus and gave substantially to the college. Carter is aware of tension among the fraternity brothers. Apparently, Isaac and Edward are rivals for the affection of Mary Clark. Up to now, the president has urged them to resolve their differences in a friendly way. I said that might be impossible in view of this morning's attempted poisoning."

"How did Carter react to that news?" Pamela asked.

"With disbelief," Prescott replied. "He was literally speechless for a moment. Then he said he would discuss the situation with trusted senior professors who were acquainted with the fraternity."

Shortly before game time, Pamela, Prescott, and the children walked to Weston Field at the lower end of Spring Street. A carnival atmosphere pervaded the place. Near the football field, vendors had set up stalls and were selling food and souvenirs to a large, mixed crowd milling about. A band of college musicians was playing popular tunes.

Pamela and Prescott and the children sat on the benches reserved for relatives and friends of the players. The judge and his nephew were also there, looking glum and disinterested. Isaac stood up and surveyed the crowd, then stared lustfully at Mary. He was a tall, heavy young man. His face was handsome, though tending to fleshy. Mary turned her back to him. He smirked.

"What was that all about?" Pamela asked quietly, "Is he threatening you?"

"He only annoys me now. A few months ago, he wanted me to become his girlfriend. I dislike him—he's a sneaky bully—so I refused. Then he started to follow me around town and spread nasty stories about me. Finally, when Edward challenged him to a boxing match and threatened to beat him, he promised to stop."

At this point, Prescott broke into the conversation. "Whitman, the referee from Harvard, has arrived." He pointed to a sportsman surveying the field. "And here comes Parker, the umpire from Yale, and Pamela's namesake, Thompson, the linesman from Princeton."

"So what will they do?" Pamela asked.

"They'll enforce the rules of the game that the teams have agreed to in advance. To the casual observer, football may look like mayhem but Whitman, Parker, and Thompson will keep it under control."

Edward arrived in his uniform and chatted with Mary Clark and her brother. Pamela shot a glance at Judge Fawcett. He was frowning at Edward and his guests. Edward ignored him and soon left to join his teammates waiting nearby. A crowd of several hundred had gathered; their excited chatter filled the cool, crisp air.

Precisely at three o'clock, the two teams jogged onto the field. The Williams men wore thick, white pullover sweaters with a purple *W* on their chests; Amherst wore purple pullovers with a white *A.* Both teams wore knee-length, loose-fitting, thick khaki pants. Thick, uncut hair was all that protected their heads. A roar of cheering voices greeted them.

The Amherst team lined up at one end of the field, eleven

strong, to kick off. Williams faced them at the other end to receive. The crowd's excitement rose to an ear-piercing pitch. At the signal from Herbert Pratt, the Amherst captain, a teammate kicked the ball to Williams, and the Amherst men charged down the field in hot pursuit.

Williams returned the ball ten yards, but made no further progress in the following plays. Edward dropped back and punted the ball fifty yards to Amherst. The Williams men raced downfield and tackled the Amherst receiver for a loss.

For most of the first half, the game remained a scoreless draw. Again and again, first one team, then the other brought the ball forward a few yards, but failed to cross the opposing goal line. In a typical play, muscular young Williams men wrestled their Amherst opponents, trying to clear a path for a ball carrier, usually Edward, the fullback. The Amherst men refused to yield, and Edward tried to force his way through. The result was a great pile of writhing bodies, as in the rugby scrums Pamela had seen years ago in England. When a team couldn't make further headway, it punted the ball to the opponents, who were likewise unsuccessful.

Toward the end of the first half, Williams gained the upper hand and forced the ball over the goal line twice for eight points and successfully kicked the ball over the bar between the twin goal posts for four extra points. The half ended with the score: Williams 12–Amherst 0.

During the game Pamela had divided her attention between the players, chiefly Edward, and the Clark children, who were following the action closely. To Pamela's surprise Mary Clark knew the game well and didn't seem repelled by its brutality. She covered her eyes at times when Edward was buried beneath a pile of Amherst players, and she was visibly relieved when he emerged unscathed.

"Edward has taught the game to me and my brother," Mary explained. "It's not my favorite sport—I prefer baseball—but I enjoy watching Edward. He's so courageous." Pamela agreed. Edward took after his father.

Pamela wondered how Prescott would react to the game's violence in view of his military experience. "It resembles battle," he admitted. "And sometimes it gets out of hand, as at Harvard and Yale, with fistfights and broken bones. But Amherst and Williams play fairly and for the sport of it. Like baseball, football teaches teamwork and builds character. Edward is a good example of the sport at its best."

At halftime the players retired to their benches on the sidelines. Many had cuts and bruises that needed attention. The grueling half hour had drained their energy. A few players appeared nearly exhausted and sat, heads down, breathing heavily. Substitutes were preparing to replace them.

The second half began like the first one with neither team able to score. However, after a quarter of an hour, Amherst was clearly tiring. At the end of a long drive, Edward forced through the Amherst line for another score.

Herbert Pratt returned the kickoff for several yards until Edward tackled him. He fell hard and lay still on the ground. His teammates carried him from the field. When the game resumed, Amherst soon recovered a Williams fumble, gained ground on a penalty, and scored its first touchdown.

Shortly afterward, Williams regained the ball. Lacking their captain, Amherst's defense weakened. Edward dashed through a large hole in the center of the line for sixty-five yards and another touchdown.

Amherst scored after a second Williams fumble. But Edward received the kickoff and sprinted eighty-five yards, weaving and dodging through Amherst defenders, for a touchdown. The extra point attempt was good.

By this time, the sun was beginning to set. Amherst was soundly beaten and agreed with Williams to end the game. The final score was Williams 32–Amherst 10. Like proper sportsmen the players shook hands, and many of the defeated players congratulated Edward on his outstanding performance. Edward inquired about Pratt, but he had already been moved to the Greylock Hotel for observation.

Prescott and Pamela, and Mary and Tom walked onto the field and greeted Edward. Though covered with sweat, grass stains, and bruises, his face shone with profound inner satisfaction. His father patted him on the shoulder and Pamela shook his hand. Mary and Tom stood shyly a step back, admiring him, until he beckoned and gave each of them a brotherly hug.

Prescott told Edward, "We'll walk you back to the fraternity house. When you're ready, we'll eat a light supper at the Greylock Hotel, then meet President Carter at the village opera house. He has invited the football club and their parents, guests, and supporters from the community to a reception and dance."

At the hotel, Pamela was the first to recognize Herbert Pratt, sitting at a table in the dining room with an Amherst teammate. During the game she had admired his valiant attempts to rally his dispirited teammates. She beckoned the others and they approached his table.

"It's good to see you up and about," said Edward solicitously as the two friends shook hands.

"Your shoulder slammed into my chest and knocked the wind out of me," said Pratt. "For a moment my heart stopped and I thought that was it. But the doctor couldn't find any lasting damage and told me to rest overnight. He'll check me in the morning." Pratt glanced at Mary, then at Edward.

"My friend, Mary Clark, from Williamstown," said Edward.

"Pleased to meet you, Miss Clark." He gave her a searching, approving look, and then asked the others, "Would you join us?"

Edward deferred to his father, who agreed, and a large table was formed, where Mary was seated across from Pratt and alongside Edward. They ordered a light meal, since there would be more refreshments at the opera house later.

Pamela had expected their conversation to focus on football, but instead Prescott led Pratt to speak about his large, wealthy, and socially prominent family in New York. They were major dealers in the oil refinery business. All the men in the family went to Amherst. After graduation in June, Pratt would go on to a career in business. Like Edward, he had a wide range of interests, including the arts.

For all his privilege, he seemed genuinely interested in Mary, a mill worker's daughter, and her hopes for a higher education. He asked about the new normal school in North Adams for the training of teachers and encouraged her to attend. "My father founded a similar school in Brooklyn, Pratt Institute, for worthy students in engineering, design, and architecture. Our programs are open and affordable to all young people."

Edward mentioned Mary's interest in drawing. "She sketches everything that catches her fancy."

Pratt gave her an encouraging nod. "Keep it up, Miss Clark. Drawing is a universal language and a key element in the training we offer at Pratt Institute, not just freehand, but also mechanical and architectural drawing."

Though a young man, he spoke with natural authority. Pamela had no doubt that he would "captain" or take charge of any organization to which he belonged.

At moments in the conversation the social and cultural gap between Mary and these wealthy, educated young men, Edward and Pratt, seemed to overwhelm her. Then she'd glance at Pamela, who would reassure her with a confident smile. Earlier in the day, after they had first spoken at length about her desire for education and a career, Pamela had told her, "You are young, healthy, and intelligent. Aim high, choose wisely, and with luck you'll get there."

As supper came to an end, Pratt's eyelids were drooping. He

gazed at Mary for a long moment, and then said, "I'll skip this evening's entertainment. I've done more than enough 'dancing' on Weston Field for one day. So I'll say good night to you, Miss Clark. It's been a pleasure. I hope we meet again." To Edward, he said, "I'll see you next November at Amherst from the sidelines on Pratt Field, if not sooner."

He bid good-bye to the others, then walked stiffly erect from the dining room.

That evening at the opera house President Carter showed Pamela and her companions into a spacious hall festooned with purple and yellow ribbons. A large banner on a wall congratulated the team. A student orchestra sat at the far end of the room playing a lively rendition of "The Mountains," the college song, plus a medley of popular waltzes.

For the occasion Pamela had groomed Mary Clark, helped her into a simple blue frock, and arranged her hair into a chignon. Edward Prescott was her escort. Other members of the football club had also invited young women, mostly from nearby colleges, and had lodged them in the village. At first sight of the crowd, Mary seemed a little anxious. But Pamela declared that her beauty was equal to any of the other young women, and in her clothes she wasn't greatly inferior. She shouldn't worry. After all, this was the celebration of a sporting event, rather than a formal affair. The other young women wore simple dresses like hers.

When it came time to dance, Edward's teammates called on him to begin. As the orchestra struck up the first waltz, he led Mary onto the floor. They whirled once around the hall to general applause. Then his teammates and their female guests joined in.

Pamela watched the young couple with amazement. Edward was as light on his feet as a ballet dancer. Mary, the machinist's daughter, followed him elegantly. They must have danced together before. When they returned, she asked them.

"Yes," Edward replied. "We often dance. It's our favorite entertainment." He turned to his father. "Now may I dance with Pamela while you dance with Mary?"

Everyone agreed. The orchestra began a schottische, and the two couples set forth, joined by most of those present.

While dancing with Edward, Pamela was reminded again how remarkable this strong young man was. On the football field he had charged through the opposing line like a bull, but following the scrimmage he had helped a dazed opponent to his feet. And after the game he inquired as to the condition of Pratt, the injured Amherst captain. Now on the dance floor he was as gentle and considerate as if she were delicate porcelain.

As their dance ended, she questioned him, "You've said that your parents were absorbed in their own differences and sent you away to boarding school. Tell me, who has influenced you most as you grew up?"

He smiled. "Even from a distance Jeremiah served as my model of courage and integrity. At school, the headmaster was like a father to me, the wisest, kindest man I've ever known."

At an intermission, Pamela asked Prescott for his impressions of Mary.

"She's a lovely young woman, well informed and mature beyond her years, and I'm pleased that Edward is fond of her."

Toward the end of the evening, President Carter drew Prescott and Pamela aside. "You may have noticed that Judge Fawcett isn't here. After the game he came up to me and said, 'You won't see my money or me on this campus until Edward Prescott and his confederates cease persecuting my nephew and apologize. I also expect you to reprimand them.' "

"What are you going to do?" Prescott asked.

"Tonight, I haven't spoken about this unfortunate development. That would spoil the party. But on Monday, with the advice of the senior professors, I'll form a committee to study the situation in that fraternity and report to me in a couple of weeks.

At this time, I don't want to prejudge the results, but I'll keep you informed."

When Carter moved on, Pamela whispered to Prescott, "I hope the college authorities will ignore the judge's threats and simply consider the facts. Edward and his comrades merely relieved the workers' distress; they didn't publicly criticize the management's policies."

"I agree entirely, Pamela. At lunch, tomorrow, I'll warn Edward of the college's impending investigation. Now we should leave after saying good night to him and Mary. They'll dance on for another hour."

"And we need a few minutes to ourselves," Pamela added.

As they walked back to the hotel, Pamela said to Prescott, "It's unfortunate that Judge Fawcett has cast a shadow on this weekend with your son. Still, through this controversy I've come to appreciate even more Edward's sterling quality. He's done what's right even at some risk to himself."

"And I'm pleased that you two have become friends. He and I have also come closer together." Without a word, they linked arms for the first time and walked quietly on at a leisurely pace. Pamela felt at ease with this greater intimacy. Over the weekend, she had come to know him so much better through his son.

As they climbed the steps to the hotel's veranda, the thought flashed through her mind, should she invite him to her room? *Not yet,* said a small voice of caution. Nonetheless, under the pale glow of a gas lantern, she embraced him and they kissed good night.

The next day, Pamela and Prescott went to the fraternity house and roused Edward on time for an early lunch at the hotel. His face still bruised, he grimaced with pain as he eased himself into a chair. "In a couple of days," he remarked jovially, "the stiffness will go away, and I'll be fine."

Prescott then told Edward about President Carter's plan to investigate the fraternity. "What do you think of it?"

The young man replied, "The college has to help the fraternity resolve this conflict. I hope the committee will agree that Isaac Fawcett was responsible for the attempt to poison me and that one of his allies was also involved, either supplying the poison or inserting it in my porridge. Our own internal investigation is nearly complete and the case against Isaac is convincing. He should leave the college. If that happens, I'll be greatly relieved."

After lunch, Edward rode with them to the station and waved a cheery good-bye. They watched from the train window as he gradually disappeared from view. Pamela turned to Prescott and asked, "What will the college do with Isaac? Expel him?"

Prescott shook his head. "It will threaten Isaac with expulsion but allow him to withdraw. In any case, Judge Fawcett is going to be very angry and lash out at me as well as at the college."

"That can't be helped," said Pamela. "Unfortunately, he'll be all the more resolved to block our attempt to exonerate Harry Miller."

CHAPTER 8

The Dark Side

New York City
Saturday, November 17

Meanwhile in New York, Harry Miller was investigating Michael Sullivan. When Harry first realized Sullivan's rigid pattern of proper behavior, he had almost despaired of ever exposing his true character and thwarting his apparent efforts to gain legal control of Theresa and her boy. Then Mrs. Donovan had reported him sneaking out late on Saturday. So, on this night, Harry hid across the street from the house in the hope of discovering Sullivan's secret.

After guests had left and the family had retired, and the servants had closed down the house, a dark figure emerged from a side door, scurried to Broadway, and hailed a cab. Convinced it was Sullivan, Harry followed him into Chelsea's Tenderloin district, notorious for its brothels, saloons, and gambling dens, as well as for the corrupt police who protected the vice in return for sharing in the profits.

The cab turned into a darkened side street and stopped in front of a large, three-story private residence close to Broadway. The shades were drawn; the building was dark, save for a small gaslight over the entrance. A servant opened for Sullivan and he disappeared inside. Harry waited nearby for a few minutes, observing a few more men arrive. Finally, realizing that Sullivan would stay for a while, Harry left to do more research, lest he walk blindly into a viper's nest.

Early on Sunday, Harry went back to his colleague, the private investigator Barney Flynn. Over morning coffee in Flynn's tiny office, Harry asked him about the private residence off Broadway.

"I know the one you mean, an elegant bordello called the Phoenix Club. Let's walk by it on the way to church."

Harry raised an eyebrow.

Barney smiled. "I have helpful contacts there."

The building appeared quiet as they approached, but shades were up and windows open. Harry caught the strong scent of tobacco and a hint of opium.

Flynn nodded. "This is an expensive den of iniquity that offers high stakes gambling, beautiful women, and various means of intoxication." An attractive woman appeared at one of the upstairs windows and drew a deep breath of fresh air. She glanced at Harry and Flynn on the sidewalk below and gave them a sleepy smile.

Flynn waved to her, then turned to Harry. "Lucretia La Belle, she calls herself. Can you believe that's her name? She's a courtesan of the better sort, the bastard daughter of one of our 'Captains of Industry.' He's a silent partner in the business and backs her financially—for him it's a piquant private joke. We'll soon see her at church, and I'll introduce you. She'll know Sullivan."

St. Martin's was a modest brick church, nearly empty when Harry and Flynn arrived. A stout, middle-aged priest in black cassock, white surplice, and biretta stepped out of the confessional box in the rear of the nave and hurried down the aisle toward the sacristy. As he passed the two men, he glanced at Harry, threw Flynn a wry smile, and asked, "Barney, who's your friend?"

"Harry Miller. A good man—once lost, now found."

The priest paused, stared intently at Harry, then nodded. "Come to the rectory anytime and we'll get acquainted."

The church filled up quickly with artisans, maids, and other servants, softly greeting each other. They were mostly Irish, thought Harry, judging from their accents.

"Look over there," whispered Flynn, and pointed with his eyes to Lucretia entering a pew on the far side. She had come alone, but she nodded and smiled friendly greetings to the congregants nearby.

"She says church is her tonic, and she comes here regularly," Flynn explained. "The priest says she's welcome but shouldn't go to Communion. That's fine with her."

Lucretia's dress was dark-hued, simple and modest but of high quality and exquisitely tailored to her beautiful form. A tasteful veil covered her hair. Her fine clothing, a certain grace in her movements, and an aristocratic bearing set her apart from the plain, toil-worn women who were the majority of the congregation.

After the Mass, Flynn steered Harry toward Lucretia, and they met at the church's front door. "Barnabas Flynn!" she exclaimed. "What a pleasure to meet you here." She gazed at Harry, her eyes dancing with curiosity. "Who's your friend, Barney? I haven't seen him before."

"He's Harry Miller, a distinguished member of the honorable fraternity of private detectives. He has come to me on a private matter that might be of interest to you. Shall we have lunch together?"

"It's my day off, Barney. Keep it light, please. My spirit needs uplifting after what I've been through last night with the dregs of upper-class male humanity."

"Harry's story will touch your tender heart, my dear. Lunch, then?"

She smiled. "Let's go to a nice, quiet place."

The Donegal was an unassuming restaurant located in a decent block of West Twenty-third Street off Eighth Avenue. A waiter standing by the door gave Lucretia a sharp, disapproving glance as she and her companions entered, but Flynn countered with a withering stare. The waiter instantly put on a courteous expression, even bowed slightly as he showed Lucretia to a table in a quiet corner. Barney gallantly eased her into a chair. With a glint of amusement in her eyes, she lifted her chin and surveyed the room, momentarily playing the role of princess in the company of a pair of scruffy attendants.

When they had ordered, Lucretia asked Harry, "Why are you interested in the house where I work?" Her tone was light, but the firm set of her jaw indicated that she wasn't being coy. She wanted a direct, honest answer.

Harry replied in the same spirit. "I'm privately investigating one of your customers, Michael Sullivan. For years he has abused his sister, whom I have come to love. Recently, he has opposed our intention to marry. I believe he also seeks custody of her nine-year-old son and would be harmful to the boy." Harry met her eye. "What do you think of Sullivan?"

The waiter arrived with their lunch: lean, thinly sliced, smoked ham on rye sandwiches with potato salad on the side. To drink, the men had Ruppert's Ale; Lucretia, a bottle of Saratoga Spa water.

When the waiter left, Lucretia returned to Harry's question. "You correctly assume that I know Sullivan, a snake disguised as a gentleman. He came to us with good character references, including one from Judge Noah Fawcett. On three different Saturday nights, he behaved like a gentleman through most of his visit, gambling moderately. But each time, late in the evening, he turned nasty toward a woman. After the first night he was cautioned. But on the second night, he was warned more severely. He also lost heavily at the roulette wheel. Last night, he gambled on credit and lost again. When he also abused a third woman, he was ejected from the club."

"What kind of abuse, precisely, was he guilty of?" Harry had in the back of his mind Michael's abuse of his sister.

"He called the women dirty whores, stupid cows, sex toys, and the like. His intercourse with them was rough and unfeeling, reeking of contempt. I called him a pig and said he could take his money elsewhere."

"And how did he react?"

"As he left, he threatened to go to his friends in the police and have us closed down."

Harry shook his head. "That might have been a bluff. He would have to weigh the risk of injuring his sterling reputation for integrity against the pleasure of revenge. I guess he would rather protect his reputation."

"I hope you're right." Lucretia rolled her eyes. "The club is nonetheless concerned. When Barney introduced you, my heart sank. I thought you might be a police detective and about to investigate us."

Harry waved off her fears. "Don't worry about the police. Your business, I'm sure, is a lucrative investment for them. However, if they were called in, they might demand more protection money. You should watch out for Reverend Parkhurst and his moral crusaders. They might close down the club and put most of you in prison."

"What use will you make of what I've revealed to you?" Her voice quivered.

"Don't worry, Lucretia. My main concern now is to prevent Michael Sullivan from hurting the woman I love or her son. I'll find enough evidence to discredit him without incriminating you."

* * *

After lunch, Harry and Barney returned to the latter's office. "I strongly suspect," said Harry, "that Sullivan has been thrown out of more than one brothel. Would you check with other madams of your acquaintance? He might have carried on this secret life for years. I'd like overwhelming evidence of his immorality."

"How would you use it?" Barney seemed concerned.

"Discreetly. I may not have to expose him publicly. That would cost him his job and deprive his aged parents of support. It would also deeply grieve them. That in turn would upset my friend, his sister Theresa. Hopefully, my threat of exposure might force him to cease harassing her and allow her to marry me without hindrance. However, I wouldn't hesitate to bring my evidence to a magistrate if Sullivan attempted to gain custody of a child, as I think he might abuse him or her. Finally, if the police were to arrest him for assaulting a woman, even a prostitute, I'd add my evidence to theirs to ensure that he wasn't let off lightly but went to prison where he belongs."

"I'm happy to do this favor for you, Harry. Well-connected scum like Sullivan get away with murder."

"While you are investigating his vices, would you also find out how he pays for them?"

"Certainly. Sullivan's salary is probably modest. If his private investments don't yield as much as he needs, he would be tempted to cheat investors who trusted in him, such as Judge Noah Fawcett."

Chapter 9

A Tammany Tiger

Monday, November 19

Early in the morning, Pamela was back at her office desk, waiting eagerly for news from Harry, when he appeared at her door. She cleared file boxes off a chair for him. "What did you learn about Michael Sullivan while Prescott and I were in Williamstown?"

"He leads a double life. On Saturday nights he visits the Phoenix Club, a high-priced bordello, and gambles away money that isn't his. My friend Barney Flynn and I suspect that he might steal from accounts at the bank, including Judge Fawcett's. We'll look for evidence of fraud."

"That's encouraging news. We may be on the right track. By the way, Prescott and I encountered Judge Noah Fawcett. As if our relationship with him wasn't already complicated, he became irate when he learned that our Edward was 'persecuting' his nephew Isaac." Pamela explained the tense situation in Edward's fraternity. "The college president will investigate. Whatever the outcome, it's certain that Fawcett is angry and even more likely to obstruct our efforts to clear your name."

As Pamela spoke of Judge Fawcett, Harry's expression was

inscrutable. He appeared to have gone beyond hating the man. When she finished, Harry remarked indifferently, "True, there'll be more venom in his bite. We can deal with that. What's our next step?"

"We should investigate the cabdriver's murder, beginning with Dan Kelly, the man who actually killed him. Did he act on his own or on behalf of another person?"

Stroking his chin, Harry recalled the official version. "The Tammany witnesses claimed that the two men quarreled outside the Tiger's Den. Tempers flared. They insulted each other. The cabdriver grew angry, cursed, and drew a knife. Kelly also drew a knife and stabbed the driver in the throat."

"That sounds like self-defense," Pamela agreed. "But can we believe that the Tammany witnesses just happened to be at the scene at that moment?"

"They were paid off," Harry replied. "Let's visit the scene and ask if anyone else witnessed the incident."

The Tiger's Den was on a narrow side street off West Twenty-third. On the sign outside, a Bengal tiger bared his teeth. As Harry walked in, several older workingmen were sitting at battered tables, playing cards, smoking, and drinking beer. Fresh sawdust covered the floor. Spittoons were strategically placed within spitting range. The foul smell of stale tobacco assaulted Harry's nostrils.

At the far end of the long, highly polished bar, two men were drinking beer and loudly exchanging views on a nearby construction project. The older of the two, a bearded, scowling giant, about forty, wore a boldly patterned green and black coat and a black derby hat and spoke with an air of authority. His younger, clean-shaven companion referred to the giant as Big Tim.

Harry stepped up to the bar. The bartender, an older man with a permanent smile on his face, was washing glasses and humming a tune. He seemed to pay no attention to the discussion at the end of the bar.

Harry caught the man's eye and spoke in a friendly way. "A Ruppert, if you please." When the beer arrived, Harry remarked, "I'm new in the neighborhood. Is it safe? They tell me that a cabdriver was stabbed here a few years ago."

"It was the winter of '87, late in the afternoon," the bartender replied. "We have fights on the street and sometimes a man is hauled to the hospital, bruised and bloody. But this time the driver died." The bartender wiped a glass, absentmindedly, recalling the incident.

"Did you know the cabdriver?"

"Yeh, Tony Palermo, a big, tough guy. He was sometimes here between fares. Used to flash a knife. 'For protection,' he'd say. He had to take customers into dangerous parts of the city. On the day he died, I was standing at the window looking out on the street and saw him quarrel with a small guy, Kelly, an occasional patron here. They began to shout at each other. Tony seemed to draw a knife. Kelly also pulled a knife and cut Tony's throat. He was probably dead before he hit the ground." The bartender put the clean glass into a rack above his head.

"Sounds like self-defense," said Harry evenly. "Did you personally see Tony draw his knife?"

At the end of the bar Big Tim rapped loudly and yelled, "Another beer, Joe! Right now!"

The bartender stiffened and mumbled to Harry, "I couldn't actually see one. His back was to me. But witnesses remembered a knife." He hurried to the tap, drew a beer, and took it to the giant. He gave the bartender a hard look and muttered something under his breath. The bartender said in a quavering voice, "Yes, Mr. Smith," and returned to Harry with a bill.

"Stranger, you'd better get out of here." His hand was shaking.

Harry flashed a knowing smile, paid for his beer, and left.

* * *

Pamela was waiting for Harry near a bakery facing the saloon. When they met, Harry described his experience inside. "The bartender started to say that the cabdriver might not have drawn a knife on Kelly, but a tough-looking man at the bar cut short our conversation."

"I'll try to find out the truth from a neighborhood lady," Pamela said. She had previously noticed a slender, elderly woman out on the street. Now she entered the bakery and Pamela followed her. The woman asked for a small loaf of bread.

"Would you like it sliced, Miss Mulligan?" asked the baker in a tone of unusual respect.

"Yes, please, Mr. Hogan." She began a conversation about his artistic display of tarts and small cakes, and then asked about his family and the state of his health and his business. When they moved on to crime and other social problems in the neighborhood, Pamela expressed interest. Miss Mulligan quickly involved her in the conversation. Pamela mentioned that her job involved searching for missing children and that she had worked at St. Barnabas Mission on Mulberry Street.

"How interesting!" Miss Mulligan exclaimed. "I'd like to hear more. But we shouldn't take up Mr. Hogan's precious time. Shall we buy our things and go up to my rooms for tea?"

"Delighted," Pamela replied. She bought a couple of apple tarts, Miss Mulligan paid for her bread, and they bid Mr. Hogan good-bye.

Miss Mulligan's sitting room was above the bakery on the street side of the building. The tea table stood at the window overlooking the street and the saloon. "Call me Florence," said Miss Mulligan as she hung her coat and hat on a rack.

Pamela gave her name and began to speak of her work. Prodded on by her host, Pamela described her recent search for Ruth Colt, a young black maid who disappeared earlier in the year from the Crawford home on Washington Square. "Unfortunately, I found her dead, the victim of a brutal murder. The most I could do was to arrange for her proper burial."

Throughout Pamela's account, Florence appeared enthralled, lips parted, eyes wide. At the end, she shook her head. "Such a sad end for the girl!" Tears filled her eyes. But she quickly recovered, set the tea table, and waved Pamela to a chair.

While tea was being poured, Pamela studied the sitting room. Shelves of books covered a long wall. Florence followed Pamela's gaze and remarked, "I'm here alone much of the day. Good books keep me company."

"May I ask for your favorite author?"

"Recently I've discovered Arthur Conan Doyle." She drew two books from a nearby shelf and handed them to Pamela: *The Adventures of Sherlock Holmes* and *The Memoirs of Sherlock Holmes.*

Pamela scanned the contents and recognized a few stories from the *Strand Magazine* that Prescott had talked about. "Isn't the author presently in this country on a lecture tour?"

"Yes, I've recently heard him here in New York. He gives a good impression of a British gentleman and speaks as well as he writes."

"What draws you to these stories?"

"The art of detection. I learn to observe things in a systematic way, like a scientist, with attention to detail. Here at my window I study people on the street. At night, I enter my impressions in a journal; sometimes I sketch interesting faces."

Pamela gestured to the saloon across the street. "What goes on there? The sign over the door says it's the Tiger's Den."

Florence studied Pamela for a moment before continuing hesitantly, "I call it the 'Devil's Den.' "

With a nod and a smile Pamela encouraged Florence to continue.

"It serves as Tammany Hall's neighborhood clubhouse. For an hour or so during the day, Big Tim Smith, the boss of this ward, meets with the block captain to consider requests for help with food or rent or various personal problems. If you are in the party's favor and vote as directed, they might help you. They also offer protection and other services for a fee. If you refuse to pay or cross them in any way, they might break your legs, smash your windows, lame your horse, drive your customers away, or generally cause you pain."

"You speak bravely to a stranger, Florence."

"You aren't a stranger, Pamela. Your reputation has gone before you among those of us concerned for the poor. In the bakery I recognized you from St. Barnabas, where I used to help out when I was stronger. Fret not, I don't speak out in public." She nodded toward the saloon across the street. "I respect the tiger's teeth and its claws."

"Nonetheless, could you tell me what you might have seen seven years ago when the cabdriver Tony Palermo was stabbed in this street?"

"I saw it all." Florence drank deeply of her tea, then explained that Big Tim demanded cabdrivers to pay an extra fee for parking a cab in front of the Tiger's Den. Palermo refused, insisting he'd already paid for a city license. "The streets belonged to everybody," he declared, and he would make sure that other cabdrivers also refused. The boss grew angry and threatened to put him out of business permanently. Palermo retorted that he could take care of himself.

"Then one late afternoon in January outside the saloon, he quarreled with Dan Kelly from Tammany Hall. You must know the rest of the story. It was written up in the papers."

Pamela nodded. "But could you tell me if the cabdriver drew a knife on Kelly?"

"I don't think so. Palermo raised his hands, perhaps to grab Kelly and shake him or slap his face or push him away. Quick as a flash, Kelly stabbed him. By that time, men had come out of the saloon and were looking on. I watched very closely. A well-dressed stranger tried to stop Palermo's bleeding. Big Tim took a knife from Palermo's belt and put it on the pavement by his outstretched hand, then reached into Palermo's pocket and pulled out what looked like bundles of money."

"How could you see all that?" Pamela was growing skeptical. Perhaps Florence spent too much time alone reading detective stories.

Florence smiled. She opened a drawer in the tea table and pulled out an opera glass. "I keep this handy."

Pamela's doubt vanished. "Had you seen Kelly before?"

"Yes, he had come to the Tiger's Den a few times but wasn't a regular patron."

"Kelly's nickname is The Knife."

Florence shuddered. "I suspected he was a professional assassin and perhaps Big Tim hired him. I decided to stay out of it."

"Did Officer Malone question you?"

"He tried. I told him I was in the kitchen when the incident happened. That's what I also told Mr. Miller, the police detective, a few days later. I heard that he got into trouble afterward for trying to open up the case—lost his job and went to prison. That was a warning to me. I've never since spoken about it."

"Why are you telling me?"

"An hour ago, I recognized Mr. Miller in the street before I went downstairs to the bakery. For seven years that murder has troubled me. I think of it every time I see the ward boss. He should be brought to trial and punished if proven guilty. I believe you and Miller are trying to rectify an injustice. I'm still fearful, but I'll talk to my friend Joe Meagher, the bartender across the street, and see what we can do to help. He knows a lot but keeps his mouth shut."

"That's courageous of you."

"It's what my brother Matt would have wanted. Many in this ward remember Matt and dislike Big Tim. They stand behind me. One day, we'll force him out of the club."

Over tea and pastry, Pamela learned that Florence was the spinster sister of Matt Mulligan, well-liked deceased boss of the ward. For years she kept house for him and carried out much of the ward's assistance to its needy residents.

"Matt was a good man," said his sister. "He got out the votes without hurting anyone. When he died, I stayed here and have continued to help the needy. They are my family. But Big Tim Smith, the new ward boss, has made my life difficult. He's a mean, greedy man, hungry for power. He demands that I spy on people and tell him how they vote. I'm supposed to stop helping those who vote the wrong way."

"Tell me more about Big Tim."

A flicker of distaste flashed across Florence's face. "He's been the boss here in the sixteenth ward for only a couple of years. Before that he was in Sing Sing."

Pamela raised an eyebrow in surprise.

Florence smiled wryly. "While alderman for Chelsea, he was convicted of fraud and taking bribes in the great 'Boodle' scandal."

"I vaguely recall," said Pamela, "that Jake Sharp's street railway company bribed several members of the Board of Aldermen for the franchise to run a line down Lower Broadway."

"Big Tim was the ringleader of the thieves," Florence explained. "A competing company cried foul and forced the district attorney to investigate. He found that Sharp had paid twelve aldermen, mostly Democrats from Tammany Hall, about $40,000 each for their votes."

"A princely sum!" Pamela exclaimed. "Each alderman could have built a mansion on Fifth Avenue and lived the rest of his life in splendor. How could they imagine that they would get away with such a huge deception?"

"Hard to fathom indeed," Florence replied. "Their lust for wealth and power overrode their common sense."

"I must leave now," said Pamela, shaking Florence's hand, "I'll go out the back door. Big Tim might grow suspicious if he learned that I was visiting you." She left her card on the tea table. "If you need help, Florence, you can reach me at the office on Irving Place or at my apartment on Fourteenth Street."

Pamela met Harry in a tearoom a few blocks away and reported on her visit with Florence Mulligan. "We may have found a new suspect, Big Tim Smith. He and Palermo had quarreled over a parking fee."

Harry nodded. "You might be right, Pamela. Big Tim looks mean enough. I can imagine him paying Kelly to injure, if not kill, Palermo. The fatal thrust to the throat might have been unintended. We need to find out how well Big Tim knew Dan Kelly. Unfortunately, Joe Meagher, the bartender, is too fearful and cautious to be of much help now."

"Then we must begin to investigate their relationship from Kelly's side."

"Right. It's a fact that Dan Kelly killed Palermo. But did he act in self-defense or for another personal reason? Or, had he acted on behalf of someone else, such as Big Tim?"

That afternoon, in a crowded lunchroom next door to Tammany Hall, Harry recognized a retired police officer sitting alone at a table and reading a newspaper.

"May we join you?" Harry asked.

The officer glanced up from his paper, blinked, and smiled. "Miller, I haven't seen you in years. Sit down. I like company." He put the paper aside and tentatively studied Pamela.

"The missus?"

"My partner, Mrs. Pamela Thompson. We're taking a lunch break."

During the meal the two men caught up on news about old mutual acquaintances. In the exchange, Harry managed to bring up Dan Kelly. "What's he doing these days?"

"He's one of the guards at Tammany Hall. You'll see him at

the main door in an hour. During elections he earns city money as a poll watcher. Eats and sleeps in Sadie's boardinghouse up the street. Otherwise, he's in Tammany Hall's poolroom."

Harry looked doubtful. "He used to be called The Knife and spent some time in jail for cutting up a guy. Has he changed his ways?"

"I guess you can say that he's now on the right side of the law," the officer replied. "I'm told that he gathers information for the police and collects payments for their protective services."

Pamela caught Harry's eye. He nodded slightly. So Kelly was now a police informer and a feared thug who forced neighborhood merchants and proprietors of gambling dens and houses of prostitution to pay into the police department's protection rackets.

After lunch, Pamela and Harry observed Kelly from a distance outside the busy Fourteenth Street entrance to Tammany Hall. He was a short, thin man, nearly bald, with sharp features and a sallow complexion. For about an hour, he studied everyone entering the building with quick, keen glances. Then another man took his place.

While Pamela went off to Sadie's boardinghouse, Harry followed Kelly into a saloon. He walked up to the bar, where the bartender offered him a beer, "compliments of the house." Kelly took the beer without a smile or a thank-you and joined a pair of ruffians at a table off to a side of the room. He appeared to give them instructions, his hands chopping the air to stress his points.

While nursing a beer, Harry noticed how most customers watched Kelly with fearful eyes and darting glances. A few others couldn't fully conceal their dislike. He didn't appear to notice. Behind Kelly's back, another man slouched in a chair, his cap pulled down to his eyebrows, and mimicked Kelly's gestures. Alcohol must have fortified his courage, Harry thought.

His beer finished, Kelly left the saloon, while his companions remained at the table. Harry picked up his glass and approached the slouching man. "May I join you?" Without waiting for an answer, Harry signaled a waiter for two beers and sat down. "I'm Harry, could I have a word with you?"

"Sure. They call me Fred."

Harry asked evenly, "I wonder why Dan Kelly gets special treatment here?"

"He has the ear of the ward boss and can do favors for people he likes. The bartender is one of them."

"Do you know Kelly well?"

"Yes, but I don't care to talk about him when I'm drunk. I'll go home and sober up. Thanks for the beer, but I couldn't drink it." He walked out the door on shaky legs. Seconds later, Kelly's two companions got up from their table and followed Fred.

As soon as they were out the door, Harry went after them.

Fred walked a couple of blocks and turned into a narrow passageway. The two ruffians followed him. Harry kept a short distance. When he rounded the corner into the passage, he saw that one of the ruffians had pinioned Fred's arms behind his back and the other had drawn a knife.

Harry dashed up to them and knocked the knife out of the ruffian's hand with his blackjack. The two ruffians fled, leaving Fred swaying on his feet. Harry caught him before he fell. "I saw that those two men meant to harm you. May I take you home?"

"I'd be obliged to you. They knocked me on the head. I'm dizzy."

Harry took him under the arm and they walked slowly to the entrance of a boardinghouse. Harry rang the bell.

The landlady opened and exclaimed, "Mr. Grant! You look dreadful."

Harry explained what had happened, then helped Fred up the stairs to his room. Harry told him, "Stay in the house. The ruffians may lurk in the neighborhood for a few days, waiting for you. Your landlady will care for you. I'll see you tomorrow. Hopefully, you'll feel better."

Meanwhile at Sadie's boardinghouse, Pamela met the landlady and identified herself as a private investigator looking for a missing young woman who was said to have known Dan Kelly. Pamela concocted the woman's name and general physical appearance.

"She's not living here," said the landlady. "Mr. Kelly lives alone in a small basement apartment. I keep track of who comes and goes. He moved in about seven years ago and is a quiet tenant who regularly pays the rent."

"Does he have any female visitors?"

"From time to time, he brings one home but she doesn't stay overnight. That's not allowed. In the first few months he used to have a particular visitor but she stopped coming. I think they had a falling out."

Pamela showed interest.

The landlady shook her head. "She's not your missing young woman. Kelly called her Alice Curran."

With this new lead Pamela narrowed her search to Alice Curran. She might have known Kelly about the time of the cabdriver's murder. Her family name was common Irish. There would be dozens of Alice Currans. Still, she might have had a brush or two with the law and be known to the police. Pamela would speak to her friend, Larry White.

Larry had come home from police headquarters for supper. Pamela joined the family meal. When the table was cleared, Larry lingered. “I think you have a question for me, Pamela.”

“Yes, have you heard of Alice Curran?” Pamela briefed him on the Kelly investigation and described Alice. “I know she’s a needle in the proverbial haystack. Nonetheless, could you find her for me?” She gave him the bits of information that she had gathered.

“I’ll try,” he replied. “I assume that she was a prostitute and might appear in police lists from 1887. But don’t raise your hopes. By now, she might have lost her wits or her life.”

CHAPTER 10

A Missing Person

Tuesday, November 20

The next morning, Pamela and Harry went to Fred Grant's boardinghouse and inquired about him. Mrs. Scott, his landlady, told them that he had been with her for several years and worked as a clerk in Tammany Hall. He had occasional visitors, all of them presentable men and women. She didn't know their names or what they did.

Pamela and Harry climbed upstairs to his room. Fully dressed, he was sitting at a table, the remains of breakfast before him. He had sobered up but complained of a headache that reminded him of yesterday's assault.

Harry introduced Pamela as a social worker and friend. "Can I be of help?" she asked Grant sympathetically. "How shocking to be attacked in broad daylight!" She offered him a small oilcloth bag filled with crushed ice. "Put this on your head. It'll reduce the swelling. Your landlady has more crushed ice for you in the kitchen. As the ice melts, the bag will leak a little. Wrap it in a towel."

He put the bag on his head and leaned back. "I appreciate

your kindness." He motioned for them to sit facing him at the table.

"Your head must still be hurting," Pamela continued. "So we won't be long. Do you know the two ruffians who attacked you?"

He nodded. "Paddy McBride and Bill Cook. They work in Kelly's protection racket."

Harry added in an aside to Pamela, "According to Officer Malone back in January 1887, they also witnessed Kelly stab the cabdriver."

"Yes, I recall," commented Pamela ironically, "they just happened to be there at the time." She turned to Grant. "Tell us why Kelly attacked you."

"He must have noticed that I made fun of him behind his back. He demands respect and resents that I've always disapproved of him. So, he set out to punish me."

"Was he going to kill you?"

"No, typically, he would have slashed my face to leave a scar. That would serve as a warning to me and others never to speak ill of Dan Kelly."

Pamela winced. "Your dislike for Kelly appears deep. How long have you known him?"

"We grew up together in Hell's Kitchen. He was born in a brothel near the docks and raised in foster homes. A runt, he learned early in life how to use a knife to survive. Over the years, he has perfected that skill. He can thrust and slash faster than the eye can follow, and he throws the knife with deadly accuracy."

"Amazing!" Pamela encouraged Grant to continue.

He smiled wryly. "Once in our youth, we went to a circus and watched a man in fancy clothes throwing knives at a pretty girl standing with her back to a large board. His knives came very close but never scratched her. Kelly went right home, drew a figure on a board, and started throwing knives like the man in the circus. He was soon good at it and tried to force neighborhood girls to stand at the board. Their parents called in the police. By that time, he was already a petty thief so the police put him away."

"Why does Tammany Hall allow such a dangerous man in its organization?"

"They think of him as a vicious guard dog that they control and can put to good use."

"We know," said Harry, "that Kelly stands guard at the entrance to Tammany Hall and watches the polls during elections. Is that all they ask of him?"

Fred fell silent. "My mouth has a way of getting me into trouble. I've already said more than I should about Dan Kelly, and not just yesterday in the saloon. I'm grateful for your visit and for the ice. I'm beginning to feel better already. I'll rest now."

Harry handed his card to Grant. "Later, you might want to talk to us again and figure out a way to protect yourself. Kelly will hear of this incident and will order his ruffians to try again to punish you. Why should you have to live in fear? He's a bully. Isn't it time to confront him?"

Grant replied with a doubtful smile.

In the Irving Street office after lunch, Pamela asked Harry, "When Fred Grant considers his situation, do you think he'll get back to us?"

"I'm worried for him," Harry replied. "He may go to Kelly, confess he was drunk when he mimicked him, and beg for forgiveness. Kelly would then ask about us driving away his ruffians. Grant would have to admit that we had helped him. Kelly might pretend to forgive him and defer punishment to a later, more opportune date."

"So, do you think we should deal cautiously with Mr. Grant?"

Harry nodded. "Kelly might use him to mislead us, even draw us into danger." Harry glanced at his watch. "An hour from now,

Kelly will return to his post at the entrance to Tammany Hall. Fred Grant will have rested, thought things over, and may have come to a decision. Let's see if he goes to Kelly."

A few minutes before three o'clock in the afternoon, Pamela and Harry hid themselves in a coffee shop on Fourteenth Street across from the main entrance to Tammany Hall. At three o'clock, on schedule, Dan Kelly assumed his place.

Pamela studied him in her opera glass. His face was a mask, devoid of expression, but his eyes were in constant motion, taking in everything around him. After ten minutes, Fred Grant appeared on Fourteenth Street, walking slowly toward Tammany Hall. Was he going back to work in his office? Pamela wondered.

Near the entrance, he stopped momentarily. Kelly noticed him and glared. Grant walked up the steps and held out a hand. Kelly ignored it, frowning. Grant seemed to plead. Finally, with a rude jerk of his head, Kelly sent him inside, presumably to wait out the hour.

Pamela said to Harry, "I feel very sad for Fred Grant. His attempt to reconcile with Kelly will not end well."

Harry nodded. "I'll ask Fred's landlady to send a message to our office when he returns. There's nothing more that we can do here."

That evening while waiting to hear from Grant's boardinghouse, Pamela and Harry searched through their law firm's files on Tammany Hall. Prescott had occasionally represented clients associated with Tammany and communicated with the organization's legal office.

"Here he is!" exclaimed Harry, handing Pamela a brief message. Five years ago, the clerk Frederick Grant informed Prescott that a client was too ill to make a court appearance.

Eventually, their search yielded a sketchy profile of Grant at work. Pamela concluded, "He checks the legal language of Tammany's business contracts and researches questions from his superior. I'd say he holds a responsible position, similar to Peter Yates's in our firm."

Harry was gazing at a message in his hands. "I agree. Grant seems appreciated. His boss, Mr. Dodd, expresses condolences when Grant lost his wife a couple of years ago."

Late in the evening, as they were about to leave the office, a messenger arrived from Mrs. Scott and reported that Mr. Grant hadn't returned.

Pamela slowly turned to Harry.

He anticipated her question. "Dead or alive, Grant should turn up in the morning. It's late. I'll walk you home now."

CHAPTER 11

Bellevue Hospital

Wednesday, November 21

Early the next morning in the office, Pamela received another message from Mrs. Scott: Still no word from Fred Grant.

Pamela said to Harry, "We should go looking for him. Where do we start?"

"First stop is the city morgue. Are you willing and able?"

"To be honest," she replied, "that's the last place in New York I'd care to visit, but I insist on overcoming my aversion. I've already learned that death is unavoidable and distressing."

The city morgue was a plain, single-story building on the huge Bellevue Hospital campus at First Avenue and East Twenty-sixth Street. Harry described Fred Grant to an attendant who led them to a room with four marble-topped tables. "Several bodies were brought in last night. To judge by the size, one of them could be Mr. Grant."

In a few minutes, the attendant returned with a cart on which a figure lay wrapped in canvas. He exposed the head. The face was flabby and dark, clearly not Grant's.

The Emergency Pavilion was a short walk away. Harry again asked for Grant. "From your description," said the attendant, "I think we may have him. Follow me." He led them down a hallway to a door and knocked lightly. A nurse opened it, raised a finger to her lips, and showed them to the sleeping man's bedside. His head was bandaged, except for the face. His legs were encased in plaster casts. "He has also been stabbed," whispered the nurse as she walked with them to a tiny parlor at the end of the hall. "We've sedated him. When his condition becomes stable, we'll move him to a room in the hospital next door. Did you recognize him?"

"He's definitely Frederick Grant. We were with him as late as yesterday. When and where was he found?"

"Shortly before midnight, a watchman at a construction site off First Avenue heard a man moaning and hurried to the scene. Mr. Grant was lying on the ground, barely conscious. To judge from his wounds and his loss of blood, he was assaulted about an hour earlier. If the watchman hadn't found him, he would have soon died. His attacker—there could have been more than one—had fled. The police soon arrived and we gave them this information. There was no identification on his person."

"Hopefully," said Harry, "we'll find out more when he regains consciousness. Now we'll identify him to the hospital authorities."

After leaving the hospital office, Pamela said to Harry, "Grant's room might contain information useful to our investigation. We must search it before the police and agents of Tammany Hall arrive. They would surely remove anything damaging to the organization."

Visibly agitated, Mrs. Scott met Pamela and Harry in the parlor. "A few minutes ago, a pair of ruffians knocked on my door and said Mr. Grant had been injured and taken to the hospital. They claimed he asked them to fetch certain things for him from his room upstairs. I recognized the men from your description and told them to leave. I wouldn't open the room until I heard from Mr. Grant himself or from the police."

Pamela reassured her. "You did well, Mrs. Scott. We've just come from Bellevue Hospital, where we saw Mr. Grant, unconscious and badly beaten, perhaps by the same two men you spoke to, Paddy McBride and Bill Cook. I suggest that we go with you to his room and find names and addresses of persons who should be notified of his situation. If we come upon any valuables, we'll put them in your room for safekeeping."

Pamela's suggestion appeared to please Mrs. Scott. She gathered her keys and they went upstairs together. While Mrs. Scott searched for money and valuables, Harry looked for a diary and Pamela browsed in Grant's file boxes. In a short while, Mrs. Scott found an envelope of cash, a life insurance policy whose beneficiary was a son living in Connecticut, and a pair of gold cuff links. She would notify his son and put the cash and the cuff links in the house safe. In a table drawer Harry found a cryptic diary. He would bring it back to the office for closer study.

An exchange of messages between Grant and Frank Dodd, senior clerk and friend, caught Pamela's eye. In a message just after Tammany's defeat in the November election, Grant complained that Dan Kelly's strong-arm tactics had hurt the club's reputation even among the Democratic Party's most faithful voters. Dodd replied that concerned members of the club should band together and get rid of Big Tim Smith and his thugs. Other targets of their criticism were too vague to identify, but reflected their negative attitude toward the current leadership and a desire for change.

"Help me decide, Harry. Should I take these messages with me? If they were to fall into the hands of certain Tammany leaders, they could harm Mr. Dodd. The remaining files are of little interest to us. Tammany can have them."

Harry reflected for a moment. "Take the personal messages. We'll arrange to return them to Dodd. If we can gain his good will, he might help us penetrate into Tammany's dark secrets."

Downstairs, they bade good-bye to Mrs. Scott, promising to visit her injured tenant and report back to her. As they left the house, they glimpsed a pair of police officers approaching, together with a man in a business suit, probably a lawyer from Tammany Hall. From where they were hiding they saw one of the officers show Mrs. Scott what appeared to be a search warrant. She nodded and reluctantly let them in.

Shuddering, Pamela prayed that the good woman wouldn't get caught in the claws of the Tammany tiger.

Back at her office, Pamela called Tammany's legal department and learned that Francis Dodd had just been called to Bellevue Hospital on an emergency.

"Tammany officials apparently withheld the news from Dodd for several hours," Harry noted. "I wonder why?"

"Kelly and his ruffians might have acted on their own. Higher officials perhaps weren't informed until this morning, sometime after we were, and then they notified Dodd. This brutal attempted murder could seriously embarrass Tammany Hall at a time when reformers are looking over their shoulder. Could Kelly be in trouble?"

"We might find out if we were to talk to Francis Dodd."

"Then, let's go back to Bellevue Hospital."

At the hospital, they found Dodd slumped down in a chair in the emergency pavilion's busy lobby. He looked surprised when they addressed him. "Have we met?" he asked, staring suspiciously at them.

"No," Pamela replied gently. "A nurse told us you were here."

"Then you must be the pair who saw him earlier."

They introduced themselves as private investigators, and

Dodd seemed to relax. A middle-aged, balding, stout man, he now gazed at them with kind but canny eyes.

Pamela asked, "How is Mr. Grant?"

"Still heavily sedated but resting quietly," Dodd replied. "Could we speak privately elsewhere?"

In a small, empty visitors' room, he asked them, "Can you tell me what's going on? Tammany Hall is suspiciously mum about this incident." Personable and intelligent, Dodd spoke like a man accustomed to the exercise of authority. As senior clerk at Tammany, he would be in charge of the office staff.

"We know part of the story," Harry replied. "Your colleague Fred Grant angered Dan Kelly." Harry described Grant mimicking Kelly in the saloon, the ruffians McBride and Cook assaulting Grant near his boardinghouse, and his attempt to reconcile with Kelly outside Tammany Hall. Dodd appeared increasingly distressed.

Pamela asked, "Did you see Grant yesterday?"

"No, he never came to the office. Kelly's men must have held him somewhere until the evening, when they attempted to kill him."

"How are the police going to avoid implicating Tammany?" asked Harry. "They will have to investigate such a serious crime."

Pamela replied, "If Fred is unwilling or unable to accuse his assailants, the police can conveniently blame a couple of tramps."

"That's likely," Dodd agreed. "Police detectives have searched the construction site and found no sign of struggle. The assailants must have attacked Fred elsewhere, then dumped him at the site. The detectives also interrogated the watchman, but he never saw the perpetrators. Fred should accuse them, but he may choose not to. There were no other witnesses." Dodd sighed. "Eventually, the police might speak to Kelly and his two ruffians, but they'll have alibis. The assault was well planned."

"Could this crime have any meaning for you?" Harry asked.

"I assume that you shared your colleague's opposition to Kelly and his kind."

Dodd grew anxious. "It's true we worked together but we didn't always think alike."

"Nonetheless, this morning Tammany dispatched one of its agents and two police officers to search Grant's rooms at the boardinghouse. Could they be looking for hidden threats to the organization's current leadership?"

Dodd began to perspire. "Oh my God! I don't know what to say."

"You have good reason to worry, Mr. Dodd, but don't despair. We anticipated Tammany's reaction and removed certain messages from your colleague's rooms that could be used against you and him. We'll return them to you at the earliest opportunity."

Dodd's lips parted in a mixture of relief and incredulity. "I'm grateful to you, but I can't help but wonder why you've become involved." He cast a glance in the general direction of the beaten man. "You surely recognize the dangers."

Pamela and Harry nodded in unison. She remarked, "We have a stake in solving a seven-year-old crime, Kelly's murder of the cabdriver, Tony Palermo. As you may recall, the police never charged Kelly. He has been free to this day to assault whomsoever he wills." Pamela met Dodd's eye. "You should help us or you could be his next victim."

"I take your point." His brow creased with concern. "Are you working for the police in any way?"

"As private investigators, we answer only to Jeremiah Prescott. However, if we can find sufficient evidence to convict Kelly, we'll bring it to the police."

"I'm beginning to understand," Dodd said. "The NYPD's cozy relationship with Tammany Hall deters police detectives from investigating this case. So how could I help you?"

"Kelly acts like a professional assassin who is sometimes out of control. We need to know who is shielding him from prosecution, and why."

Dodd reflected for a moment. "Such a person would have to come from Tammany Hall's upper levels and hold sufficient power to influence the police. That would most likely be Big Tim Smith, the ward boss in Chelsea in charge of Tammany Hall's finances and security. He oversees Kelly and the guards and the watchmen."

Harry added, "Kelly's protector may also come from outside, a Tammany ally."

"I understand," Dodd said. "I'll search for a trail of money to Kelly. If I find a significant connection, I'll contact your office. In the meantime, I'm concerned for my colleague Fred. He's in grave danger here."

"Yes," said Pamela. "Kelly could arrange to have him suffocated so that he couldn't witness against him. I'll speak to Larry White, an honest cop. In the summer we worked together on a missing person case that earned him a promotion to the NYPD's detective bureau. He might provide protection for Fred, at least until he gives testimony." She asked Dodd, "By the way, have you heard of a woman in Kelly's life called Alice Curran?"

Dodd rubbed his chin, trying to recall. "Kelly knew a girl by that name in Hell's Kitchen, a fiery redhead with a hot temper to match. Smart too. She married a dockworker. I don't know what happened to him, but she and Kelly got together later. I haven't heard of her in several years."

Pamela remarked, "Officer White has been looking for her and may have more to tell me."

Pamela sat down to supper with the White family. After the meal, when the children left with their mother, Pamela asked Larry about Alice Curran.

"I found her this afternoon," he reported. "She runs a brothel in Brooklyn. An officer from our vice squad says she's one of the smartest madams on the Barbary Coast."

"Where's that?" Pamela asked.

Larry smiled. "It's the nickname for the rough area of Brooklyn Heights between the East River docks and the U.S. Naval Yard. Alice's brothel is on Sand Street, between a saloon and a pawnshop. Her customers are mostly dock workers and sailors from all parts of the world."

"I want to talk to her. How can I best do that?"

"You could call on her at home on Cumberland Street facing Washington Park, about a mile from the brothel. Or, you could chance to meet her walking in the park in good weather. As a last resort, you could ask for her in the Sand Street brothel. In that case, take Harry along."

"Thanks for the tip. Harry and I will begin on Sand Street tomorrow morning."

Chapter 12

Brothel Madam

Thursday, November 22

"Before we approach Alice Curran, we should know the kind of business she's operating," said Pamela to Harry. "You check the saloon to the left. I'll visit the neighborhood." They were standing on Sand Street across from the Sailor's Nest, Curran's four-story brick hotel. In the sign above the entrance a lightly clad young woman fanned a recumbent sailor, while another knelt at his feet and pulled off his boots.

Next door, Mickey Finn's Grog Shop was already open at nine when Harry walked in. Dockworkers lined the bar, drinking beer and eating raw oysters and dark bread. Others from the same shift were being served at tables. To judge from their conversation and the stains of perspiration on their shirts, the men had already loaded a ship. This was breakfast.

Two men quietly sitting at one of the tables looked like the decent, hardworking sort. "May I join you?" Harry asked. They studied him and nodded. A waiter soon served their food and took Harry's order.

Harry felt at ease with these men. One of his companions in Sing Sing had been a dockworker from Brooklyn serving several years for aggravated manslaughter, the consequence of a barroom brawl. He had often spoken about life on the docks and had taught Harry the local slang and peculiar inflections.

"You're new here," said one of the men. "Looking for work?" asked the other.

"Actually, I'm looking for a room. What's it like in the hotel next door?"

The two men smiled wryly at each other. The older one said, "Well, friend, that depends on the kind of accommodation you're wanting. If it's a clean room with a pretty girl at a fair price, you won't find a safer place or a better bargain in Brooklyn."

Harry feigned surprise. "Here on Sand Street? Its bars and seamen's dives are notorious for their vice and violence."

"You're right, friend. Dangerous trash drifts ashore here from all four corners of the earth. Late at night, you could be killed for the penny in your pocket. But Alice runs a safe house. No need to worry, as long as you're inside."

"How does she manage?"

He tapped his temple with the index finger. "She's just a tiny woman but she's fearless and has a good head for business—only lets decent guys in, mostly ships' captains and first mates. If anyone makes trouble, her bouncers need only stare at him and he'll slink away."

"Does she live here?"

"She has an apartment in the building and a house on Washington Park a mile away. Her movements are hard to predict. I can't tell you for sure where she is at the moment. In the afternoon, she's usually at home."

Meanwhile, Pamela watched people going in and out of the hotel. A woman, perhaps in her thirties, left with a bundle under her arm and started down the street. Her businesslike air intrigued Pamela, so she followed her. The woman stopped in front of a small shop, pulled a key out of her apron pocket, and entered. The sign above the door said MARIA STELLA, SEAMSTRESS & TAILOR.

Pamela lingered outside for a few minutes and then entered the shop. A little bell chimed, and the woman came out of a back room. "How may I serve you?" She spoke with a strong Italian accent. Though a few years past the full bloom of her beauty, she was still an attractive woman: thick, dark brown hair; clear, fair complexion; shapely figure.

"Could you show me samples of your work?"

Maria drew a gown from a clothes rack and held it up for Pamela's inspection. "The hem was torn. I repaired it."

The work was perfect, and Pamela said so. She learned that the woman had come from Milan with her husband, a tailor. He took sick and died, leaving her alone and penniless. She ended up a prostitute in the hotel across the street. Alice Curran discovered her talent and helped her open this shop. Curran also directed the hotel's business to her and promoted her work in the community.

"I thank Miss Curran every day. She saved my life."

Pamela purchased thread, promised to recommend her work to friends, and said good-bye.

She met Harry coming out of the grog shop and they compared notes. "Alice Curran seems to be an enlightened, enterprising lady," she remarked. "Where is she staying?"

"She's at home. While you visit her, I'll hurry over to Bellevue Hospital. When Fred Grant regains consciousness, I must question him before someone from Tammany Hall shuts him up for good."

In the afternoon, Pamela took the elevated train to Cumberland Street in Brooklyn and walked a short distance to Washington Park. Uncertain what to say during this visit, Pamela strolled thoughtfully through rows of leafless chestnut trees, past two small ponds, and up to the park's highest point. There she gazed at Curran's home, a tasteful, three-story brownstone townhouse, similar to others in the block, clearly an affluent neighborhood.

She pondered the best approach to take, if she were to find Alice at home. Should she slyly pretend to be soliciting contributions to a charity? The little she knew of Alice suggested that she would respond best to candor.

Squaring her shoulders, Pamela set out across the park to the house and climbed up the steps to the front door. To the left and right were narrow, plain glass lights where a person inside, hidden by curtains, could observe the caller. Pamela had put on her best blue woolen street dress and a matching cap. She lifted her chin a little higher and rapped on the door. Seconds later, the curtains stirred, then they were still for a couple of minutes. Finally, the door opened.

"Who are you and what is your business?" A tall, blond amazon, apparently the housekeeper, stood in the doorway, searching Pamela with skeptical blue eyes. A domestic maid was behind her.

Pamela gave her name. "I'm a private investigator for Mr. Jeremiah Prescott and I'd like to speak to Miss Alice Curran about circumstances surrounding the death of the cabdriver Tony Palermo seven years ago. Mr. Francis Dodd has directed me to her."

"I have to inquire if Miss Curran is at home." The accent was Scandinavian. "Please wait in the hall. The maid will stay with you."

While the housekeeper was away, Pamela tried in vain to make conversation with the maid, a plain, dark young woman of mixed race. She seemed to understand what Pamela said, but had been instructed to watch, not speak. Obliged to wait, Pamela studied the furnishings in the room: photographs and paintings of all types of ships, a seaman's whistle, a naval telescope, a rack of canes with curiously carved heads.

After several minutes, the housekeeper returned. "My mistress can see you in twenty minutes. Is that convenient?"

"Yes, of course, I realize that I arrived unannounced."

"Then follow me."

The housekeeper left Pamela in a small parlor off the entrance hall. Within minutes, the maid came with tea and sweet biscuits. As silent as earlier, she poured for Pamela, then stationed herself near the open door to the hall.

While drinking the tea, Pamela momentarily feared that it might be drugged, though its taste was normal. She couldn't imagine why Curran would do such a thing. So, Pamela again examined the woman's ambiance. Expertly carved models of exotic ships were displayed in glass cabinets, complete with tiny figures of the crews. Since Curran was in the business of serving seamen, the nautical theme didn't surprise Pamela. Nonetheless, she felt that these things were tokens of appreciation and friendship. She had expected to find expressions of a more vulgar sensibility in a brothel madam's house.

Promptly as promised, the maid announced that Miss Curran was ready and led Pamela into a study. A woman sat at a writing table, beckoned Pamela forward, and dismissed the maid, who shut the door behind her.

Curran's appearance was extraordinary. Her body was small, thin, and severely hunched; her head was disproportionately large but refined, and reminded Pamela of a British aristocratic lady. Her rich auburn hair was darker than the flaming red that Dodd had spoken of. Perhaps it had faded with age. She was about forty.

Leaning forward, arms resting on the table, Curran briefly studied Pamela with deep-set, lively green eyes. "Have you been talking to Frank Dodd about me?"

"Yes, he gave you a good report. We met him at Fred Grant's bedside in Bellevue Hospital."

Curran raised an eyebrow. "An illness?"

"No, he was stabbed and beaten and is unconscious."

"Grant's a good man. Sorry to hear of his misfortune. You said you wanted to talk about the death of Tony Palermo seven years ago. Where's the connection to Grant—as if I couldn't guess."

"Dan Kelly. Fred appears to have insulted him."

"You said 'we' as if you have a partner."

Pamela nodded. "His name is Harry Miller."

"Oh, I see. Miller was a police detective investigating the Palermo case and got in trouble." She leaned back, reflecting. "So what are you trying to do?"

"Clear Harry's name. He was framed and spent four years in prison. The conviction still hangs over his life."

"What do you want from me?"

"Whatever you know about that incident, in particular, who hired Dan for the killing. I'm sure he didn't act on his own."

"I owe Dan a great deal, so I speak reluctantly of his sins. He and I found each other while growing up on the West Side in Hell's Kitchen. With his knife he protected me from schoolyard bullies, as well as vicious predators. In return, I taught him to read and write and to distinguish right from wrong. He was grateful, perhaps even fond of me."

She drew Pamela's attention to a birdcage off to one side, covered with a dark cloth. "Danny's old canary is having a nap. It's about time for him to wake up and entertain us. Would you remove the cover? The cage is open."

Pamela put the cover aside and came face to face with a bright yellow canary. At first, he tentatively twittered, then burst out in joyous song. A few seconds later, he flew out of the cage and landed on Alice's shoulder.

"Danny bought him eight years ago and loved to pet him—trained him to perch on his shoulder. When he went to work for Tammany Hall, he couldn't take proper care of him, so he gave him to me."

She offered her finger and the bird perched on it. "I saw Danny's best side. As he grew older, however, I could guide him less and less." A hint of regret appeared in Curran's eyes. Her mind seemed to drift back in time. Without asking, she poured more tea into their cups.

"When I took over the old hotel on Sand Street, Danny came with me as a bouncer and companion. I probably would have failed without him. Then, one day, he told me that a customer from Tammany Hall had offered him a job as a guard with higher pay and greater responsibilities. I told him to take it. He could always come back to me."

She paused for a sip of tea. "A few months later, he paid me a visit. There was a worried look on his face. I asked, was Tammany Hall treating him right?

" 'That's not the problem,' he replied, 'the pay is good and the work is interesting.'

" 'Then, what's bothering you?'

"He looked me in the eye and said, 'I've been told today to kill a man. He's causing major trouble for the organization. I'll receive an extra $200.'

" 'That's a lot of money, about as much as I would pay you in a year. If you refuse, what will happen?'

" 'I'll lose my job and maybe my life.'

" 'But, if you do it,' I said, 'you will be Tammany's slave for the rest of your life. It's not worth it. Tammany's man could always deny being involved in the killing and turn you over to the police. Quit the job and come back here.'

"He said he'd think it over. I was pretty sure he'd take the two hundred. I haven't seen him since—though I've kept track of him."

"Do you have any idea who paid him?"

"He didn't mention a name."

"May I ask who was your customer from Tammany who persuaded Dan to become a guard?"

"I don't know. Dan didn't tell me. But if you can somehow get into Tammany's financial records, look for a special payment of $200 to Dan Kelly for services rendered in January 1887."

While Pamela visited Alice Curran at home in Washington Park, Harry hastened back to Bellevue Hospital in the city. He was relieved to find one of Larry White's officers guarding the door to Fred Grant's room. A sign read NO VISITORS. The officer remarked, "A couple of police detectives came up to me this morning and asked to see the patient. I said he was still unconscious. They insisted. I pointed to the sign. They seemed annoyed."

The nurse on duty said Grant's vital signs had improved during the morning, and he should awake soon. "I'll check." She was in the room for only a minute. When she came out, she said, "He'll speak to you now. Don't tire him."

Harry entered quietly, sat, and waved a greeting. Grant's eyes were dull and half-open, his speech slurred, but he managed to ask, "Did you catch the bastards who did this to me?"

Harry leaped to his feet and called in the officer and the nurse. Grant seemed about to identify his assailants. Harry asked him, "Who attacked you?"

"Kelly lured me into a basement room and watched while McBride and Cook tied me up and blindfolded me. Hours later after they left, I heard two men enter the room—Dan Kelly and Big Tim Smith, to judge from their voices. Smith beat me; Kelly broke my legs and stabbed me. I passed out. When I came to, they had untied me and removed the blinders from my eyes. They must have thought that I was dead. I kept my eyes closed, but I recognized their voices. They laid me on a canvas cloth. Shortly afterward, I heard their voices at a distance and smelled tobacco smoke. My vision cleared for a few moments and I finally saw them. The rest is a blur. I remember being lifted up, hauled away, and dumped somewhere."

To be sure that he had heard Grant identify his assailants, Harry asked, "Did McBride and Cook beat you?"

"No, Dan Kelly was the one who cursed and stabbed me and broke my legs. Big Tim Smith punched my head. McBride and Cook weren't in the room."

Harry added, "But they probably moved you to the building site."

When Grant began to tire, Harry said, "That's enough for now. I'll continue when you've improved."

Outside the room Harry wrote out Grant's statement and had the officer and the nurse sign as witnesses. Larry White could begin to build a case against Kelly and Big Tim, and search for McBride and Cook, who might have already disappeared into the city's underworld.

Back in the office on Irving Place, Pamela found Prescott at his desk, an open file before him. He smiled brightly and pointed her to a seat facing him. "Tell me about Alice Curran."

"I was frankly surprised," Pamela began. "I was expecting to meet a coarse, greedy, and sly old whore. Alice is a kind, intelligent, shrewd businesswoman." Pamela went on to describe how Dan Kelly evolved from a slum boy, defending Alice as well as himself, into a paid Tammany assassin. "Alice couldn't tell me precisely who hired Dan to kill the cabdriver, but she gave me the price, $200. She hasn't heard from Dan since."

"Congratulations. You've brought the investigation a step forward. Pass your information on to Larry White. I look forward to hearing from Harry." He reached into the file box and handed her a document.

"It's a memorandum dealing with Ambrose Norton, the clerk in Michael Sullivan's office. My associates and I have agreed to hire him as a trust officer. He would bring useful skills to our firm. The next step is to engage him in our plan to uncover Tammany Hall's financial secrets. For the time being, we shall all observe strict secrecy."

"How do you envisage Norton's specific role?"

"He should search for evidence that Sullivan and/or Judge Fawcett acted illegally in the cabdriver's case. Perhaps the judge through Sullivan accepted money to convict Harry."

"Why would Sullivan and Fawcett take such great risks?"

"Tammany may have made an offer the judge couldn't resist."

"Then we'll go to the Cooper Union this evening and speak to Mr. Norton."

Pamela found Norton again in the great reading room, concentrating on a salmon-colored page of London's *Financial Times*. She sat down with a magazine opposite him, cleared her throat, and passed a note over the table: *Can you meet me in the café in ten minutes?*

He glanced at the note and lightly nodded.

Ten minutes later, he sat down with Pamela. She told him, "We're going to speak with Mr. Prescott this evening. He has rented a small office in the neighborhood. Our investigation must be kept as secret as possible, or there will be dire consequences. Follow me out. Are you ready?"

"Yes," he murmured. His eyes darted about the room, seeking Tammany spies. Pamela got up and left. Outside, she glanced over her shoulder. Norton was following her.

They climbed the stairs to a room above a tailor's shop. After introductions, Prescott said, "My associates and I are prepared to offer you a position as trust officer in our firm. Here is a printed agreement. The only condition is that you help us investigate the murder of the cabdriver Tony Palermo seven years ago and the possible complicity of Michael Sullivan and Judge Noah Fawcett. Are you willing?"

"Yes, I am," he replied with a shaky voice. His neck muscles were tightening. "What is the state of the investigation thus far?"

Prescott described the cabdriver's murder, the corrupted police investigation, and Harry's foiled attempt to reach the truth. "Recently, we have undertaken this private, secret investigation and opened several promising lines of inquiry. This afternoon, Mrs. Thompson learned that someone in Tammany Hall offered Dan Kelly $200 to kill Palermo. Could you search for evidence that Tammany also may have paid Judge Fawcett to cover up the crime?"

Norton was listening intently. "Such a transfer would certainly be disguised. Sullivan created dummy accounts for the judge to mask suspicious deposits and withdrawals. While searching for them, I might also turn up evidence of fraud." Norton began to bite his lip, appearing to weigh his options. "This is a larger, more complicated, and more dangerous investigation than I anticipated."

Pamela felt sorry for him. By joining the investigation he would take on great risks. But the alternative was a menial, dead-end job for life.

He drew in a deep breath. "I'll start my part tomorrow. God help me."

CHAPTER 13

Secret Accounts

Friday, November 23

Ambrose Norton arrived at the bank, a changed man. He was still on the company's payroll and about to work on its familiar premises. But, as he surveyed the rooms, he now felt like a stranger and a thief. Through a half-open door, he saw Sullivan already at his desk, the morning newspaper laid out before him. The office boy was coming with the morning tea.

As Norton entered the room, Sullivan glanced up and grunted, "Morning, Norton," and handed him a clipping. "File it under 'railroads.' " The boy set the tea to the right of the newspaper and added the customary dose of cream and sugar. Sullivan stirred the tea absentmindedly, his eyes focused on the news of the day. To judge from his intermittent grunts he wasn't pleased.

"That idiot Cleveland!" he finally exclaimed. "He still refuses to take over the Hawaiian Islands."

Norton understood that Sullivan was referring to the president's refusal to approve the U.S. annexation of the sovereign kingdom of Hawaii, where a gang of wealthy American sugar planters in collusion with the American ambassador and a company of U.S. Marines had recently overthrown the royal government and deposed Queen Liliuokalani. Cleveland had recently said it would be shameful for the U.S. to seize a small, peaceful nation by guile and force. Moreover, the coup was illegal under international law.

For investors in sugar, like Sullivan, the annexation of the islands meant increased opportunity for profit. The planters' sugar exports to the continental U.S. would be exempt from the U.S. tariff.

"Indeed," said Norton in a noncommittal tone. He actually had followed the story in the press at the Cooper Union, and he agreed with the president. His special emissary to the islands had determined that, contrary to the planters' claims, the monarch had not threatened American lives or property. Weakened by disease or reduced to near slavery on the great plantations, the common people sympathized with the monarch and her attempts to help them. However, they were powerless to save her. Norton felt a strong urge to contradict Sullivan, but this wasn't the right time or place.

Norton hung up his coat, sat down at his desk, and began to sift through his in-box, quickly dispatching the routine items. He needed to set aside time for prying into Sullivan's desk whenever an opportunity presented itself.

That moment came at noon when Sullivan was going out to lunch. Norton distracted him with a last-minute question about a complicated investment. Afterward, Sullivan left in a hurry and neglected to lock the desk drawer. Norton rushed to the drawer, seized the secret green account book, and searched the entries for January 1887. When he came upon a cash payment of $350 for services rendered, January 20, he almost shouted for joy. Fortunately, Sullivan had used obvious initials, T. S. for the giver, Tim Smith, and N. F. for the receiver, Noah Fawcett.

At one o'clock, Norton returned the book to the desk drawer. A quarter hour later, Sullivan walked into the room. Norton breathed a sigh of relief. He would call Mrs. Thompson's office from a nearby phone and report his discovery.

Pamela had just hung up her coat when a call came in. A hurried voice said, "Norton here. I've searched S's account book and found a transfer of $350 from Smith to Fawcett's secret account, dated January twentieth, 1887, for services rendered. If need be, see me at the usual place."

She read the notes of her conversation with Norton to Harry when he returned from Bellevue Hospital.

Harry scratched his head. "The payment looks suspicious. Encourage Norton to pursue that lead."

"I'll do that soon. Now tell me, how is Fred Grant?"

"Doing poorly. The doctor heavily sedates him to ease the pain. While I was there, the police detectives returned with a Tammany lawyer. The nurse allowed them only one question: 'Who beat you?' Fred struggled through the pain. You could hardly hear him, but he managed to say, 'Dan Kelly and Tim Smith.' The lawyer asked, 'Are you really sure?' Grant closed his eyes, his face contorted in pain. A detective insisted, 'Do you want to press charges?' Grant moaned pitifully. The nurse stepped in. 'That's enough! I said, one question! Can't you see he's in pain?' "

"Incredible!" exclaimed Pamela. "What clods!"

"Tammany is really worried. When we left the room, I said to the detectives, 'You know Kelly and Smith. Lock them up. Their thugs assaulted Fred once already, this past Monday. I'll testify to that.' "

"How did the detectives react?"

"The old one said, 'Mind your own business.' The young one added, 'Mr. Grant has only given us two names. We don't know if he's of sound mind. He hasn't lodged a complaint. We don't know if he wants to.'

"By that time, I was seeing red. I asked the three of them,

'Are you going to leave Kelly and Smith free to come here and finish him off?'

"The old detective told me to watch my lip or he'd haul me into the station house and teach me a lesson. I thanked him for the advice. He didn't catch my irony."

"Is Fred safe in the hospital?"

Harry nodded. "The doctors and nurses are vigilant, Fred's best line of defense. They distrust the police and Tammany Hall." He paused. "By the way, let's pay Barney Flynn a visit. He has researched Michael Sullivan's nightlife and has news for us."

Late in the afternoon, Flynn was in his office at his writing table, a bottle of whiskey and a half-filled glass to his right. He glanced at the bottle. "I need to relax. It's been a nasty day. Can I offer you a shot, Harry?"

"Some other time, Barney."

Barney turned to Pamela. "Sorry, ma'am, I've nothing here that's fit for a lady."

"Don't apologize, Barney. As a private investigator, I'm not quite ladylike. Still, I don't need a drink just now. What have you to tell us?"

He sipped from the glass and let out a sigh of pleasure. "I checked with the gambling dens that Sullivan has frequented on Saturday nights. He owes them thousands of dollars and his credit is zero. The Phoenix Club is easily the most familiar and the least hostile to him. This afternoon after lunch he returned to his bank and nearly cleared out the judge's largest secret account."

"What does this mean?" asked Pamela.

Harry replied, "Sullivan will probably put the money into a desperate gamble at the Phoenix Club to restore to Judge Fawcett's account what he has stolen over the past year or so. The only other way that he could quickly restore the money would be to rob a bank."

Barney nodded, then continued with his report. "After taking the money, Sullivan invested a few dollars in a pocket double-barreled derringer pistol and two bullets, should he lose. That's a likely way out for the failed, high-stakes gambler. Tomorrow night, Mrs. Thompson and I will observe him up close. Harry, you will be out of the picture, since he'd recognize you."

"Right. I'll go to the Sullivan house on a rescue mission while you two are watching Michael destroy himself."

Barney shook his head. "We'll try to prevent him from killing himself or anyone else. Alive and threatened with going to prison, he could be persuaded to expose your wrongful conviction."

Pamela asked Barney, "How come you know so much about Sullivan's fraud?"

"That's a professional secret," he replied with a coy smile. "But I'll tell you that banks with Tammany Hall accounts pay the staff poorly, so I've recently been able to hire a well-placed clerk in the Union Square Bank. This week, he checked Sullivan's accounts for me. I'll send you the bill. Prescott should be happy to pay."

As Pamela and Harry left Barney's office, she remarked, "How callously banks seem to deal with our money! Secret accounts invite fraud."

Harry agreed. "Since banks have weak regulation or oversight, the temptation to cheat is often irresistible. Sullivan's addiction to gambling has caused him to recklessly overreach. Had he been more prudent he could have skimmed the judge's account indefinitely."

"In my view," Pamela concluded, "The judge and his partner in crime deserve each other."

That evening, Prescott asked Pamela out to supper at the Jolly Clam, a little fish restaurant on Fourteenth Street. After they ordered clam chowder, the house specialty, she described Sullivan's reckless misuse of Judge Fawcett's money to feed his gambling addiction. "We believe Sullivan is heading into a crisis tomorrow night."

As she was speaking, she noticed that Prescott was struggling to pay attention and looked distressed. At that moment, the waiter came with the chowder.

When he left, Pamela asked solicitously, "What's bothering you, Jeremiah?"

"Sorry. It's my son, Edward. That nasty controversy in his fraternity has deepened. The faculty committee appointed to investigate agrees that rat poison was in Edward's porridge, but they can't determine how it got there."

"Couldn't they find a single credible witness?"

"Credible? No. However, one of Isaac Fawcett's allies in the fraternity claims to have seen Edward furtively put a powder in his porridge. That could have been the rat poison."

"Or harmless sugar."

"Judge Fawcett insisted that the poisoning was faked in order to blacken Isaac's reputation and force him out of the fraternity. Edward must have known all along that the poison was there. That's why he never tasted it and instead concocted the tale about the finicky cat."

Pamela remarked, "Fawcett is trying to spread the controversy to the alumni and the wider campus community and force the college administration's hand."

Prescott nodded. "To fan the flames, my ex-wife, Gloria, echoed Judge Fawcett's complaints. She told President Carter that I have filled our son's mind with subversive notions about the rights of working men and women. She also called me a negligent father who has encouraged Edward's imprudent relationship with Mary Clark, the former mill worker's daughter. In Gloria's opinion, Edward should be confined to the college campus and placed under supervised study until he recovers his senses."

"Do you think that her opinions influenced President Carter?"

"Yes, at the least, he has to take them seriously since they are supported by Fawcett and prominent men of like mind, some of them alumni."

Pamela gazed sympathetically at Prescott. "This conflict could disrupt Edward's studies. What can you do to help him?"

"I'll take an early morning train to Williamstown and plead Edward's cause with the college authorities." In a light-hearted moment he added, "I might even play the detective and solve the mystery of the poisoned porridge." The chowder finished, he signaled the waiter and paid the bill.

Out on the street, Prescott offered Pamela his arm and asked, "May I walk you home?"

She gave him a tender, affirming glance.

As they strolled down Fourteenth Street, he asked her, "Are you nervous that you must cope with the Sullivan crisis as it comes to a head tomorrow?"

She patted his arm. "Rest easy, Jeremiah. I'll be ready."

CHAPTER 14

Desperate Measures

Saturday, November 24

The next morning, Pamela went with Prescott to Grand Central Station and waved him off to the Berkshires, praying that he would resolve his son's problem. Then she went to the Phoenix Club and informed Lucretia that Michael Sullivan now had money and would likely come to her club that evening. "He might be armed," Pamela warned.

Lucretia sighed. "I'll receive him reluctantly and cautiously. He wouldn't be the only one in the club carrying a hidden derringer."

Pamela expressed surprise.

"You should know, Pamela, that my guests come and go through dangerous streets late at night, and most of them feel safer with a pistol in their pocket."

"I understand, Lucretia. But how do you keep them from using their pistols at the gaming tables?"

"If a guest loses heavily, or shows bad temper, my women watch him more closely. To borrow a line from William Congreve, they are trained 'to soothe the savage breast.' Still, exposure to violence comes with running an illegal enterprise like mine, where men wager large sums of money while drinking whiskey. If the threat of violence is more than my women can deal with, I trust my bouncer to intervene."

She hesitated, reflecting for a moment. "I don't expect Sullivan to be violent. Still, as an added precaution, may I hire you and Barney to watch over him tonight?"

Pamela agreed that she would pose as a hostess at the club, and Barney would be a guest. After exchanging messages with Harry and Barney, she spent the rest of the morning at the club and became familiar with the staff and their operation.

Early that evening, as Pamela emerged from her apartment building, a wide-eyed Harry exclaimed, "You look *beautiful* tonight!"

"What did you expect, Harry? The drab, boardinghouse Pamela? Tonight, I'm off to work in a high-class brothel." Harry chuckled.

That afternoon, Lucretia La Belle had come to Pamela and dressed and groomed her in a red satin gown with a low neckline and a string of pearls.

At the waiting coach, Barney Flynn stepped forward to greet Pamela. In contrast to his usual scruffy appearance, he now wore a well-tailored dark evening suit. He bowed like a gentleman and lent an arm as Pamela climbed inside. Then they rode to a sheltered place where they could observe the Sullivan house.

Harry followed them in a separate coach as far as the Sullivan house. When Michael left, Harry would attempt to rescue Theresa and her son. At about eleven in the evening, Sullivan predictably stole out of his house. Pamela and Barney drove after him to the club and parked nearby to observe him.

At the door a porter stopped him from entering, but then admitted him when he showed a pocketful of money. Barney waited a minute and then followed Sullivan into the house.

Pamela entered the club by the back door. La Belle's servant directed her to a private room with a one-way window into the gaming room. For several minutes she watched the activity before her until she felt comfortable enough to play her role.

She placed herself inside the gaming room by the pantry door, pretending to oversee several beautiful women who were moving among the tables with trays, offering drinks and cigars to dozens of rich-looking men playing roulette, faro, and poker. A pungent, blue haze filled the room; the level of noise was high. Sullivan approached the roulette table, Barney close behind him.

For an hour Sullivan played at the roulette wheel, laying chips tentatively on the green cloth–covered table, as if trying to get a feeling for the game. Finally, he took a stiff drink of whiskey to screw up his courage. At that moment, a commotion broke out at the wheel as players left the game while others tried to push up to the table. In the ensuing melee, Sullivan was jostled.

Barney signaled Pamela to come closer, then he brushed against Sullivan, picked the pistol from his coat pocket, and slipped it to Pamela. She hurried away to the women's restroom, substituted blanks for the bullets, returned to the gaming room, and gave the pistol back to Barney.

By this time, Sullivan was rapt in the game, drinking heavily, and wagering hundred-dollar chips with abandon, losing more often than winning. Barney slipped the disarmed pistol back into the gambler's pocket unnoticed.

Pamela watched amazed as Sullivan became increasingly desperate and compounded his losses, apparently unaware that he was doomed if he continued. She and Barney left the gaming room to watch Sullivan through the one-way window for a while, lest he notice their constant near presence. She asked Barney, "Has the success of the judge's investments given Sullivan an inflated sense of his ability to gamble?"

"Yes," Barney agreed. "Sullivan thinks he's a financial genius. But he lacks the intuition and skills of the more successful professional gamblers, like those you saw during the summer at the casino in Saratoga Springs. Whiskey has also made him careless tonight. He'll soon run out of money and attempt to shoot himself."

Pamela shuddered. "We'd better go back into the gaming room."

Twenty minutes later, Sullivan threw his last chips on the table. The wheel spun, and he lost. For a long moment, he stood stock still, staring at the wheel. As the croupier raked in the chips, he glanced anxiously at Sullivan. The men around him drew away and grew ominously silent.

"I want to win back my money," Sullivan said to the croupier in a high, shrill voice. "Give me a thousand dollars in chips." He drained his glass, set it on the table, and signaled a waitress to fill it.

Just then Lucretia entered the room. The croupier caught her eye and beckoned. Barney whispered to Pamela, "Trouble is afoot."

A bouncer slipped into the room behind Lucretia and they advanced on Sullivan. He met them, unsteady on his feet, his face contorted in a mixture of anger and grief. "Give me more chips!" he shouted, slurring the words.

"You've had too much to drink, Mr. Sullivan, and are in no condition for gaming. I must ask you to leave." Her voice was soft but her expression firm. She glanced over her shoulder and nodded to the bouncer, who took a step forward.

Suddenly, Sullivan reached into his pocket and drew the pistol to his temple. As he was pulling the trigger, Barney grabbed his arm. The shot's explosive charge grazed Sullivan's head, leaving behind the scent of scorched hair. Stunned momentarily, he stood still, while Barney wrestled the gun from his hand. The bouncer quickly manacled his arms behind his back.

At the pistol's sharp report, a few patrons rushed to the doors or ducked under tables, but others stood shocked and amazed as Sullivan slumped inert into the bouncer's arms.

Barney passed the gun to Pamela and then examined Sullivan's head. "He's not bleeding. The blast has merely scorched his hair and knocked him out." As Barney and the bouncer were carrying Sullivan from the gaming room, Lucretia announced, "After that excitement, gentlemen, a round of drinks is on the house and let the games resume."

Pamela checked her watch as Sullivan opened his eyes. They appeared unfocused. He was lying on a sofa in the small, bare parlor and had been unconscious only two or three minutes. She beckoned Barney, who was studying Sullivan's little pistol in the light of a gas lamp.

"He's awake," she said as he raised himself on one arm and gradually took note of his surroundings.

"Who are you?" he asked querulously.

Barney pulled up a chair and sat next to Pamela. "We're private detectives, hired by Madam La Belle. She thought you might come to gamble and cause trouble. She was right."

Sullivan was becoming lucid. "I don't feel well. I'm going home. Take off the manacles." He began to look angry.

Barney cautioned him. "We've discovered that you had embezzled the money that you lost tonight. That's why you tried to kill yourself, right?"

Sullivan's lips worked nervously from growing awareness of his predicament.

His inquisitors stared silently at him until he was compelled to speak.

"What do you want of me?" he asked. "If any money is missing in my accounts, I'll pay it back."

Barney replied, "The sum you stole is a small fortune. You can never pay it back. You will have to throw yourself on the judge's mercy."

As Barney's reference to the judge sank into Sullivan's mind, his spirit seemed to deflate. "Why didn't you let me kill myself?" His gaze moved from Barney to Pamela, apparently for sympathy.

She disappointed him. "You can still undo some of the evil that you and your associates have done. For a start, you could tell us or the state's attorney general or a grand jury how Judge Fawcett got the money that he was hiding in a secret account. How has he spent that kind of money over the years?"

"I'm beginning to understand," Sullivan remarked, a cunning look in his eyes. "You may be working for Reverend Parkhurst or Senator Lexow or the other reformers. If any money is missing from the judge's account, Ambrose Norton must have stolen it. I shouldn't have trusted him with so much responsibility."

"I followed you to the bank," said Barney. "Together with the bank teller, I witnessed you withdrawing the money. Your signature is on the receipt."

Sullivan was silent for a long moment, then he said in an even voice, "I want to go home now. Remove the manacles."

"We'll wait a few more minutes," said Pamela, "until Madam La Belle gathers statements from patrons who witnessed your suicide attempt. Then we'll call police detective Larry White and explain what has happened. When he arrives, we'll release you to him and hand over the statements from the witnesses, together with your pistol and a warning that you are a danger to yourself as well as to others. Until then the bouncer will look after you." She nodded to Barney and they left the parlor.

As they entered the gaming room, Pamela and Barney met Lucretia. She appeared calm and collected. "I figured that the police would be called. So I hid the roulette wheel and other evidence of illegal gambling. Until the police leave, my guests will enjoy penny ante poker, with good food and drink and conversation with my young ladies."

A few minutes after midnight, Larry White arrived with a patrolman. Barney gave Larry the derringer. The officers briefly inspected the scene of the attempted suicide and followed Pamela to the parlor. Sullivan was still lying on the sofa, eyes half closed with fatigue. The bouncer released the manacles and helped Sullivan to his feet. The patrolman brought him out to the Black Maria in the street.

As the police wagon was about to leave, Larry said with a wink to Pamela, "We'll hold Sullivan in the station house until later this morning. He should be sober by then and can go before a magistrate. Since at least a dozen men and women witnessed the incident, the news will spread quickly and soon reach Sullivan's bank and Judge Fawcett."

Pamela was relieved. She had been anxious about Harry and Theresa, but she now felt they would be in a safe place long before her brother was released.

CHAPTER 15

Rescue

Saturday, November 24

Meanwhile, late in the evening back at the Sullivan house, Harry had waved Pamela and Barney off to the Phoenix Club, then he got out of his coach, hastened across the street, and sneaked through a narrow passageway to the rear of the building. He whistled, and the door opened.

"Harry, is it you?" came a soft, anxious voice.

"Yes, Theresa. Is the coast clear?"

She let him in and threw herself into his arms. For a long moment, he held her tight, breathed in her scent. She whispered, "Mr. and Mrs. Sullivan and Mrs. Donovan are asleep, and the maid has the night off. She's supposed to return at breakfast. I'm packed and ready to go. Shall I get my son, James?"

"Not yet. We'll search Michael's study for an hour at least. This may be our best opportunity, but we must be quick." Harry thought that if Michael were to kill himself tonight, Tammany Hall would immediately attempt to secure his personal papers, the secret green account book, and possibly related messages, as they had tried in a similar way in Fred Grant's case. Harry felt stressed, because he really didn't know if or when Michael might come home.

He and Theresa stole through the house to Michael's study, where Harry quietly picked the lock. Once inside, Theresa pulled drapes over the windows, and Harry lit a gas lamp on the writing table. Its drawer was also locked but easily picked. The green account book was waiting for him. He stuck it in his pocket.

"Michael is a man of habit," Harry whispered. "He must keep a diary. Do you have any idea where he might hide it?"

"Mrs. Donovan has seen a plain beige notebook on his table."

"That could be a diary. We must find it."

They surveyed the study, trying to figure out where this cunning, secretive man might have hidden the daily record of his vices and crimes. The study was on the first floor of the house, near the front door. On one side, a large bow window looked out over the street. A tea table and chairs stood nearby. On the other side, built-in bookcases were interspersed with framed prints and photographs. Opposite the entrance was Sullivan's large writing table and behind it a wall of file cabinets and a door to the next room.

"What's in there?" Harry asked, taking a step toward the door.

"His bedroom," Theresa replied, a bitter tone in her voice. Harry understood that Sullivan had assaulted her there several years ago and the memory was still painful. It was best not to remind her.

He turned back toward the writing table. "Your brother would hide a diary close to where he used it."

The table had two side drawers. The left one was filled with writing supplies. The right side contained only a large box of cigars and a box of matches, but beneath them was a false bottom. A diary for the year 1894 was hidden there.

"Where could the diaries for other years be?" he asked Theresa.

"Possibly behind the bookcase," she replied. "A skilled cabinetmaker built it." The case was made of fine brown mahogany and capped by fancy, decorated molding. But, on close inspection, Harry couldn't find any secret levers or panels. A quick search of the rest of the room was also fruitless.

Reluctantly, he nodded toward the bedroom. "Sorry, I have to look in there."

She cast her eyes down and murmured, "I'll wait out here."

Harry found the old diaries hidden in a locked closet, together with Sullivan's collection of pornographic photographs and books. He brought the diaries into the study.

Theresa looked distressed. "Sit at the tea table and rest," Harry suggested. "I'll browse in the diaries."

"Let me read them," she insisted, "I want to see what he says about me."

"Not now, Theresa," he cautioned. "I'll take the diaries and we'll read them later. Rouse your boy now. We'll go as soon as he's ready."

While Theresa was upstairs, Harry carefully removed every visible trace of their presence from the study and the bedroom. Though Sullivan, if alive, would soon miss the diaries and the secret account book, he might not know for sure whether they were taken by Theresa or by agents of Tammany Hall, somehow alerted to his thievery.

Harry had just finished cleaning up when Theresa walked into the study with James, each carrying a traveling bag. The nine-year-old boy looked very sleepy. Still, he said, "Hi, Harry. Mom says you're taking us to Aunt Patricia's house. Why are we going in the middle of the night?"

"We had to wait until your uncle Michael was away. He wants to keep you here. We can talk about that later. Now we'll leave quietly so as not to disturb your grandfather and grandmother."

The boy nodded and took his mother's hand. Harry opened the study door, stepped into the hall, and listened. "Someone is stirring upstairs. Wait! Now I hear steps in the stairway." He closed the door and locked it. Theresa started to question. "Hush," he whispered and shuttered his lantern.

"Is anyone there?" an elderly, cracked voice called out in the hall.

Harry's heart was pounding. He feared a confrontation with Mr. Sullivan, an old, frail, obstinate man in his nightshirt. He could refuse to let them leave and stand in their way. What could Harry and Theresa do then? Harry wouldn't use force; Theresa could tearfully threaten never to speak to her father again. The old man might call him a thief and her insane, a bad mother to James, and raise an alarm. The police would come and . . . Harry's mind was running wild.

The old man tried the study door and muttered, "It's locked, good." He shuffled away. Harry waited a few minutes, his ear to the door. He heard the stairs creaking. Finally, a door closed on the second floor.

Harry drew a deep breath and let it out slowly. "We're ready to leave now, Theresa." She was crying softly, but she clutched his hand. With him leading the way, they moved silently through the hall to the back door. Harry picked up a bag that Theresa had hidden there and they slipped out into the cold.

The night was dark. They felt their way through the narrow passage and crossed the dimly lighted street. Harry helped Theresa and James into the coach, stowed the luggage, and climbed into the coachman's seat. As he cracked the whip, it suddenly dawned on him that Michael or his father could accuse him of home invasion, burglary, and kidnapping a child. Then he reflected that he was saving Theresa and James from the imminent threat of Michael, a desperate man, armed with a pistol. Life was often a choice between risks.

* * *

At dawn, Pamela awoke, groggy from barely three hours of sleep. She hastened her toilette and ate a quick breakfast, anxious to learn whether Harry had managed to free Theresa and her son from the Sullivan home. As she was finishing the coffee, a note was slipped under her door. *Meet me in the parlor. Harry.*

With a jumble of questions in her mind she hurried downstairs. Harry was haggard and unshaven, his suit rumpled, but he summoned a weary smile. "I left Theresa and James at Larry White's apartment—they should still be resting. Then I went to the Phoenix Club and found its gaming tables going full tilt. Lucretia had heard from Larry White at the Chelsea police station house that Sullivan insisted on going home, but Larry wouldn't let him go until a magistrate released him."

Pamela gazed at Harry. "Why don't you go home and sleep? Larry will look after Sullivan. I'll check on Theresa and James."

By the time Pamela reached the White family apartment, Theresa was alone, eating breakfast, looking snug and warm in her sister's bathrobe. Trish had gone to Sunday Mass with the children, including James. Larry would join them later for lunch and a visit to Huber's Fourteenth Street Museum. Its popular Curio Hall's huge collection of freaks and stuffed animals, including a giant boa constrictor, should entertain the children for hours.

"How do you feel, Theresa?"

"Light-headed and joyful, Pamela, as if I've been freed from prison. I'm savoring the moment and not thinking of tomorrow."

"And James?"

"He's quiet, feels uneasy, and doesn't understand why we left home like thieves in the middle of the night. He probably also misses the attention his uncle Michael paid to him."

"You should know that Michael is in police custody." Pamela described the violent incident at the Phoenix Club and

Michael's arrest. "His addiction to gambling has led him to embezzle a large sum of money from Judge Fawcett's account. The outlook for his future appears dire."

"God forgive me, Pamela, but I can't shed a tear for my brother. He has brought this trouble on himself. Too bad that it will shatter his father's illusions of him as a golden boy. He must now see his son for what he is, a base, ruined man. That may be more than my father can bear."

"How will your mother react?"

Before Theresa could reply, someone knocked on the door out in the hall.

"I'm not expecting anyone at this hour," said Theresa, signs of anxiety suddenly appearing in her eyes. "Could it be the police?" She began to tremble. "You answer the door, please, Pamela."

Pamela put a hand on the woman's shoulder. "Don't worry, I'll handle this." She went to the entrance hall, opened the door a crack, and said loudly enough for Theresa to hear, "Welcome, Mrs. Sullivan. It's good to see you. Please come in."

Martha Sullivan was a petite, once-pretty woman, who looked now as if she hadn't slept during the night. Her face was drawn, her eyes red from weeping. And she seemed uncertain how she would be received. Theresa entered the hall, gazed at her mother for a moment, and then embraced her.

Pamela stood aside, deeply touched. Finally, she took Martha's coat and they sat around the kitchen table. Pamela prepared the tea.

"Were you hurt badly that I left home?" Theresa asked tentatively.

Martha's lips tightened with the stress from a painful memory. "I was deeply saddened, Theresa, that the situation in our family had become intolerable for you—and nearly for me as well. You had no choice but to flee in the dark of night. I wasn't surprised. Our maid had spied on you and warned me that you were making suspicious preparations. I said that was nonsense and gave her the night off to get her out of the house."

"Have you heard about Michael being arrested?" Pamela asked, while pouring the tea.

"Yes, I know all about it. Larry wrote to me from the station house." She added, "I was upset, but really not surprised. I've known for some time that he sneaked out on Saturday nights, to drink and gamble—or worse. On Sunday mornings, he looked jaded. I tried to warn my husband, but he wouldn't hear of it and still refuses. He claims that enemies of Judge Fawcett and Tammany Hall have falsely accused Michael of vice and embezzlement, but the judge will defend him, and in the end everything will be all right. I think it's foolish to trust the judge. He looks and talks like a gentleman but he's a wicked man and will betray Michael."

Theresa frowned.

Martha nodded. "I'll speak frankly. Your father has always been prone to believe what suits him. He has gotten much worse as he slips into senility."

She drew a deep breath and gazed at her daughter. "I've come here this morning, Theresa, to assure you of my love. Mr. Miller seems to be a fine man. You and he are fortunate to have found each other. Don't rush into marriage. Take the time to become true friends."

As she left, she sighed, "I fear for Michael."

That evening, Pamela met Prescott at Grand Central Station upon his return from Williamstown. He hadn't eaten, so they stopped at a small, quiet restaurant for a light supper. Pamela was eager to hear the outcome of the controversy concerning Edward and his fraternity. But first Prescott would want a report on the latest development in the Sullivan crisis.

"Michael Sullivan seems to have disappeared," she began,

after the waiter had taken their order. She went on to describe Michael's attempted suicide at the Phoenix Club and his arrest. "Larry White stayed with him at the station house and has kept me informed. Late this morning, a police magistrate released him. He told the magistrate that he would go home, but instead he went to Judge Fawcett's mansion on Fifth Avenue. Larry followed him and watched until dusk, but Sullivan didn't emerge. Larry left, assuming that the judge had put Sullivan up for the night."

"That's possible," Prescott remarked. "Fawcett would surely want to punish Sullivan but would hold back until he had thoroughly questioned him about the secret account at the Union Square Bank and Trust, and possibly certain Tammany Hall matters. That could take hours."

The food arrived, spinach bisque with a pitcher of white wine. When the waiter left, they raised their glasses in a toast to Lady Justice. Pamela added, "May she correct the wrong done to our friend Harry."

"Amen," said Prescott. "Tell me about Theresa."

"She's fine," Pamela replied. "Harry freed her and her son, James, from the Sullivan house. They will stay with me tonight. I'll find a small apartment for them tomorrow in my building where I can keep an eye on them. Michael might still be a threat. Now tell me, what happened in Williamstown? Was Edward's case resolved?"

Prescott nodded. "Yesterday afternoon, President Carter met with the faculty committee investigating the recent tension at the fraternity and the attempt to poison Edward. The fraternity president and two other seniors at the meeting reported that Isaac Fawcett and Edward were rivals for Mary Clark's affections. They were also competing for the office of fraternity president, but Edward's athletic success gave him an advantage. Consumed with envy and jealousy, Isaac had recruited a fraternity brother, also resentful of Edward, to poison his breakfast porridge and make him sick before the Amherst game. Isaac slipped the poison into the bowl while his accomplice distracted the cook."

"How did the student investigators prove their case?"

"They closely questioned the accomplice's roommate. Out of fear, he had initially given the rogues an alibi. Now, he was sorry and told the truth."

"So what was the final outcome?"

"The faculty committee accepted the students' report and recommended that Isaac and his accomplice be expelled. President Carter agreed. He would call them to his office on Monday and give them his decision, then inform the judge by letter."

"That should free Edward of a great distraction from his studies."

"True, but Isaac Fawcett's disgrace will enrage his uncle, the judge. He will blame us and make our efforts to clear Harry's name even more difficult."

"That can't be helped. We'll prevail nonetheless."

CHAPTER 16

Suspicious Death

Monday, November 26

Early the next morning, Pamela was at breakfast with Theresa and James, when the landlady came with a message. "Mrs. Thompson, police detective Larry White is calling for you. Shall I send him up?"

"Yes, please do," replied Pamela, and turned to her guests. "Larry White is coming. Are you ready to see him?"

"You don't suppose he's been sent to arrest me?" asked Theresa, a nervous tremor in her voice.

Pamela shook her head. "He and I may have business to discuss. He'll be pleased to see that you and James are here, safe and well."

Within a minute there was a knock on the door and Pamela let him into the entrance hall.

"I have news for you," he said, a cloud of concern lingering on his face. Then he instantly brightened. "But first, I'd like to give my best wishes to Theresa and James."

Pamela led him into the kitchen where Theresa was standing, eyes shining and lips parted in expectation. "Larry, it's so good to see you." She embraced him and presented James, who greeted him shyly. They gathered at the table, Pamela served coffee, and James recounted yesterday's adventures in Huber's Museum. Today, he was trying to imitate the ventriloquist.

After a few minutes of family conversation, James was sent to read a book in the parlor. Larry then gazed tenderly at his sister-in-law. "This may be hard to deal with, Theresa, but I must tell you that your brother, Michael, is dead. Workers found him under a dock in the East River, early this morning. I've just informed your parents and your sister."

At the news, the young woman's hands flew to her face. But she quickly composed herself. "I can't say I'm sorry that he's gone. He was the bane of my life. But I would have wished him a better end."

Pamela asked, "How did it happen?"

"No witnesses have come forward. When found, he had been in the water several hours and was fully dressed. The strong tidal current could have carried him some distance from where he entered the water. I saw no obvious signs of malicious violence on his body. There were bruises to his head, but they might be due to him striking objects in the water, especially around the docks."

"Suicide?" Pamela asked.

"A reasonable conjecture," Larry replied, "since Michael had attempted to kill himself the night before. Financial reverses had apparently made him despondent. The investigation has only just begun. At this point, I wouldn't rule out foul play. I'll talk to Judge Fawcett, possibly the last person to meet Michael."

Late that afternoon, Larry White stopped at Pamela's office with news. He had found Fawcett at home in his study, apparently distressed. An acquaintance had told him about Sullivan's death in the East River.

"Was he surprised to see you?" Pamela asked.

Larry nodded. "I explained that I was charged with investigating the death, a routine procedure when there were questions about the victim's motive and no witnesses. I had to fill in gaps in the record of Michael's movements. Then I asked the judge to describe Michael's visit with him."

"Did he object?"

"He appeared offended that I would question him like any ordinary person. Still, he explained that Michael had seemed deeply disturbed about certain financial irregularities in the account that he managed for the judge at the Union Square Bank and Trust. A large sum of money appeared to have gone astray. Fawcett had told him that this was neither the time nor the place to discuss the matter and assured him that they could work out the problem after he had rested. He left in a cab early in the evening. It was dark."

Pamela asked, "Did the judge seem aware that Michael had attempted to kill himself several hours earlier in a bordello, after losing a very large sum of money?"

"When I told him what had happened at the Phoenix Club, he pretended to be surprised."

"Isn't that suspicious? Someone from the Phoenix or the police station must have told him."

"That's true. For whatever reason, the judge was holding back. Still his servants agreed that he was home all night."

"Nonetheless," Pamela insisted. "He might have arranged for someone else to kill Michael."

At that point Harry entered the room, lines of concern on his brow. "Theresa has told me that Michael's body is found. She and Trish are deeply concerned about their parents. Mr.

Sullivan is too feeble, mentally as well as physically, to manage their finances. Michael had handled everything. Mrs. Sullivan is alert but lacks experience and self-confidence."

Harry turned to his prospective brother-in-law. "I realize that Patricia has her hands full, but she knows how to manage a household. Could you arrange the transfer of Michael's power of attorney to her? Theresa would like to share the burden and could quickly be helpful."

"That sounds like a reasonable arrangement," Larry replied. "I'll discuss it with the sisters. I'm also concerned about Michael's personal papers that might shed light on his suicide."

"Don't worry," said Harry. "When Theresa and I left the Sullivan house, I brought with me Michael's secret account book and his diaries and other papers that might prove relevant to your investigation."

Larry quickly perceived the value of this revelation. "Michael had an insider's knowledge of Tammany Hall and that may have contributed to his death. For the present, let's keep these papers to ourselves. Where have you stored them?"

"They are secure in my office."

"Keep them there for the time being. Now we should visit the Sullivan home, together with Theresa and Patricia, and see what we can do for their parents. Mrs. Donovan will look after little James."

The Sullivans' maid admitted the visitors into a parlor. Seeing Harry and Theresa, she grew embarrassed, as she realized their new, dominant position in the family. "I'll fetch Mrs. Sullivan," she stammered.

Martha Sullivan arrived shortly and said, "I'm so glad you came." After James had left for the kitchen, Mrs. Sullivan turned to her daughters. "Your father has been in a daze since

Michael's disappearance. He lies in bed most of the time, or wanders about the house talking to Michael's ghost. The servants and I are at a loss what to do."

Before Pamela closed the parlor door, she surveyed the hallway. The maid was nearby, busily dusting a lampshade. Pamela stared at her severely, and she scurried away.

Theresa took the lead. "We can help you, Mother. This is our plan." She went on to explain the need to transfer Michael's power of attorney to her and her sister. They would become responsible for the household's oversight and its finances.

Still standing by the door, Pamela sensed a movement outside and raised a warning hand for Theresa to stop. Pamela then suddenly opened the door and came face to face with the maid.

Mrs. Sullivan rose from her chair, strode across the room, and confronted the woman. "You must leave this house immediately. We will send your things and your wages to whatever address you give us."

For a moment, the woman seemed defiant, but then glanced at Larry White, who had come up behind Mrs. Sullivan, and at Pamela. Finally, the woman said sourly, "Then I'd better go."

Pamela saw her to the door, returned to the parlor, and said to Martha, "Your maid used to spy for Michael, so now she's apparently doing the same for Big Tim at Tammany Hall."

"What a relief to get her out of the house!" Martha exclaimed.

Pamela assured her, "With extra help, Mrs. Donovan can temporarily fill the maid's place until a new one is hired, a mature woman who will respect you and help you oversee the household. Meanwhile, Theresa and Patricia will put the family finances on a sound footing."

Martha turned to her daughters. "What will you do about your father? If he comes out of his daze, he could object to the whole idea."

Patricia replied, "At that point we'll have to engage a doctor to assess Father's state of mind and certify him incompetent."

That would be a wrenching moment for the family, thought Pamela.

After supper, Pamela returned to the Irving Place office and reported to Prescott. As she spoke, he nodded with approval. At her conclusion, he reached into a cabinet for a bottle of whiskey and offered a shot to her. She declined. Then he poured one for himself and saluted her.

As he sipped from the glass, he said apologetically, "I'm sorry, Pamela, the burden of the investigation will increasingly fall on you. Harry must spend more time with Theresa and her son and bring the Sullivan family through its crisis. I also need his help in a complicated divorce case that I've just undertaken—frankly for the money. A Fifth Avenue matron wants me to win a large financial settlement from her philandering, wealthy husband. My commission will fund Harry's exoneration and replenish the firm's pro bono fund."

She waved away his concern. "I'm pleased that you trust me with this investigation, Jeremiah. It's what I really want to do. The key to Harry's exoneration lies in the Palermo killing seven years ago. A crucial piece of evidence has thus far eluded us, not to mention the NYPD."

Prescott cocked his head at a skeptical angle. "And what might that be?"

"A missing witness whom we know only by his initials, H. C., the passenger who left his shiny black portfolio in Palermo's cab. According to the cabdriver's landlady, he had found evidence in the portfolio that was very damaging to someone at Tammany Hall. When Palermo tried to extort a large payment for that evidence, he was killed. Mr. H. C. probably knew the significance of that evidence as well as the person it compromised. In sum, he's likely the key to our investigation."

Prescott nodded thoughtfully. "That's a reasonable conjecture. How do you propose to find H. C.?"

"Tomorrow, I'll speak to Fred Grant and Francis Dodd and hope they might point me in the right direction."

Chapter 17

An Abandoned Spouse

Tuesday, November 27

Late the next morning, with a heightened sense of responsibility, Pamela set out for Bellevue Hospital. Fred Grant had been there a week and might have recovered enough to be questioned. When she arrived, he was sitting up alone in the room, a book in his lap.

"I'll be mercifully brief," Pamela said. "Can you recall a man at Tammany Hall in January 1887 who carried a black portfolio with the initials H. C.?"

Grant struggled with the question for a long moment. "That might be Howard Chapman, a lawyer who handled Tammany contacts with utility companies and railroads. Though I never met him, I've heard he was a presentable Columbia College man about forty, valued for his ability to negotiate complex, favorable deals with the best of lawyers representing the business community. He left under a cloud, a year or two before I arrived at Tammany Hall. Francis Dodd might know more about him and should be here in a few minutes."

Seconds later, Dodd walked in, and Pamela repeated her question.

"I did routine office work for him," Dodd replied. "He greeted me by name, but kept a distance between us and never confided in me or sought advice." Dodd explained that Chapman had disappeared shortly after the cabdriver's homicide. Seven years later, no one seemed to know where he or his black portfolio had gone.

"Have you heard why he left?" Pamela asked.

Both men shook their heads. Dodd said, "Occasionally he smelled of cigar smoke and liquor in the middle of the afternoon."

"That's common enough at Tammany Hall," commented Grant wryly. "Why don't you look up his wife? She still lives somewhere in Tammany's neighborhood."

As Pamela left the hospital, she reflected on Chapman's possible addiction to strong spirits. Perhaps his mind was already befuddled when he climbed into Palermo's cab with the black portfolio. Still thirsty, he might have stopped the cab at the next saloon and gone in, leaving the portfolio behind. Several shots of whiskey later, he would have forgotten about the portfolio and Tammany Hall, and the cab was long gone.

At the Limerick, a restaurant on Fourteenth Street where Tammany members gathered, Pamela recognized Edgar, an old waiter who used to serve her. She asked if he had known the missing lawyer.

The waiter nodded. "He was a generous tipper. One day, he vanished, leaving his wife behind." He gave Pamela an address to Ellen's apartment off Fourteenth Street near Tammany Hall.

"She lives there, sickly and alone," the waiter said. "She used to come here occasionally, and we'd chat. I've heard that her savings have nearly vanished in the present economic depression. She must be desperate." He looked over his shoulder and lowered his voice. "In the seven years since her husband disappeared, Tammany Hall has given her no help, and she has probably grown bitter."

On the way to Mrs. Chapman's apartment building, Pamela reflected that the woman would surely be skittish toward a stranger knocking on her door. Pamela would put off until later any mention of her search for the missing husband.

The apartment was on the first floor of a brownstone town house. In response to Pamela's knock, Mrs. Chapman opened the door only as much as the security chain would allow and peered through the crack. "Who are you?" she asked in a cultivated voice, her brow wrinkled with distrust and fear.

"I'm Mrs. Pamela Thompson," she began softly. "I live in the neighborhood across from Union Square. Edgar, the old waiter at the Limerick, just told me that he hadn't seen you lately and was wondering if you were all right. He suggested that I call on you. It's almost teatime. May I treat you to a cup at the café down the street?"

Mrs. Chapman released the security chain and studied Pamela. Over the years working at St. Barnabas Mission, she had perfected a kindly, gentle manner to reassure abused, lonely, poor middle-aged women.

The fear in Mrs. Chapman's eyes slowly diminished, replaced by curiosity. "Are you the lady who searches for lost girls? I heard about you last summer."

"Yes, that's one of the things I do."

Except for her drawn expression, Mrs. Chapman was an attractive woman. Close to Pamela's age, slender, with refined facial features, she could have sat for one of John Singer Sargent's society portraits.

She beckoned Pamela into the entrance hall. "You can tell Edgar that I thank him for asking about me. I simply can't afford to eat out. And I shouldn't accept your invitation to tea since I can't return the favor." Her shoulders sagged under the weight of disappointments and defeat.

Pamela gently waved aside her protest. "I don't like to sit

alone in a café. Your company would please me and incur no obligation. Please call me Pamela."

She smiled timidly. "Since you put it that way, Pamela, I'd be delighted to join you. You may call me Ellen."

They sat at a table in a quiet corner of the café where they could speak without fear of being overheard. A waiter stopped by, and they ordered a pot of tea, biscuits, butter, and orange marmalade.

"Tell me about yourself, Pamela."

"I've been in situations similar to yours, Ellen. Not so long ago, I too lost everything—husband, property, social standing, and worst of all, my young daughter, Julia. Somehow I kept my self-respect and began to rebuild my life. I enjoy sharing my experience when it might encourage others."

The dull, defeated look disappeared from Ellen's eyes. The food and drink arrived. The waiter poured and left. The two women added cream and sugar to their tea, spread butter and marmalade on the biscuits, and raised the cups in a toast. Ellen ate and drank with relish.

"Please continue your story," she said, her voice growing lively. "It does seem to resemble my own."

Pamela touched on her social work at St. Barnabas Mission, her daughter's death and her husband's suicide, and her year managing a boardinghouse in a slum. "Then a good man came into my life, trained me to guard jewelry at Macy's and to find lost persons. In the summer of '93 in the Berkshires I helped a wealthy woman deal with a thieving butler and a difficult husband."

Pamela paused. "Now tell me about yourself."

Ellen nibbled on her biscuit, eyes gazing inward. "My husband left me suddenly, early in the morning, a complete surprise, seven years ago. He had to go into hiding immediately because someone at Tammany Hall was going to kill him. He promised that I would hear from him, but I never did. Most likely he died that day, and his body has never been found. Still, for years I hoped he might return, or at least contact me. After grieving for a while, I should have left this place and begun a new life, but I felt stuck with nowhere to go, nothing to do. The shock of losing him seemed to have killed my spirit. My friends also abandoned me. You kept your self-respect. I lost mine."

"How have you managed to survive?"

"Howard was very clever in financial matters. Much of his money disappeared with him. But he left behind large investments that he had recently put in my name. If he went bankrupt, we'd have financial resources to fall back on. I lived on the dividends until the national economic depression last year drove several of my railroad companies into bankruptcy."

"That was unfortunate," Pamela granted. "But, when the country's economy improves, you might receive dividends again. Until then, you will need assistance. I'll enquire at St. Barnabas and find out what can be done for you."

Ellen gazed at Pamela with admiration. "You seem able to solve problems, your own and others'." She hesitated. Pamela encouraged her with a smile. She drew a deep breath. "Could you find out what has happened to Howard? The truth would give me peace of mind and the freedom to move on. I've asked the police but they were no help."

"I could try. Tell me more about him." Pamela filled their cups.

Ellen nodded thanks, stirred in a little sugar, and took a sip. "We had a good life together. He was a handsome, well-mannered gentleman, kind and amusing in a self-centered way, and a rich, successful lawyer. We often dined in fine restaurants and attended the music halls, enjoyed expensive wines and elegant clothes, and vacationed in Newport and Saratoga Springs. His financial interests took him across the country to California, and he took me along."

"Did you have children?"

"No, he claimed they would be a distraction to his work. To be fair, I didn't want any children, either. My health has always been delicate."

"Why did he go to work with Tammany? With his talents and his privileged Columbia College background, he must have had good social connections. He could have chosen to enter a prominent private corporation."

"At Tammany Hall he became rich quickly. He liked the rascality of Tammany and shared its disdain for the snobbishness of the uptown society he was raised in. He also admired Tammany for what it did better than any other organization in the city—win elections." She finished her tea. "Shall we go up to my apartment and continue our conversation?" She seemed pleased with Pamela's interest.

Pamela gladly accepted her invitation. This was going better than she had anticipated.

Ellen showed Pamela into a parlor with a view out over the side street. The room looked bare. A bookcase of empty shelves stood against a wall. Next to it, a large vitrine displayed a fine collection of porcelain, but half of the shelves were empty. Furniture was sparse.

Ellen followed Pamela's gaze. "I've recently sold my crystal ware. The porcelain will go next. Over the past year, I've also sold the sofa as well as my silverware and the dining room table and chairs." She smiled wryly. "At this rate, I'll soon be sleeping on the floor in a much smaller apartment."

Pamela pointed toward several framed photographs standing on the mantel. "Is your husband in one of them?"

"This is he, ten years ago." She handed Pamela the picture of a man in his early thirties, dark-haired, clean-shaven, and handsome, except for a weak chin and a cunning look in his eyes. She recognized him as one of the Columbia alumni that her late husband, Jack, used to invite home after football games in the autumn, ten years ago, for cigars, strong spirits, and loud conversation.

"And here am I from the same time." Ellen brushed a little dust off the picture of a beautiful young woman in a fashionable white gown.

While studying the picture, Pamela remarked, "You make a good-looking pair and appear happy. I hope we can improve your lot." Pamela looked at Howard Chapman more closely. "May I ask, how well did he deal with strong spirits? I see no sign of abuse in this photograph. Still it's a common, often hidden problem among men of all social classes and can cause abnormal behavior."

"It's perceptive of you to ask," Ellen replied. "Both his father and his mother drank to excess and died young. Howard picked up the habit at Columbia but held it under control through most of our marriage. However, in the year before his disappearance his drinking became excessive and his behavior erratic. He hid bottles of liquor in the apartment and pretended he didn't have a problem. When I asked what was wrong, he said he was under great pressure at work."

"Can you think of anyone at Tammany Hall who would have wanted to kill him?"

Ellen hesitated, as if uncertain how to reply. "I don't want to say anything that would get him in trouble with the police."

"I don't work for the police. While I search for your husband, I'll report only to you. I happen to believe that the day before he disappeared, he had witnessed a Tammany Hall assassin kill a cabdriver. Is that what he told you?"

Ellen had turned pale. "Yes," she murmured. "He said it was a dreadful, complicated story and he didn't have time to explain. He was very nervous."

"Have you subsequently figured out how he got into that situation?"

She nodded. "I found his secret journal and his personal Tammany files dealing with the Broadway Railway's attempt to bribe the city's aldermen. Howard was in the middle, negotiating with both parties. I assume that something went wrong and Howard was blamed. I know that eventually many of the aldermen went to jail or fled to Canada."

"I can explain, Ellen. Your husband made a costly mistake: While carrying a large bribe from the railway company to the aldermen at Tammany Hall, he got drunk and left his portfolio with the money and certain compromising papers in a cab. The cabdriver found the portfolio and tried to extort a ransom from Tammany. Someone there ordered that the driver be killed. Your husband feared that he knew too much and would also be killed. Even if he escaped the assassin, he would be arrested by the police and convicted for his apparent part in the 'boodle'."

"Is his situation still hopeless?" Ellen asked weakly.

"I don't think so," replied Pamela. "At the time, he was in grave danger of a violent death or imprisonment. But seven years have passed. Reformers have pulled out some of Tammany's teeth. If your husband is alive, he could return home safely. With a clever defense attorney, like my friend Jeremiah Prescott, he should also avoid prison."

"How can I help you bring that about?" Ellen asked.

"May I see his journal and his personal Tammany files?"

"Yes, follow me."

Pamela went with Ellen into her husband's study, a small, cozy room with a window looking into a courtyard. The vanished occupant had arranged the furniture to serve his private interests rather than Tammany business. A large map of the United States in the 1880s, depicting the country's railroad system, hung on one wall. Shelves of file boxes covered another wall.

"His private papers?" Pamela asked, glancing at the boxes.

"Yes," Ellen replied. "Howard kept all his business papers in an office at Tammany Hall, and his successor must have cleared them out. I've examined everything here, but I've put it all back as it was."

"Has anyone else been in this room?"

"No," she replied emphatically. "Shortly after Howard's disappearance, a Tammany agent came to my door and asked to search my husband's office for whatever might belong to Tammany Hall. I told him that I'd already checked and there was nothing."

Pamela studied Chapman's writing table. There wasn't a speck of dust and no clutter of papers.

Ellen noticed. "I clean the surface every day. Even though the window is tightly closed, fine coal dust seeps in. If I didn't wipe it off frequently, it would cover the table with a thin black film and stain the sleeves of his clean white shirt. He was very concerned about his appearance."

Pamela sat down in Chapman's chair at the table and gestured for Ellen to sit facing her. "I'll look for clues to where he might be, dead or alive. Tell me what he was wearing when he left."

"I kept a diary," Ellen replied, "but I don't have to consult it now. I recall clearly my last image of him. It was January. He wore a winter coat and hat, over a dark business suit and white shirt. All his clothes were of the highest quality. He used to say, 'Appearance counts.' He wanted to be considered respectable and trustworthy even though he worked for Tammany Hall."

"Was there anything distinctive about his appearance or his personal effects?"

"Howard always wore an expensive gold pocket watch from Tiffany on Fourteenth Street that I gave him nine years ago. A gold chain attached it to his vest. Inside the cover is engraved, FROM ELLEN ON OUR FIRST WEDDING ANNIVERSARY. When he walked out the door, he was carrying his favorite black leather portfolio in one hand and a small satchel in the other."

"That sounds like a man going on a routine business trip for a night or two."

"That's true. He often left the apartment in that manner."

"It could also mean that he wanted to conceal his true purpose." Pamela surveyed the room. "Assuming that your husband is alive and hiding, I'll put myself in his shoes. He feels he must flee or be killed. Tammany has eyes and ears everywhere in New York City. Where else can he go where he would be safe and comfortable? That should be a distant place where he wouldn't be recognized, yet one that he has visited or read about. Can you think of a few such places?"

"We visited California twice, Florida once. He enjoyed their warm climate and good prospects for investment. On his own he went to Montana and Colorado on business trips to study the mining industry." She hesitated momentarily. "Perhaps you should look at his journals for which place he might have preferred."

She pressed a hidden lever in the bookcase, opened to a small room, and pointed to a neat row of books. "You may sit at his table and read them. Put them back when you've finished. I'll be in the parlor if you have questions."

After a couple of hours browsing in the journals, Pamela told Ellen, "If I may, I'll come back tomorrow and work through the day until I'm fairly sure where he might be hiding."

* * *

The next morning, Pamela studied Chapman's journals, travel scrapbooks, and private investment files. At noon, she and Ellen went to lunch at the Limerick. Edgar the waiter greeted Ellen warmly and served them. Afterward, Pamela returned to Chapman's study and consciously applied the science of detection to his disappearance. In the journals Chapman revealed his overriding passion for the sport of making money; he also enjoyed spending it on his wife as well as on himself. Pamela soon recognized patterns in his behavior and could anticipate how he might deal with a future problem—like fleeing from certain assassination.

She repeated the procedure the next day and again took Ellen to lunch at the Limerick. This time Edgar seemed tense as he approached their table.

"Do not appear alarmed," he murmured as he handed menus to the two women. "One of Dan Kelly's spies is following you." The waiter's eyes pointed to a small, bald man near the door who appeared to be reading a copy of the *New York World*. A blond woman joined him and ordered coffee. Soon she too was gazing furtively at Pamela.

"Do you recognize them?" Pamela whispered to Ellen.

"He's the supervisor in my apartment building. She's a German woman. They live together. Even after seven years, Tammany still spies on me."

They ate lunch as if the spies weren't there and ignored them as they left the restaurant. Nonetheless, Pamela was alarmed. Dan Kelly might force Ellen to have nothing more to do with her. She would thus lose access to the missing husband's papers. So she now took copious notes.

Late in the afternoon, as Ellen came into the study, Pamela waved a hand over the journals and file boxes piled neatly on the table.

"If your husband is alive, he's in Los Angeles."

"Have you picked that city out of a hat?"

"No. The city intrigues him. He's familiar with nearly all its nooks and crannies. His comments are more enthusiastic than on any other place. Furthermore, although he has been there twice, he doesn't mention a single person who would recognize him. If he were to change his name and disguise his appearance, he could find a comfortable niche in society and not have to live like a fugitive."

Ellen looked skeptical.

Pamela handed her a thin folder of miscellaneous notes. "These suggest that he had recently thought of moving to Los Angeles, even before the cabdriver's murder. He writes that he wanted to get away from the shabby intrigue and simmering violence at Tammany Hall and strike out on a new path."

As Ellen studied the notes, a troubled expression grew on her face. "He never spoke to me about it. I apparently wasn't in his plans. Was he going to leave me even before he knew of the threat to his life?"

That thought had passed through Pamela's mind, but she didn't wish to burden Ellen with distressing speculation. "The notes tell us only that he's most likely in Los Angeles—if he's alive. I'll leave now and figure out how to proceed. Los Angeles is a bustling city of sixty-five thousand people, nearly three thousand miles from here. It wouldn't be easy to find him."

Pamela packed the notes into her portfolio, together with a file of Chapman's private papers concerning Tammany officials and businessmen and their dealings with various city utilities and surface railway lines. She would study them later.

On the way to her office in Prescott's building on Irving Place, she became aware that Dan Kelly, The Knife, was following her. His spies at the Limerick must have tipped him off to her visits with Ellen Chapman. He apparently had concluded that the two women were conspiring against Tammany Hall.

To evade him, she slipped into a teashop, where she was well known, and ordered hot tea.

As she was about to drink, Kelly entered and sat brazenly facing her at the table. "Give me your portfolio," he demanded. "It may contain things that don't belong to you."

"What's in my portfolio is none of your business," she said loudly. "Now leave me alone."

He tilted back in his chair, took out his knife, and began to trim his nails. "I'll count to three, bitch," he said loudly enough for everyone to hear. A nervous silence fell upon the room.

Without warning, Pamela tipped the table over him, knocking him backward sprawling on the floor, soaked with hot tea. As he was falling, the knife flew out of his hand. Pamela kicked it across the room.

For a moment he lay there, stupefied and speechless. Then, cursing her, he scrambled to his feet. Before he could strike her, she pulled a blackjack from her bag and hit him hard on the temple. He fell senseless to the floor.

Anticipating trouble, the proprietor had sent a boy to fetch the neighborhood patrolman. Within minutes, Kelly was hauled away handcuffed. The proprietor kindly escorted a shaken Pamela the rest of the way to her office on Irving Place.

Pamela realized that the police would soon release Kelly. She went directly to Prescott and reported the incident.

"Do you think you can deal with him?" he asked, his brow creasing with concern.

"Yes, he'll be less arrogant in the future, and I'll be more careful." She went on to describe what she had discovered at Ellen Chapman's apartment. "I'm confident that, if her husband is alive, he's living disguised and under a false name somewhere in Los Angeles."

"He would be a valuable witness for us," Prescott remarked. "Finding him could be difficult but not impossible. I'll send your information to the Los Angeles Pinkerton Agency today and ask them for a quick search. That could still take several days."

"In the meantime," Pamela said, "I'll check on the crisis in the Sullivan family." She paused for a moment with an afterthought and shook her head. "I regret now that I've drawn Kelly's attention to Ellen Chapman. He may try to intimidate her."

Chapter 18

The Hostess

Saturday, December 1

The next day, Pamela set off for the Sullivan home, hoping to meet Harry Miller. He was now staying there and would be familiar with the latest development in the family's ongoing crisis.

A sturdy, middle-aged woman met her at the door. "I'm Mrs. Carlson, the new maid. Please come in, Mrs. Thompson." She showed Pamela into the parlor. "I'll fetch Mr. Miller for you."

The woman made a good first impression. To judge from her accent and her alert blue eyes, she was Swedish and exuded competence. Reassured, Pamela followed Mrs. Carlson into Michael Sullivan's former study, now temporarily serving as Harry's room.

A few minutes later, Harry arrived and slumped into a chair. "By now, Mr. Sullivan should be settled into his new quarters at the nursing home and no doubt is complaining. His wife and her two daughters are there, trying to console him." Harry shook his head. "These have been difficult days for all of us."

"How has Mr. Sullivan reacted to Michael's death?"

"At his wife's insistence, he read the newspaper account of

the discovery of Michael's body, but he refused to believe that his darling son was dead and called constantly for him. When Michael didn't come, the old man wept pitifully and accused his wife, Martha, and his daughters of lying to him. As his frustration mounted, he screamed and threw things at them. Finally, exhausted, he stared at the wall and refused to speak or eat."

"How have his wife and daughters coped with him?"

"He's more than they can handle. Martha is distressed and sleeps poorly. Trish is overburdened with demands at home. Theresa has always disliked her father. His erratic behavior provokes feelings in her akin to hatred. The family's best solution is the nursing home that will care for him in the short term. Monday, we'll begin the process of declaring him mentally incompetent."

"That's sad. Under the best of circumstances, the old man would be a heavy burden on his family." Pamela sighed. "Shall we move on? Any progress in the investigation of Michael Sullivan's death?"

"Yes," Harry replied. "Larry White would like to talk to you. He has questioned Judge Fawcett's servants again. Catherine, the distant cousin, seems to be holding back information, presumably fearing reprisal. Larry believes you are acquainted with her. Maybe she'll open up to you."

Pamela found Larry at the University Athletic Club near Madison Square. Prescott had secured him as a boxing instructor on Saturday mornings and had invited him to lunch. She joined them in a small private dining room. Women weren't allowed in the rest of the club.

Hours of exertion in the gymnasium this morning had given Larry a fresh, ruddy complexion and a strong appetite. He and Prescott ordered steaks; Pamela asked for a small piece of broiled salmon.

Boxing was far too brutal a sport to interest Pamela, but she politely asked Larry about his work at the club.

When he blushed and stammered, too modest to speak of his prowess, Prescott stepped in. "Larry is in excellent condition and skillful with his fists. Among middleweight boxers, he could more than hold his own. He has many disciples in the club."

Pamela searched Larry's face. "He must be an artful dodger—if I may use Dickens loosely. After hours of boxing he still looks as handsome as ever."

Larry smiled at her teasing. "Here in the club we use soft, padded gloves. No one gets hurt."

When the food arrived, the conversation shifted to the investigation into Michael Sullivan's death. Pamela had put Larry in touch with Ambrose Norton, Michael's clerk at the bank. They were working together on Michael's diary, his secret financial accounts, and other private files from his home.

"Did Michael's death create a problem for you?" Pamela asked.

"It's not as serious as you might imagine, since Norton had previously copied or summarized the most relevant material."

"What have you learned thus far?"

"To support his habitual gambling Michael has been skimming the judge's money for at least a year. In his last entry in the diary, Friday evening, the twenty-third of November, when he was planning that massive theft from the judge's secret bank account, he asked himself, 'What would the judge do if he were to find out?' Michael answered, 'The judge would sputter and fume, but he wouldn't do anything because I'd threaten to reveal his secret crimes to the police.' "

"Doesn't that throw more light on why Michael went from the police station directly to the judge rather than to the Sullivan home?" asked Pamela.

"I agree," replied Larry. "Michael wasn't casting himself on Fawcett's mercy but was trying to deter the judge from going to the police and charging him with embezzlement."

"That's extortion, a powerful incentive for the judge to kill Michael Sullivan."

"Correct. But did the judge act on that motive? He has an alibi for that night. And that leads me to ask you, Pamela, to investigate Catherine Fawcett."

Pamela was taken aback. "Isn't she the judge's cousin who manages his household and his philanthropy? I've met her through St. Barnabas Mission. She's an upstanding woman who has served the judge for years."

Larry nodded. "That's her, though 'upstanding' is perhaps merely the public's perception. In fact, the character of anyone working closely with Judge Fawcett is likely to be tarnished. The snickering and backbiting that I heard from other servants probably means that the judge sleeps with her."

"What aroused your suspicions?"

"When I questioned her, she acknowledged having seen Sullivan at the mansion but hadn't noticed anything out of the ordinary. Over the years, he had occasionally come on business. The servants said much the same. But I felt strongly that Miss Fawcett appeared unusually anxious talking to me and was perhaps trying to hide something."

"Your intuition is reliable," remarked Pamela. "I'll investigate her for a few days while waiting for word from the Pinkertons in Los Angeles. Tell me more."

"I'll lend you her file. She lives in the judge's Fifth Avenue mansion in an apartment of her own and regularly takes Saturday nights off."

"Years ago, she and I had a good relationship. I'll arrange to see her today."

* * *

Late that same afternoon, chilled to the bone, Pamela waited on Fifth Avenue across from Judge Fawcett's elegant brownstone mansion. She recalled Catherine's thick black hair, blue eyes, slender, attractive figure, and gracious manner that made her stand out among women in the judge's household—and attracted their envy. The cook and the housekeeper were dowdy, older women; the maids were plain, untutored girls.

Finally, Catherine left the mansion from a side door in a fur coat and hat and hailed a cab. Pamela caught the next one and followed her closely a short distance to Carnegie Hall at the corner of Seventh Avenue and Fifty-seventh Street. To conceal her identity Pamela pulled her hat down low over her forehead and wrapped a scarf over her chin.

At the ticket office Pamela edged close enough to hear Miss Fawcett ask for tickets reserved in her name. When Pamela's turn came, she asked for a nearby seat. After paying for the ticket, she glanced at the program. Only then did she realize that this evening the Oratorio Society of New York was going to present Joseph Haydn's greatest piece of choral music, *The Creation.* Walter Damrosch would conduct the New York Symphony Orchestra. Pamela thanked her good fortune. Tonight, she would combine business and pleasure.

Meanwhile, she kept an eye on Miss Fawcett, who had begun to walk down Seventh Avenue. It was six o'clock. The program didn't begin until eight. Pamela followed her at a safe distance, though the woman seemed too preoccupied to notice her.

At an English teashop a short distance from the hall, Miss Fawcett glanced at a menu in the window, walked in, and sat down at a table set for two.

Peering through the window, Pamela wondered, was this a rendezvous?

A waiter approached the table with a familiar greeting and gestured to the empty chair. Miss Fawcett shook her head, and he removed the extra setting. She apparently would dine alone. To judge from the look on her face she wasn't disappointed.

Pamela thought this the right moment to enter the shop. As she drew near, Miss Fawcett looked up from the menu and their eyes met. After a momentary hesitation, Miss Fawcett smiled in recognition. "What a delightful surprise to see you, Mrs. Thompson! What brings you here?"

"Haydn's *Creation,*" she replied, reproaching herself for the partial deception. Her main reason for coming was to spy on Miss Fawcett. "I look forward to hearing Walter Damrosch and the New York Symphony and the Oratorio Society. This should be a glorious evening."

"I agree," said Miss Fawcett, her face lighting up at the prospect. "I shall be there too." She glanced at the empty place in front of her. "Would you please join me?"

Pamela agreed gladly. The waiter returned with another setting and took their order for tea and a light supper.

The two women renewed their acquaintance from St. Barnabas Mission. Several years ago, Pamela had solicited funds from Miss Fawcett. She then joined Pamela in seeking support from other wealthy women. Pamela offered a brief sketch of her life since then. Miss Fawcett nodded sympathetically at Jack Thompson's financial crimes and suicide.

Pamela finished her account as their omelets arrived. Miss Fawcett suggested that they use their Christian names and Pamela agreed.

Pamela asked, "May I ask how you have fared since we last met?"

Catherine shrugged noncommittally. "I still serve as hostess for my cousin, the judge, and dispense his philanthropy."

"I can imagine that the role of a hostess might be challenging, as well as enjoyable. What does the judge expect you to do?"

"Arrange dinners—some intimate, others grand—for fellow

judges, lawyers, prominent politicians and businessmen. Wives and female friends are sometimes included. I also oversee the house and the servants. By 1887, I was also acting as his personal secretary: making travel arrangements, composing, editing, and even signing many of his letters and legal documents."

Pamela looked askance. "Really?"

Catherine nodded. "Yes, Fawcett finds paperwork tedious and gladly pushes it off onto me."

"That sounds like quite responsible work. I trust he appreciates your skill and discretion."

Catherine shrugged. "I also listen patiently to him rant on about the lazy poor, the ungrateful and unruly workers in his Massachusetts textile mill, and our incompetent Democratic president, Grover Cleveland."

"You must be busy. Is the work rewarding?"

"At first it was. Now I find less satisfaction in it." She paused and drew a breath. "But I don't want to spoil your evening and mine with complaining. Shall we speak of the concert? Where will you be seated?"

Pamela showed her the ticket.

"Would you consider joining me?" Catherine asked. "The judge has reserved the seat next to mine, but he won't be coming. You could take his place and return your ticket."

"What an inspired idea! I accept."

In the hour that remained before the concert, Pamela prompted her companion to speak of herself, beginning with her love of music. She entertained the judge's guests on the grand piano in the mansion's music room. He sometimes asked her to play popular tunes on a small piano in her apartment. Every year, he subscribed to seats at the Metropolitan Opera House as well as the Carnegie Music Hall.

"Does the judge have a serious taste for music?" Pamela asked.

Catherine shrugged. "He's proud of his handsome, dignified appearance and big, deep, rich voice. Music, like philanthropy, gives him an opportunity to dress up and present himself to the city's social elite as a wealthy, cultivated gentleman. His interest in music is shallow and vulgar. The best part of a concert for him comes before it starts when the lights are on and people are chattering and gawking at each other. When the lights go out and the music begins, he quickly grows bored and he fidgets until the intermission. Then he wanders about the hall, seeking out important people and exchanging a word or two with them. When the concert resumes, he hurries from the building to his club for a drink and a smoke."

"Does he simply abandon you in the middle of a concert? How rude!"

Catherine nodded. "But don't feel sorry for me. I enjoy the music much more when he's not sitting in the next seat. I stay to the end and take a cab home." She studied Pamela curiously.

"Do you have much music in your life?"

"My friend, Jeremiah Prescott, and I occasionally attend the Met and Carnegie Hall. I'm also fond of the sacred music of Bach and Handel in a religious setting as in the Church of the Ascension near my former home in New York."

"Is your Prescott a good companion?" Catherine asked slyly.

"Yes, he appreciates serious music and especially enjoys Mozart. But his personal taste runs mainly to lighthearted Viennese operettas, like *The Gipsy Baron*. They help him escape from his demons. He avoids grand operas with tragic themes. 'As a soldier in the war,' he once said to me, 'I observed too many deaths that were truly tragic in contrast to the often false, or pathetic, operatic variety.' "

"You are fortunate to have such a friend," Catherine said with feeling, then signaled the waiter for the bill. "Our supper has been lovely. Now it's time for the music."

* * *

The auditorium was rapidly filling up, and the musicians were already tuning their instruments. Pamela and Catherine settled quickly into their seats. The chorus, some sixty men and women, filed in behind the orchestra. The musicians and the chorus grew still. An expectant hush came over the audience. Finally, Walter Damrosch, the conductor, walked onto the stage, followed by the three soloists.

Pamela glanced at her program. Lillian Blauvelt, soprano, was the Archangel Gabriel; Charles Herbert Clarke, tenor, was the Archangel Uriel; and Emil Fischer, bass, was the Archangel Raphael. Pamela pulled out her opera glass and studied them, beginning with the young soprano.

Catherine leaned toward Pamela and whispered. "Miss Blauvelt is only twenty-one, born in Brooklyn. She's very pretty and truly sings like an angel."

Damrosch raised his baton and the music began.

For the next hour and a half, the three archangels—in recitative and glorious arias—described God creating the universe and man out of the primeval chaos. The chorus added powerful, awestruck commentary and joined the trio in great bursts of divine praise. The oratorio concluded with the chorus singing a mighty "Praise to God."

Pamela thoroughly enjoyed the music though Catherine sometimes seemed distracted. Her lips parted in awe at the young soprano's powerful, limpid depiction of God creating light. At less compelling moments, however, Catherine seemed to slip into a troubled inner place that brought her close to tears.

When the concert ended and the crowd surged toward the exits, the two women remained in their seats for a few minutes, savoring the music, and agreed that it had exceeded their expectations. Then Catherine searched Pamela's eyes and asked, "Would you care to join me for tea in my apartment? It's not too late, is it? The weather is mild for this time of year. A cab would take us there in five minutes."

"What a perfect way to end a delightful evening!" Pamela replied, wondering what had prompted Catherine's invitation. Did she need to confide in someone?

Chapter 19

Confession

Saturday, December 1

Pamela and Catherine entered Fawcett's mansion by the side door, climbed up a private stairway to the next floor, and entered a parlor. A piano stood to one side, a folder of sheet music nearby. A photograph of the judge in judicial garb hung on a wall. His expression was stern, as befitted a zealous guardian of the law. Pamela also detected a hint of self-importance in the thrust of his jaw.

Catherine followed Pamela's gaze and remarked, "This evening, Judge Fawcett went to a meeting at Tammany Hall, saying he'd be gone overnight."

"Does he belong to that organization?"

"No, but he offers legal advice there when asked. Make yourself comfortable while I go to the kitchen and hurry the tea along. It should be ready in a few minutes."

A tea table had been set for one person. Apparently, Catherine had expected to be alone. The tableware was common silver plate; the cup and saucer were plain chinaware. The tablecloth was likewise clean and serviceable. Pamela saw no sign of luxury in the room, other than the piano. This evening, Catherine wore a decent, tasteful, but inexpensive gown. Her jewelry was similarly plain.

Earlier, the servants' insinuations had led Pamela to wonder if Catherine might serve as the judge's mistress. He could afford one. Thus far, Pamela hadn't noticed any of the usual outward signs of a rich man's "kept woman," such as fashionable clothes and diamond rings, expensive porcelain and furniture. Catherine's surroundings suggested that she was merely a privileged servant.

Catherine returned with another table setting and small pastries. After flashing Pamela a nervous smile, she went back for the tea. Finally, they sat down at the table and Catherine poured, her hands trembling. She offered Pamela a pastry and then took one herself. For a few awkward minutes, they ate and drank quietly. Pamela began to feel apprehensive. They had spoken little since arriving at the apartment.

Suddenly, Catherine put down her cup, covered her face with her hands, and began to sob. Her sobs became convulsive, and Pamela's concern mounted. She rose, put an arm on the woman's shoulder, and asked softly, "What can be the matter?"

"My life is a mess," stammered Catherine, brushing away her tears. "This morning the judge gave me three weeks to leave this apartment and his service. 'It's time for a change,' he told me. 'I've found a more suitable hostess.' "

"Is she rich or young or both?"

"I know her. She's a few years younger than me. Her father is a wealthy, socially prominent businessman with connections to Tammany Hall and has brought her to the house on visits. It's rumored that Fawcett plans to marry her. He's probably with her tonight instead of at Tammany Hall."

"Would it help if you were to tell me how you got into this situation?"

Catherine nodded. "Thank you. I need to bring things out into the open that have burdened me for years, and there's no one in my circle of acquaintances that I can talk to."

"Start from the beginning." Pamela pushed her cup to the side and gave Catherine her full attention.

"I was raised in a well-to-do family," Catherine began. "My father, a Union officer, was killed in the war, and my mother remarried. Unwanted at home, I grew up in boarding schools where at least I received a sound, general education. My stepfather lost his money in the Depression of 1873 and could no longer support me. Upon finishing high school in 1874 without a dowry, a suitable marriage seemed impossible. For the next five years, I supported myself as a wealthy lady's travel companion. Arthritis had weakened her hands, so she hired me to write for her. If I may brag a little, my penmanship is beautiful. My mistress dictated to me all her correspondence and her journal. For the following five years, I was housekeeper for a rich elderly couple and managed their finances. During that decade, I learned a great deal about domestic service, but marriage remained a remote prospect."

"How did you meet Judge Fawcett?"

"In 1884, he had just bought this Fifth Avenue mansion and was looking for the right person to manage his enlarged household. A mutual acquaintance recommended me. At the interview the judge and I discovered we were distantly related. He liked my credentials and offered me a good salary and this comfortable apartment."

"How did you feel about him at the time?"

"At first I liked him. He seemed to be a generous, interesting, and attractive man."

"Did you think of him as more than an employer?"

"Because he was rich, presentable, and single and I was desperate, I thought of him as a prospective husband. In fairness to him, he never hinted at marriage, neither then nor later."

"When did your experience begin to turn sour?"

"Already in 1887, certain traits of his character disturbed me. At first, he pretended to be high-minded, even in private. But he soon let down his guard with me. Many of the letters he dictated seemed to approve bribes and other Tammany wrongdoing. I came to believe that he was also taking bribes to render verdicts favoring Tammany's interests. That puzzled me because he was already rich and the sums were small. What mattered most to him was Tammany's support for his election."

The conversation had come to the point where Pamela could ask, "Do you recall when he became involved in the Tony Palermo murder case?"

Catherine nodded. For a moment, she averted her eyes, apparently embarrassed. "One day, the judge called me into his study. 'You are very clever at handwriting,' he said with a smile of appreciation. 'I want you to study the handwriting in these reports, then practice imitating the author until no one can tell the difference. I may ask you to determine certain cases of fraud or extortion.' The exercise intrigued and challenged me. I was also flattered that he considered me capable of what might become a serious responsibility."

"Were you really that skillful?"

"He had reason to think so," she replied. "Early in our relationship, he had entrusted his own signature to me in routine correspondence. No one could detect the deception. I've always been interested in handwriting and what it tells us about a person. By studying the judge's handwriting I gained insights into his character, for example, his compulsive need to shine."

"What were those reports he asked you to imitate?"

"A police detective was reporting ordinary investigations and requesting reimbursement for expenses. His name was blacked out. At the time, I saw nothing improper in my assignment. Then, a few days later, the judge came with what appeared to be another exercise, a police detective's extortion letter to Mr. Tim Smith in Tammany Hall, demanding a thousand dollars to end an investigation into a suspicious death of a cabdriver. The judge said to me, 'Copy this letter, using the handwriting that you learned before.' "

Pamela frowned.

"Yes, the request seemed odd," said Catherine. "But I did what he asked."

"And, then?"

"When I finished the message, the judge came back to me with a signature, 'Harry Miller.' The judge said, 'Copy this to the message and give it to me.'

"His request made me deeply uneasy and apprehensive. This looked like extortion, a serious crime. To protect myself I made an exact copy of the signed message, wrote down a summary of my conversations with the judge, and preserved all of my preparatory work on the project."

"You were aware of becoming involved in something possibly illegal, weren't you, Catherine?"

"Yes, in a way, but I wasn't sure until I heard about the judge convicting Miller of extortion. I told the judge how I felt. He replied that Miller was guilty as sin. 'He had verbally demanded the money. But the law required written proof so we had to manufacture it.'

"I didn't look convinced. He gave me his stern look. 'Just do what I tell you and keep your mouth shut and you won't get into trouble.' "

Pamela frowned. "Was there no one you could have turned to?"

She shook her head. "I felt bad for Mr. Miller—I still do. I was afraid to tell anyone, certainly not the police: They're in bed with the judge. I believed I could be charged as an accomplice in his wrongdoing. If accused of fraud, he could have said that I acted on my own for gain. As the author of the forgery, I would be charged with offering false evidence to the court. The way the judicial system works, I could have gone to jail while the judge remained scot-free."

"Why have you confided in me?"

"When police detective White questioned me a second time, I realized that I might be in trouble. I had overheard the judge complain earlier that reformers like Reverend Parkhurst were after him. The Lexow Committee up in Albany was also likely to investigate him, like others connected to Tammany. Mr. Sullivan's recent death had made matters much worse for me. Detective White appeared at our door, and the judge instructed us servants to say we knew nothing. I grew desperate."

She paused, gazing at Pamela. "Your appearance at the concert wasn't accidental. Detective White must have sent you. He's an honest cop and a fair-minded man. He was giving me an opportunity to open up on my own terms."

"Fair enough," said Pamela. "What would it take for you to describe to a magistrate how you unwittingly copied the fraudulent extortion letter that put Harry Miller in prison?"

"I must have a strong, clever lawyer to support and defend me."

"Mr. Jeremiah Prescott, my boss, could be your lawyer. He's familiar with the complicated circumstances of the cabdriver case and is prepared to represent you, and others like you, who are innocently ensnared in Judge Fawcett and Tammany Hall's criminal enterprises."

Catherine leaned back, crossed her arms, and appeared to mull over Pamela's proposal. Then she pondered aloud, "Having given me notice, the judge will surely fear that I might betray his secrets. The servants will keep track of my movements, and he may hire a spy like Kelly to follow me—or worse. Still, I must do something to save myself or face ruin." Her brow wrinkled with this effort of reflection. Finally, she said, "Tomorrow is Sunday. As usual, I'll go to the early morning service at Saint Thomas Church a few blocks away on Fifth Avenue at Fifty-third Street. That shouldn't look suspicious. But I'll see you and Mr. Prescott there, and we'll find a safe place to talk, God willing."

Chapter 20

The Forger

Sunday, December 2

Shortly after sunrise, Pamela and Prescott joined a flock of warmly dressed servants from the great mansions of the neighborhood and climbed up the steps to the church's main entrance on Fifth Avenue. A brisk, cold wind hurried them into the building. A sprinkling of the faithful was already in the pews. This was the First Sunday of Advent, the beginning of the Christmas season. Even the early morning service would be well attended.

The sun's rays struggled through the stained glass windows into the tall, vaulted nave. As she walked down the main aisle, Pamela searched for Catherine Fawcett among the many shadowed faces in the pews. "I'll wear a blue bonnet with a pompom," she had said.

She had also instructed Pamela to carry a walking stick and wear a black veil. Prescott should walk behind her. "I usually sit up front near the chancel. One of the judge's servants also attends this early service and will be observing me. We mustn't arouse her suspicion. She would carry it back, exaggerated, to the judge, and he would make my life even more miserable. As you pass by, ignore me. After the service, I'll leave by a side door to the right and speak to the sexton—as I often do. Allow a minute to pass, then follow me."

Near the chancel, Pamela finally recognized Catherine, then glanced around but couldn't detect an obvious spy. A minute later, the sexton lit the altar candles. The celebrant entered the chancel together with two acolytes and began to intone the opening prayers in beautifully cadenced English. The reading of Psalms and Scripture and the homily on the Gospel moved the service forward at a measured, stately pace appropriate to communal divine worship. At the confession of sin Pamela thought she heard Catherine softly sobbing.

When the service ended, the sexton extinguished the candles. As he left the chancel, he seemed to glance toward Catherine and slightly nod. A minute later, she got up and followed him. Pamela and Prescott waited a minute and joined her at a table in the sexton's little room. The sexton studied them briefly, then went back into the church to prepare for the main service later in the morning.

"Can you trust him?" Pamela asked Catherine.

"Yes. We meet frequently in my charitable work. He seeks out needy people in the parish—typically elderly or infirm former servants struggling to live on meager pensions in basements and cold attic rooms—and we visit them together. I told him the gist of my present situation and said I wanted a place to meet you. He offered this room."

Pamela asked Catherine, "When did the judge return last night?"

"Shortly after you left, he came to my apartment in an ugly mood. Apparently his fiancée had denied him her bed, so he demanded to crawl into mine. I said no, I was ill. He cursed and shook his fist. For a moment, I thought he would assault me, but he suddenly grew weary and went to his room. Despite the uncertainty of my future, I'm looking forward to leaving his service."

"His fiancée might be a match for him and have her own way," Pamela remarked. "Now tell Mr. Prescott about your forgery of the extortion letter that incriminated Harry Miller years ago."

Catherine glanced at Prescott hesitantly until he encouraged her with a smile. Then she told him how the judge had tricked her into imitating Harry's handwriting and signature.

"Did you keep a copy of the letter?"

"Yes, I also kept the drafts where I practiced Mr. Miller's style of writing." She drew them from her bag and handed them to Prescott.

He held them up to the light from a gas lamp and compared the drafts with the final copy, addressed to Mr. Timothy Smith and dated January 20, 1887. "Well done!" Prescott remarked, "I understand how the police could truly believe that Harry had written the forgery."

Pamela objected, "Still, after the 'boodle' was exposed and Smith went to prison, you'd think the police would have taken a second look at Harry's case."

Prescott shook his head. "In their eyes Harry nonetheless appeared guilty of extortion, not to speak of insubordination, even though the extortion was being practiced on a criminal like Smith. Judge Fawcett must have had a strong reason to trick Catherine into creating this forgery. It was risky. He could easily have lost his reputation and gone to jail. Somehow, Harry's investigation seriously threatened him."

Pamela waved a dismissive hand. "Alderman Smith might have feared that Harry's investigation would also have exposed the 'boodle.' So he may have offered Fawcett a large bribe, or threatened to withdraw his electoral support."

Prescott glanced sympathetically at Catherine, who appeared

uneasy about her role in the widespread corruption being discussed. "You are an innocent pawn in Fawcett's criminal game—but in a dangerous situation. Would you like me to defend you free of charge?"

Catherine's face grew taut with anxiety. "Why would you do that?"

"Your testimony as to the fraudulent character of the extortion letter would go a long way toward exposing and correcting a great injustice committed on my associate Harry Miller."

For a moment she chewed nervously on her lip, then she softly said, "I accept your offer and will help Mr. Miller."

He pointed to her papers that Pamela was holding. "We'll keep these safely in our office. Now tell us, how well did you know Michael Sullivan?"

She drew a deep breath, her voice barely audible. "Since Mr. Sullivan controlled the judge's bank accounts, he and I met occasionally to discuss the judge's philanthropy."

"What happened in Fawcett's study on the night Sullivan disappeared?"

Catherine flushed. "When Detective White questioned me, I was less than honest in my reply that I knew nothing. I had in fact overheard a quarrel between the judge and Mr. Sullivan.

"An acquaintance at the Phoenix Club and a clerk at the local police station had earlier called us to report Sullivan's heavy gambling losses and his attempt to shoot himself. The judge was at church, so I received the messages. When he returned home and learned what had happened, he tried to appear calm. 'We'll soon discover the truth,' he said. But I could see in his eyes that he was very disturbed."

"How did he react when Sullivan showed up at his door?" asked Prescott.

"He pretended to be solicitous. 'You look exhausted,' he said. 'What has happened?'

"Sullivan said he had lost a lot of money at the Phoenix Club.

When he had protested, the police were called and brought him to the station house. The judge appeared to listen sympathetically and said, 'Catherine will see that you are properly fed and rested, then we'll talk.'

"After eating, Michael went to rest in a guest room. Meanwhile, I returned to the judge's study. He was on the phone and told me to wait outside. I overheard him speaking loudly to the bank's trust officer at home. The judge told him to forget about his Sunday afternoon nap and go immediately to the bank and check the secret accounts. The trust officer must have made excuses—like the building and the offices were locked and so on. The judge swore a mighty oath and shouted, 'Get back to me in an hour or I'll have your hide,' and he hung up."

"What happened next?"

"A few minutes later, he opened the door and beckoned me in. 'You've probably heard more than you should have,' he said to me. He looked so angry that I felt weak in the knees. I said that whatever I heard was confidential. He told me to hold Mr. Sullivan for an hour or two. 'Steal his clothes if you have to.' Then he told me to put a call through to Tammany Hall. He had tried once before but was unsuccessful—it being Sunday afternoon.

"I made several vain attempts on the phone in his study while he sat at his desk, furiously fingering through his file boxes, muttering to himself. Finally, one of the guards at Tammany answered—he didn't give his name. The judge took the phone and waved me out of the room. 'I don't want you eavesdropping, Catherine.'

"I said, 'Yes, sir. I'll check up on Sullivan and then join the cook for tea.'

"A few hours later, the bell rang in the kitchen. I hurried to the study. The judge said, 'Bring Sullivan here.' His voice was low and icy. I could tell that he had already convicted Sullivan and was going to pass sentence on him. On my way to the guest room, I was expecting Sullivan to have come to a clear understanding of his folly and be prepared to throw himself at the judge's feet, like a prodigal son. To my surprise, he looked as if he had a powerful weapon in his hand and was ready for battle.

" 'The judge wants to see you now,' I said simply. 'Follow me.'

"As I showed Sullivan into the study, the judge stared at me severely. 'That will be all, Catherine. Go to your apartment and stay there until I call you.'

"I didn't dare disobey him, but on the way, the porter asked me what was going on. I told him what I knew, and he said he could eavesdrop safely through the vents in a basement room below the study. Afterward he told me he had heard much of the quarrel. The judge had shouted that he would put Sullivan in prison for a very long time. Sullivan had responded just as loudly, 'Then maybe we'll share a prison cell. If you accuse me to the police, I'll tell them all I know about your financial misdeeds. And I have proof.' "

"How did the judge react?"

"He spoke in a soft voice that the porter couldn't hear. Soon, the judge called me to his study. 'Mr. Sullivan is waiting for a cab.' He was standing off to one side with a smirk on his face. I asked the porter to go out on the street and watch for the cab. In a few minutes, he came back and said it was outside. Sullivan climbed in and the cab set off. That's the last I saw of him."

At that point, the sexton returned. Catherine thanked him for the use of the room. As she left, Pamela patted her hand and told her to keep in touch. She smiled nervously.

"What do you think, Pamela, can we count on Catherine to testify in court that Judge Fawcett had her forge the crucial evidence against Harry?" Pamela and Prescott were in a teashop on Fifty-third Street and had ordered tea and scones.

Pamela shrugged. "The odds are poor, aren't they? Tim Smith at Tammany Hall would surely try to bribe her to remain silent and, if that didn't work, he would threaten her with beating or death. The NYPD, like Tammany Hall, also has to protect its already badly damaged reputation and prevent a reversal of Harry's conviction. They can't be counted on to protect Catherine."

"Regrettable but true nonetheless," Prescott admitted. "When she has reflected on the forces against her, she may refuse to deal with us anymore or testify in court."

Pamela added, "Even that might not be enough to satisfy certain people in Tammany Hall. I fear for her."

Their tea arrived and was poured. As Prescott was adding sugar, he asked, "Have we learned any more this morning concerning Michael Sullivan's disappearance?"

Pamela nodded. "Judge Fawcett was in a mood to strangle Michael that evening. I doubt that he followed Michael and personally pushed him into the river. However, his Tammany call is suspicious. He could have engaged an experienced assassin like Kelly."

"That sounds likely to me." Prescott stirred the sugar into his tea and bit into a scone. "Pass this information on to Larry White and go back to our trusty contacts in Tammany Hall."

"Yes, Fred Grant is probably still recovering at Bellevue Hospital from his ordeal and too weak for questions. But his colleague, Francis Dodd, will work tomorrow. I'll catch him before then."

CHAPTER 21

Suspect Judge

Monday, December 3

Pamela rose early, dressed quickly, and hurried to the Limerick restaurant. Edgar, the elderly waiter, had told her that Francis Dodd ate breakfast there before going to his office at nearby Tammany Hall. With luck, she might catch him and persuade him to investigate Judge Fawcett's mysterious call to Tammany Hall on the evening of Michael Sullivan's disappearance.

A few minutes before eight, she hid herself across the street from the restaurant and waited in the cold for Dodd, hoping that Kelly would not chance to appear at the same time. As a church bell struck eight, Dodd approached the restaurant alone. Pamela dodged nimbly through traffic and intercepted him at the door.

"What a surprise, Mrs. Thompson!"

"May I speak to you privately?" Pamela nodded toward the restaurant. "Perhaps Edgar could find a quiet, private room for us. I don't want Kelly to see us together."

Dodd was taken aback but quickly recovered. "You must have a delicate matter to discuss. Edgar will show us to a non-smoking room. Kelly and his gang wouldn't be there."

The room was half filled, mainly with young female office workers. Pamela and her companion sat at a table that offered privacy. After they ordered breakfast, Dodd remarked, "By the way, the police never charged Kelly and his thugs, McBride and Cook, with the assault on Fred Grant ten days ago."

Pamela frowned in mock surprise. "Really?"

"I agree, Mrs. Thompson, that the police are at least predictable. The investigating officer claimed that Mr. Grant was in no condition to identify his assailants."

"No surprise there." Pamela then asked, "How is Fred?"

"His legs are slowly healing though they cause him much pain. Nonetheless, he will leave the hospital today on crutches and convalesce in safety with his son in Hartford." Dodd paused nervously. "Will our conversation have to do with Kelly?"

"Yes. I want to know if he was on guard duty at Tammany Hall, Sunday evening, eight days ago, and might have received a phone call from Judge Fawcett's home." She explained that Fawcett spoke to an unnamed guard, presumably concerning Michael Sullivan, who afterward got into a cab and disappeared. McBride and Cook left New York the next day. "A suspicious coincidence, isn't it?"

Dodd nodded. "I'll look at the schedule to see if Kelly or one of his thugs was on duty that evening. I'll also check the telephone logbook. The guard should have noted the receipt of Judge Fawcett's call. I'll contact you after work later today."

"Would you also discreetly browse in Tammany Hall for loose talk concerning Michael Sullivan's death? It must have caused a stir. He was known there."

In her office on Irving Place, Pamela stared at the forged extortion letter that had disgraced Harry and cost him four years in prison. She was baffled that a prominent magistrate like Judge Fawcett would so brazenly violate his oath to uphold the law.

She added the letter to the already large pile of evidence on her desk concerning Fawcett. Clearly guilty of fraud and judicial misconduct, he was also an increasingly serious suspect in Michael Sullivan's death. Pamela leaned back in her chair and pondered what Fawcett's next move might be. Would he harm Catherine?

A familiar voice outside in the hall reminded Pamela that she hadn't seen Harry Miller for a week. Prescott had sent him to Newport, Rhode Island, to search for the hidden assets of that rich businessman entangled in an ongoing divorce case. Representing the man's wife, Prescott needed an accurate account of the family's wealth in order to win her a fair share.

Pamela opened the door and called out, "Harry, come! I have something for you."

He walked toward her, a tentative, expectant smile on his face. Gone was his wry look of the past. His reconciliation with Theresa and his newly harmonious relationship with her mother had sweetened his outlook.

She beckoned him into the office and handed him Catherine's copy of the extortion letter. "Do you recognize this?"

He glanced at it and then recoiled as if it smelled bad. "Indeed," he said. "This is the forgery that put me in Sing Sing for four years. Did you sneak into the courthouse archives and steal it?"

"No, Catherine Fawcett gave it to me. It's her exact copy of the original that she wrote seven years ago."

For a moment Harry stared at the letter, lips parted. "Incredible!" he exclaimed. "It really looks like I wrote it. I know she was the judge's cousin and lived with him. Still, why did she do this?" He slapped the letter with mounting anger. "Did he pay her?"

"No, Harry, he tricked her." Pamela showed Harry the samples of his own police reports that Catherine had used to master his handwriting style.

"I must admire her skill," said Harry. "At the time, I thought that someone in the NYPD had fabricated the letter or had hired an expert. I couldn't imagine that a criminal court judge would stoop so low."

"It beggars belief," Pamela agreed. "When Catherine finally realized the judge's deception and how he had used the letter to convict you, she was sorry but felt trapped and fearful. He could have severely punished her if she spoke out."

"The bastard!" Harry grimaced, struggling again with his anger.

Pamela thought, how wise of Prescott to assign Harry to other duties, far removed from Judge Fawcett. Harry's sense of the injustice done to him was still raw. She measured her words. "There's hope at last, Harry. Catherine has come to know the judge better and to detest him. With Prescott's support she is also less fearful. She'll explain the forgery to a prosecutor when we've built a strong case against the judge."

Harry drew a deep breath, gazing at Pamela. "I thank you for sharing this with me and trying to clear my name. I know only too well the danger you face in challenging Tammany Hall and the NYPD." His lips quivering, he pressed her hand and left the room.

Late in the morning, Larry White came to Pamela's office, took off his overcoat, and sat down with an expectant look on his face. "Have you found anything for me?"

"A piece of the puzzle, Larry," she replied. "Catherine Fawcett spoke of a loud quarrel between the judge and Michael Sullivan." Pamela went on to describe the judge's anger at being embezzled and Sullivan's unrepentant, belligerent attitude and his threat to implicate the judge in Tammany's financial crimes.

"What can we draw from their quarrel?" Larry asked.

Pamela replied cautiously. "No doubt the judge had a strong motive to kill Sullivan but might not have had the opportunity. Sullivan was alive when he left the judge's house and climbed into a cab. I hope to learn later today whether the cab was a trap, perhaps set by the judge."

"At least, Pamela, we can conclude that the judge is a major suspect in Sullivan's death. For now, however, our suspicion must be carefully guarded. Over the years, the judge has built powerful connections to the business community, the police, and Tammany Hall. The evidence against him must be overwhelming before we can safely attempt to expose his crimes."

"I agree," said Pamela. "Our friend Harry's fate should teach us prudence." She reached into the pile on her desk for Catherine's forged extortion letter and handed it to Larry. "I doubt that you were expecting this. It comes from Fawcett's mansion."

He glanced at the letter and frowned, apparently recognizing it almost immediately. Harry must have earlier described it to him. "Who gave this to you?"

"Catherine Fawcett. It's a perfect copy of the one she made for Judge Fawcett seven years ago that he used to convict Harry."

Larry looked troubled. "I'm surprised that she would knowingly take part in such a flagrant fraud. It seems out of character."

"She's innocent, Larry." Pamela showed him Catherine's studies of Harry's written routine reports and her successive drafts of the extortion letter that more and more resembled Harry's handwriting.

"She has the skill of a masterful counterfeiter! We could use her in the detective department to uncover fraud."

"That letter is the tip of an iceberg, Larry. Over the past ten days I've gathered more evidence of Judge Fawcett's wrongdoing." Pamela handed over Fred Grant's diary and his personal correspondence with Francis Dodd, his disgruntled colleague at Tammany Hall. "In my summary of this material, I've pointed to the judge taking bribes in return for reducing or dismissing charges, serious as well as trivial, against Tammany officials and clients. The bribes are also entered in Sullivan's secret papers."

She allowed her companion several minutes to browse through the papers. "Quite sordid," he remarked. "I'm surprised that the judge would risk his sterling public image."

Pamela waved off that objection. "With his deep rich voice, thick silver hair, handsome appearance, and the talents of an actor, he plays the role of a dutiful magistrate to perfection. In addition he's intelligent and knows the law and how to break or bend it safely."

Pamela picked up Michael Sullivan's secret green account book. "The judge could more easily appear clean because he paid Sullivan to do his dirty work. I found this account book in Michael's study at home. It records a $350 payment into the judge's secret account at the Union Square Bank and Trust Company from Big Tim Smith at Tammany Hall."

"That would be the bribe that persuaded Fawcett to convict Harry."

Pamela nodded. "I am also investigating a different payment earlier in January, seven years ago. Dan Kelly told his friend, Alice Curran, that someone at Tammany Hall had offered him $200 to kill the cabdriver Tony Palermo."

"Who was that person?"

"I suspect he was Big Tim Smith. He's Kelly's boss and a brutal, ruthless man, but I can't yet prove that Smith made the offer and actually paid Kelly. I need the testimony of a key witness who disappeared seven years ago, Howard Chapman."

Pamela reached for the remaining documents in her pile. "These are Chapman's private papers. You will recall him from the case of Tony Palermo, the murdered cabdriver."

"Yes, Chapman was the Tammany lawyer who left his portfolio in Palermo's cab. He disappeared soon afterward and hasn't been seen since."

Pamela explained, "His sudden disappearance suggests that he wasn't merely an ignorant or careless courier but a significant part of the conspiracy to silence Palermo. The plot might have unfolded more violently than he anticipated. He protested, was killed, and his body hidden. Or, he felt threatened, fled from the city, and changed his identity."

Larry tilted his head in a skeptical gesture. "What do Chapman's papers tell us?"

"They lead me to believe that he fled. From his journals, travel scrapbooks, and private files, I can imagine him in Los Angeles. He would have changed his appearance and taken a new name. According to his wife, he left with a large sum of money, so I'd guess he is presently a prosperous dealer in California real estate. He may even have married bigamously."

Larry looked doubtful. "From your description of the erstwhile Howard Chapman, I conclude that he may still believe that Tammany and /or the police would destroy him if he were to return to New York. Furthermore, he has probably sunk roots in Los Angeles, or wherever he is, and would not want to pull up and leave."

"I agree," Pamela said. "Finding him and bringing him back to New York is obviously a daunting task. Nonetheless, I should try. Chapman likely knows who ordered Dan Kelly to kill Tony Palermo. I need his truthful testimony in court in order to satisfy the demands of simple justice and to vindicate Harry Miller's conduct in this case."

"I wish you well," said Larry, "and I'll help where I can. I'll be waiting to hear from you later this afternoon concerning Judge Fawcett's call to Tammany."

Late that afternoon, Frank Dodd came to Pamela's office. "I've dug up information concerning Sullivan's death that Detective White will want to hear."

"I'll call him. He's expecting word from me."

Larry arrived shortly and asked Dodd, "What have you learned?"

"The guards on duty on the night that Michael Sullivan disappeared are my friends and spoke freely. Early in the evening, one of them heard the phone ring and called Kelly from the poolroom. A few minutes later, he returned agitated and rushed up to an off-duty cabdriver, Andy Singleton, who was playing pool with McBride and Cook. Kelly said he had sudden club business and needed to hire the cab and the driver's badge that evening. He would return the badge, horse, and cab in good condition."

According to the guard, Singleton protested that it was against cab company rules. Then Kelly held out a dollar bill. Singleton had been drinking, so he took the bill and said, "Don't scratch the paint."

Pamela remarked, "Kelly would have left with McBride and Cook about the time Sullivan was preparing to leave Fawcett's house."

"That's likely," said Larry. "But how do we know that Kelly actually picked up Sullivan?"

"I learned it from another guard," Dodd replied. "Late that night, McBride returned the cab, horse, and badge to the cabdriver's stable. The next morning, as Singleton was checking the passenger seat, he found a fine linen handkerchief embroidered with the initials M. S. He cleaned it and gave it to his wife Mary."

Pamela said, "I'm sure the embroidered initial is Mrs. Sullivan's work, a gift to her son."

"That's the key!" Larry exclaimed. "The handkerchief connects Kelly and his men to the disappearance of Michael. I'll immediately retrieve it from the cabdriver. Mrs. Sullivan will confirm its identity."

Pamela gazed at her companions. "Gentlemen, we may conclude that Kelly hired McBride and Cook to knock Sullivan on the head, and throw him into the East River to make it look like suicide. Thank you, Mr. Dodd. You've been most helpful."

Dodd remarked gruffly, "I owed it to Fred. At least this time, Kelly and his thugs might pay for their crime."

Chapter 22

The Journey West

Tuesday, December 4–Monday, December 10

Over coffee at breakfast, Pamela planned her next step. While Larry White was piecing together the story of Michael Sullivan's last hours, she would follow the westward tracks of Howard Chapman, her key witness to the death of Tony Palermo. She felt increasingly sure that Chapman was hiding in Los Angeles. By this time, the Pinkerton detective might have found him.

At the office, she found Prescott shifting through a pile of paper, his door half open. He seemed to be concentrating intensely. Pamela hesitated to interrupt him, but he never seemed to mind seeing her.

Pamela rapped lightly. "May I disturb you?"

He looked up, blinked, and then smiled. "Of course, come in." He patted the pile before him. "These documents identify the hidden treasure of my client's cheating husband. I'll happily push them aside for the moment." He pulled up a chair for her.

"Thanks. I've come to the point in the Palermo case where I need to speak to Mr. Howard Chapman, the absent witness. Have you heard from California?"

"Let me check. The clerk has just brought in the mail." Prescott fingered through a pile, pulled out a lengthy telegraph, and scanned it. "Yes, Paul Gagnon, the Pinkerton agent, has tentatively confirmed your hunch that Chapman is living in the Los Angeles area under the name Hugh Carey. Since leaving New York, he has grown a beard, lost hair and put on weight, and wears eyeglasses."

"In other words, he looks like many other men of his age," Pamela remarked archly.

"Present company excluded, my dear." Prescott stroked his clean-shaven chin, ran his fingers through his full head of pepper-gray hair, and flexed his lean, muscular arms.

She indulged him with a fond smile. "You are an exceptional man."

"You are perceptive. Now, the more telling clue is that Mr. Carey arrived in Los Angeles shortly after Chapman left New York. The detective has also noticed an Eastern accent and years of legal training in his speech." Prescott handed her the message.

Gagnon explained that Southern California's rapid economic growth had attracted men with Chapman's characteristics early in 1887. However, Carey had come alone, others had family; Carey appeared to be rich, refined, and cultivated, others did not. Carey was a canny, successful investor in the area's real estate and had earned a certain respect among businessmen.

As she returned the message to Prescott's desk, she remarked, "Your Mr. Gagnon has studied Carey only briefly and mostly from a distance. He hasn't confronted him, admittedly out of concern that he might panic and flee to Mexico. I would have wanted a sharper identification."

"Still, do you think Carey is your man?" Prescott asked doubtfully.

"All things considered, he might be. That he continues to use the initials H. C. is a telling clue to me. Still, the only way to be certain is to go to Los Angeles, observe Mr. Carey, and perhaps confront him. If he is in fact Mr. Chapman, I'll try to persuade him to return to New York and give testimony before a magistrate. If Carey's not my man, I might still be lucky and find him in Los Angeles."

Prescott reflected for a moment, his gaze inward, his fingers tapping on his desk. "Ever since telegraphing the Pinkerton detective, I've thought of sending you to Los Angeles. I'm confident that you could carry out such a project. Mr. Chapman doesn't appear dangerous. Equip yourself for the other challenges you can foresee. The trip could be quickly arranged. An express train runs daily."

"How long might I be gone?"

"I'd say, devote a month to the trip—five nights in a sleeping car each way and two or three weeks of investigation in Los Angeles. The Pinkerton will help you. Harry and I can't go since we are committed to the ongoing divorce case and other business. Fortunately, our recent and pending stipends are handsome. The firm can afford to send you first class. Still, you should probably have a traveling companion. Do you have someone in mind?"

"Yes, your son Edward's friend, Mary Clark."

Prescott was taken aback. "Really? She's a sweet girl but she's only eighteen and has never been outside Berkshire County. Wouldn't she be a hindrance rather than a help?"

Pamela shook her head. "If I were to need brawn or technical assistance, I could call upon our Los Angeles Pinkerton detective, Paul Gagnon. But I sense that Mr. Chapman might respond well to a subtle, persuasive approach where Mary could be an asset. She's the kind of attractive, guileless person that Chapman might readily relate to."

"Really? How can you be so sure of her worth? You hardly know her."

"In fact, I know her quite well. She's a strong, intelligent young woman. At her mother's premature death, Mary became head of the family. She has coped with a dispirited, unstable father and an insecure younger brother in conditions of severe poverty and become wise beyond her years. She will welcome the relief and the challenge of this trip."

"Those are encouraging signs of maturity," Prescott remarked. "Are there more?"

"Yes, there are," replied Pamela. "During last month's visit in Williamstown, I observed Mary several times and under various circumstances. She has also consulted me on delicate questions of female health. Since she wants to be a teacher, I encouraged her to broaden her outlook, while still young, and not tie herself down too early to a husband and family. She was very receptive. We've corresponded regularly ever since. Recently, we've been discussing a visit to New York City during her school's winter holiday. She would stay with me like Brenda Reilly and Francesca Ricci and my other foster girls. Instead of the New York visit, I'll now offer her the trip to Los Angeles."

"What about her family? You claim that she holds them together. Her father is unemployed and inclined to drink. Her brother seems to depend on her for guidance and for help in his schoolwork. How can they manage without her?"

"Last week, Mr. Clark finally found employment as a machinist at the factory on Water Street in Williamstown. Edward helped them move into a house nearby and continues to give moral support to Mr. Clark and son Tom. They can live without Mary for a month and will appreciate her all the more when she returns."

Initially, Prescott had listened to Pamela with a slightly bemused expression on his face. Now he looked penitent. "I realize that I've neglected Edward these past few weeks. I must write to him and catch up on his news. Thank you for the interest you show in Mary. It will make her a better person and more helpful to my son. Consult her about the trip, so that we can make the arrangements as soon as possible."

Late Monday afternoon, the tenth of December, Pamela and Mary boarded the Lake Shore Limited, a Chicago express train, at Grand Central Station. The young woman's exhilaration was contagious. Pamela felt as if she too were embarking on a great adventure. Prescott had seen them to the station and waited with them. Finally, a great clanging of bells and hissing of steam announced the train's departure. The two women waved goodbye to Prescott and set out on their three-thousand-mile journey across the continent.

Mary's leaving her father and brother had been tearful. But they had stoutly supported her. "We'll be fine," they had said in unison at the North Adams station as she boarded the train for New York City on Sunday. She had then stayed overnight with Pamela to make final preparations for the trip.

Mary's most serious problem had been to persuade her high school teachers to allow her a two-week leave of absence from classes before and after the Christmas holiday. Initially, they had balked. Then, satisfied with Pamela's credentials as mentor and chaperone, the teachers worked out together a plan of reading and writing that would make this trip a worthwhile educational experience. The young woman would bring along a few books and a supply of paper and pencils, ink, and pens. The teachers expected her to keep a daily journal and compile a scrapbook of sketches, maps, and detailed descriptions of interesting persons and places.

As the train gathered speed, the two women stood at the window, fascinated by the city's skyline. When they reached open country, there was less to catch their eye. As hours passed, the train's rocking motion and the light, rhythmic click of its wheels calmed their initial excitement.

The late autumn view from their window was bleak. Leafless trees stood like skeletons against a lowering gray sky. The Hudson River's open water appeared restless and cold and threatened to engulf the tiny boats plying its surface. Farmsteads, hamlets, and small towns seemed to vanish in the blink of an eye. Eventually these impressions blurred and the ride became routine.

The Pullman sleeping cars on their train were arranged in sections open during the day and closed off by curtains at night when porters converted the seats into berths. In view of the journey's length, Prescott had paid extra for one of the few closed compartments. Its sliding door offered greater privacy and a quieter ride. The room was small but ingeniously arranged. The two women sat facing each other on comfortable, upholstered sofas. A portable table stood between them.

Mary brushed a wayward lock of black hair from her brow, cocked her head, and asked, "Why are we going to Los Angeles?"

The question's direct thrust momentarily took Pamela aback. The two women had earlier spoken mostly about the trip's educational opportunities for Mary, the grandeur of the Rocky Mountains, and the exotic beauty of Southern California. Pamela had mentioned that this trip was also part of an ongoing search for a missing man, but she hadn't gone into detail.

Mary rephrased her question. "Could you tell me more about the person you're searching for? He must be terribly important if you would travel three thousand miles—and pay first-class fare—to find him."

"A perfectly reasonable question," Pamela replied. "The missing person is Mr. Howard Chapman, a key witness to a murder that took place seven years ago." Pamela went on to describe the most significant details of the cabdriver case and their connections to Tammany Hall. "If I find Mr. Chapman, I'll try to persuade him to tell a court who killed the cabdriver and who covered up the crime. If Chapman cooperates, the court might then eventually clear the name of my friend and partner, Harry Miller."

"I understand," said Mary. "Though I've never met Mr. Miller I feel sorry for him. His experience of injustice resembles my father's punishment for challenging Judge Fawcett's cruel policies toward the Blackinton mill workers. I know I'm supposed to study while on this trip, but can I also help find Mr. Chapman?"

"You help by adding to my disguise, Mary. Society is suspicious of a single woman traveling across the country by herself. You and I look like an aunt and her niece on a trip together. No one is likely to pry. If people do ask, we'll tell them that I'm a family friend who helps poor women and children in New York City. That's true after all. As far as anyone is entitled to know, we're going to Southern California to see its sights and enjoy its weather."

"I see. We must keep secret that you are really investigating Mr. Chapman. If he were to find out, he might cause trouble or run away."

"Precisely. I also anticipate calling on you occasionally to be my eyes and ears in Los Angeles. Perhaps you will come up with ideas or cheer me up."

"That sounds like something I'll enjoy, and I look forward to helping poor Mr. Miller. He was badly treated."

Pamela reached into her portfolio. "Study this photograph of Howard Chapman so you'll recognize him when you see him." Pamela handed her the ten-year-old photograph of Chapman. "He'd be about forty now and probably heavier, bearded, and nearly bald."

Mary held the photograph up to the light and examined it from various angles. Then she focused a magnifying glass on the picture. "What's this thing hanging on his vest?" She handed the glass to Pamela.

"A watch chain," Pamela replied. "The watch is an expensive gift from his wife."

"Why hasn't he tried to bring her out to California?"

"For her sake I hope to find the answer," Pamela replied. "They seemed compatible. She has waited seven years for him to return. What do you think of him?"

"Rather handsome and clever. I'll sketch his face, then I might figure him out."

"Could you also make a sketch of him that might resemble how he looks today?"

"I'll start now." She pulled a sketchbook and a pencil from her portfolio and set to work on the table.

After an hour, Pamela laid down the novel she had been reading, stood up, and stretched.

Mary put her sketchbook and pencil aside. "What are you reading, may I ask?"

"Helen Hunt Jackson's *Ramona,* a novel I found in Chapman's apartment. To judge from his many marginal notes, he must have read it closely, a year or two before leaving New York. His notes could offer clues to where he might be and what he's doing. The novel, by the way, has sold thousands of copies."

"Why is it so popular?"

"It's a bittersweet story of a mixed-breed young woman in Southern California, many years ago. Hunt depicts a warm, lush place, a paradise to us Northerners who must suffer through several months of snow and ice and bitter cold. Ramona's love for a California Indian in a harsh, unfeeling society ended tragically. American settlers and politicians forced the native people from their lands. Many sank into despair. A few years ago, Hunt laid out the brutal facts in a book, *A Century of Dishonor.*"

"May I read *Ramona* when you have finished? The book sounds a little like Mrs. Stowe's book, *Uncle Tom's Cabin*, about black slaves before the Civil War. Will I see the Indians?"

"You might see a few. Unfortunately, there aren't many left. Now, stand up and stretch, then go back to your studies."

An hour later, a porter named Charles came through the car ringing a small bell. A tall, slender, young black man, he had helped them settle into their compartment. At their open door he announced that dinner was being served. His speech had a soft, melodious Southern accent.

"Are all Pullman porters black men?" Mary asked, wide eyed. Apparently, this was her first close contact with a black person. The northern Berkshire textile mills depended on immigrants from Quebec for cheap labor.

"I believe that's true," Pamela replied. "Pullman porters are dependable, skilled men, though I doubt that they're paid as well as they should be. They must rely on tips. As we learned in the recent railroad strike, Mr. Pullman is as unfeeling and stingy toward his workers as Judge Fawcett."

"But why are porters so very black? Can't Mr. Pullman find any other men for the job, the Irish, for example, or even men of mixed race?"

"You raise good questions, Mary. Mr. Pullman claims that the black race, more than any other, is naturally disposed to service. He recruits his porters mostly from the descendants of household slaves in Georgia and the Carolinas, who for generations were trained to pay close, respectful attention to their masters' wishes. Pullman passengers are led to think of the black porters in a similar light and expect the same kind of deferential service."

Mary nodded but seemed uncomfortable with Mr. Pullman's outlook. "This arrangement appears to work well for the company. I just wonder how the porters feel about it. Like the textile workers back home, the black men need the money, so they have to put up with the indignity."

"That's true," Pamela agreed. "However, Charles speaks like an educated young man. He will probably soon move on to a job more in line with his ability."

"I would like to think so," said Mary in a tone both sad and doubtful.

Dinner was served in the next car. A black headwaiter showed them to a table covered with fresh white linen and clean, polished tableware. The food proved equal to what Pamela would expect in a fine New York hotel. She and Mary shared their table with a middle-aged married couple, Mr. and Mrs. Carroll, returning to Los Angeles after visiting their son in New York.

The husband remarked, "We tried to persuade him to move out to Los Angeles. It's 'a land of milk and honey,' as the Good Book says. We made the move years ago and have never regretted it. But his wife has close family ties in New York and wants to stay put."

Pamela led the conversation to the good impressions of Southern California that she had gained from *Ramona.*

Mr. Carroll shook his head dismissively. "It's a mushy, far-fetched romance about a couple of good-for-nothing Indians. But it has certainly promoted tourism. People want to see where Ramona lived, as if she were a real person."

His wife added, "Or they come to enjoy the sun and the sea and the beautiful flowers."

Pamela shifted the conversation to possible mutual acquaintances.

Mrs. Carroll eagerly rattled off a long list of names of new Californians with New York roots.

"Have you heard of Mr. Hugh Carey?" Pamela eventually asked.

"Of course. He's a wealthy local businessman. The paper announced his marriage just before we left Los Angeles. His first wife had passed away years ago in New York."

Pamela struggled to conceal her surprise, wondering whether Chapman was now a bigamist.

Back in their compartment, while Mary sat at the table and wrote the day's impressions into her journal, Pamela remarked, "If our Howard Chapman has taken a second wife, it might be harder for us to persuade him to return to New York. He would have to face a new charge of bigamy. We could threaten to denounce him to the police. But his wealth and reputation would enable him to delay or frustrate extradition."

Mary cautioned, "It also doesn't seem consistent with Chapman's secretive character that he would risk exposing his disguise in Los Angeles with a well-publicized marriage. If he were lonely, he could just move in with a woman. The more prominent he becomes, the more likely his true identity would be detected."

Pamela agreed. She asked herself if she was pursuing the right man.

At nightfall, Charles, the black porter, appeared at the door and announced that he would make their beds. Would they leave the room for a few minutes? Rather than stand outside in the narrow aisle, they walked to the salon at the far end of the car, Mary leading the way. Her slender body adjusted gracefully to the rocking motion of the train and caught the eyes of fellow passengers, especially the males.

At the sight of Mary, Pamela choked, as she frequently did, whenever a young, charming, and pretty woman recalled her deceased daughter, Julia. She would have been Mary's age.

In the salon a handsome young man offered Mary his seat.

She declined with such a lovely smile that he grew confused with pleasure. "We'll stand, thank you," she said brightly. "We've walked here for the exercise."

When they returned to their compartment, their beds were ready. They changed into nightclothes, Mary climbed into the upper berth, and Pamela turned out the gaslight. While waiting for sleep to come, she conjured up a familiar image of Prescott, gazing fondly at her. She thanked him over the distance for providing such comfort on this long, westward journey.

CHAPTER 23

The California Limited

Tuesday, December 11

As the train approached Cleveland, Ohio, Pamela and Mary were at breakfast in the dining car. To the north was a dull gray vista of Lake Erie under a low, leaden sky. To the south was a barren lakeside park where killing frosts had stripped all color from its flowerbeds. Even their thin cover of snow was gray.

Pamela sighed. But what could one expect in December? The ride had been rocky during the night. Mary hadn't slept well and had left their compartment this morning in a sour mood. Fortunately, their dining car's bright lights, luxurious furnishings, and courteous, helpful waiters had lifted her spirits.

The California couple, the Carrolls, joined their table. The husband glanced out the window, frowned, and muttered, "I can't wait to get home. Why would anyone freely live in this part of the country?"

"It's not all bad," offered Mary, once again her naturally enthusiastic self. "I read yesterday that Mr. Pullman built a clean, comfortable town in Chicago for his workers, complete with proper houses, stores, churches, and public gardens, as well as a modern railroad car factory."

Pamela asked with a hint of irony, "Doesn't that arrangement sound a little like Judge Fawcett's village, Blackinton, in Williamstown? There are also limits to Mr. Pullman's benevolence: He doesn't allow black porters like Charles to live in his town."

Mary reflected for a moment, and then nodded. "Yes, I suppose both places are run like an old Southern plantation. The master controls the keys to your life. You'll only be happy as long as you do as you're told and don't complain."

When Pamela and Mary returned to their compartment, the beds were stowed away and the table was set up again. Their porter, Charles, came by within minutes and whispered, "Mrs. Thompson, during the night, a man asked about you. I told him that we don't give out information about our passengers."

"Can you describe him?" Pamela was immediately concerned.

"He's small, bald, and expensively dressed and has a smooth look on his face. His question sounded suspicious, so I described him to other porters. They told me his name is Daniel Kelly. He's traveling alone and has a berth in one of the other sleeping cars on this train."

"Thank you, Charles," said Pamela, as levelly as she could manage, considering the distressing news. This Tammany assassin would hover over her and complicate her mission. She said to the porter, "I know Mr. Kelly, a dangerous man who should be kept at a safe distance. Thank you for this information." She gave the porter a generous tip.

He bowed politely and pocketed the money. A grave expression came over his face. "From time to time, ma'am, we have passengers who seek to prey upon others. I'll say a few words to the conductor. We'll steer Kelly away from this car. If he acts suspiciously, the other porters will tell me, and I'll keep you informed. Now, rest easy."

When Charles left them, Pamela turned to Mary, who had

listened intently. She was pale. "Don't worry, Mary. I trust our porter. We'll be safe."

Pamela poured water from a carafe and offered it to Mary. When the young woman appeared to have calmed down, Pamela remarked, "I'm frankly not surprised to hear that Kelly is following us. He believes we will lead him to Howard Chapman. His testimony in the cabdriver's case could send Kelly and his boss, Tim Smith, to prison for many years."

Mary looked puzzled. "How did Kelly find out about us?"

"Ellen Chapman may have inadvertently mentioned to someone that we are on the trail of her husband. I'm sure that Tim Smith has ordered Kelly to do what he must to prevent Chapman from returning alive to New York."

"Are we in danger?" Mary asked, with a trace of anxiety.

"Not yet," Pamela replied, feeling less certain than she sounded. "Kelly must want us alive and well until we lead him to Chapman. After that, I can't predict what he might do."

The rest of the trip to Chicago was uneventful. Mary returned to her studies and wrote in her journal. Pamela tutored her for a while and read *Ramona.* At four-thirty in the afternoon, the train pulled into Chicago's LaSalle Street station for a three-hour layover. Pamela telegraphed Prescott the news about Kelly, then she and Mary caught a cab to the Santa Fe Railroad's Dearborn Street station.

In the cab Pamela remarked, "We'll have time for a leisurely meal at the station's Fred Harvey."

"What's that?" Mary asked.

"It's one of a chain of restaurants in stations west of Chicago along the Santa Fe line. Our fellow passengers have praised the Dearborn Fred Harvey for its cleanliness and excellent meals. We'll find out for ourselves."

Comfortably seated in a spacious dining hall, Pamela and Mary shared an order of broiled fresh perch caught that day in

Lake Michigan. Fresh oranges concluded the meal. Their waitress, like all the others in the room, was an attractive, well-mannered, young white woman in a long black dress with starched white apron and collar, black stockings and shoes. She wore no cosmetics and her hair was caught up in a net.

Wide-eyed with curiosity, Mary glanced frequently at the young woman and at her companions serving other tables. Finally, she remarked, "Our waitress is so courteous and efficient! Do Harvey restaurants employ only young women like her?"

"Yes," Pamela replied. "The 'Harvey Girls' are unique. In high-class American restaurants, as in the Grand Union and other great hotels in Saratoga Springs, waiters are generally white or black men and vary in their age, appearance, and level of cultivation."

As Pamela and Mary were about to finish their meal, an older woman, dressed like the young waitresses, came to their table and inquired whether they were pleased with the service.

"Yes indeed," Pamela replied and added, "The Harvey Girls are outstanding. How do you do it?"

The older woman smiled and explained, "We hire only single American women of good character, train them to serve efficiently and graciously, and pay them well. They receive free room and board and live and work under my supervision. All the Harvey restaurants have a similar arrangement."

When the supervisor left, Mary remarked thoughtfully, "Mr. Harvey appears to treat his young waitresses with a certain respect. They respond with excellent service that pleases his customers and increases his profits."

Pamela nodded. "Mr. George Pullman could have avoided last summer's costly strike had he followed Harvey's example."

As Pamela and Mary were walking on the station platform, about to board the Santa Fe's California Limited, Pamela glanced up at a sleeping car window. Dan Kelly was staring at her. Their eyes locked. Pamela felt like she'd been stabbed. An instant later, his face disappeared but remained fixed in her mind.

Back in the compartment, the door closed, Mary turned to her school assignments. Pamela helped her to get started and then read *Ramona* for an hour to drive Kelly from her mind.

Later, as they prepared for bed, Mary remarked, "I would have loved to see the Mississippi River."

Pamela glanced at the timetable. "We are scheduled to cross at three in the morning. If you are awake then, look out the window. You might see the lights of Fort Madison, Iowa, or a riverboat. But please let me sleep."

As Pamela was about to extinguish the gas lamp, Mary said, "This may sound silly, but something is bothering me."

"Don't be shy. Tell me about it."

"I've been thinking that Kelly might suspect you are carrying secret papers concerning Chapman, like his Los Angeles address. If our porter were to fall asleep, couldn't Kelly sneak into our compartment, strangle us, and steal the papers?"

"Your idea isn't entirely far-fetched," Pamela replied gently. "Kelly could reasonably believe that we know where Chapman is to be found. If it were convenient, he would indeed steal my portfolio and might strangle us. However, I've warned our porter that we're concerned for our safety during the night and promised him a tip in the morning if we were still alive. He laughed heartily and declared he will protect us. But for added security, Mary, I'll keep this thing handy. I've used it before on Kelly." She displayed the blackjack, tucked it under her pillow, and turned off the light.

At breakfast Pamela and Mary again sat with the Carrolls, those well-informed and eager ambassadors of their Los Angeles. Mrs. Carroll warned Mary that young men in the dining car had noticed her beauty and were trying to catch her attention. "I smelled alcohol on that one." With her eyes she pointed across the aisle to a red-haired young man ogling Mary. She calmly ignored him.

After breakfast, Pamela and Mary returned to their compartment. The beds were already stowed away and Charles had left. Pamela started Mary at her studies and wrote again to Prescott, describing Kelly. He seemed to be biding his time. Then she went looking for the porter. They should soon reach Kansas City where he would deliver her message to the telegraph office in the station. Charles was certainly literate and could read what she had written. In any case, he would be discreet.

She found him in a tiny, open compartment at the end of the car where a porter could sleep on a cot and keep his supplies. Charles was sitting at a small table, bent intently over a book.

Pamela knocked gently, so as not to startle him. Nonetheless, he sat straight up, closed the book, and swiveled toward her. Irritation flashed on his face, followed instantly by his habitual deferential smile. "How may I serve you, ma'am?" he asked, rising from the chair.

"I'm sorry to disturb you, Charles." She felt genuine regret for breaking into one of the few moments of leisure in his day. Pullman porters were notoriously always on call.

His almond-shaped, golden brown eyes seemed to glisten in response to the consideration she had shown him. Most passengers never bothered to learn his name and called him "boy" or "George" when they wanted his service. He might never before have heard a passenger say to him, "I'm sorry."

Then a line of doubt creased his brow, as if he suspected she was mocking him. But Pamela's kindly smile and level tone of voice seemed to ease his concern. Pamela's mother had trained her early in life to spare the feelings of servants. Consideration was owed to their common humanity and was essential to a well-ordered society. As an adult, she embraced her mother's wisdom and practiced it in her own household.

"Charles, please take this message to the station's telegraph office and pick up any messages there for me." She handed him a dollar bill. "That should more than cover the cost," she added. "Keep the change."

He stared at her for a moment. His customary reserve seemed to melt. Then he straightened up, bowed slightly, and said, "I'll take care of the matter, ma'am."

"Thank you," she said, politely smiling. "Now please go back to your book."

He gazed at her for a second with a twinkle in his eye and nodded.

In Kansas City the train changed engines. There was confusion in Pamela's car as some passengers left the train, and others came on board. Pamela and Mary remained in their compartment, stretching stiff muscles and looking out the window. A strong wind blew coal dust and smoke over the platform.

Shortly after the train set out again at eleven in the morning, Charles came to their compartment. "I've delivered your message, ma'am, and I picked up one for you from Mr. Prescott. Here's the change." He handed her the message and a couple of coins.

She waved the money back. "Put it toward your schooling, Charles." She hesitated. "May I ask, what is your full name?"

"Charles, ma'am, I'm Charles Hart." It sounded more like a declaration than a simple reply.

"You're a student, aren't you?"

He glanced over his shoulder. Reassured that no one was watching or listening, he smiled shyly. "I've taken time off from school to earn money for tuition. In January, I'll return to Hampton Institute in Virginia for my last semester. I want to be a teacher. Now I must go."

With an ache in her heart Pamela watched him leave. He seemed so earnest. She hoped she had encouraged him. Slowly, she closed the door and then read Prescott's message aloud to Mary.

> PAMELA. I'M CONCERNED ABOUT KELLY. TAKE CARE. DODD FOUND INCRIMINATING MESSAGES BETWEEN BIG TIM AND JUDGE FAWCETT. PRESCOTT.

Pamela reflected silently on the message until she noticed Mary becoming anxious.

"Don't worry, Mary. We've taken enough precautions to protect ourselves. I'm concerned about Ellen Chapman, Florence Mulligan, Frank Dodd, and the others helping us. They are more exposed to Big Tim's wrath than we are."

At lunch Pamela and Mary again shared a table with the Carrolls. As they waited for the waiter and the lunch menu, Mr. Carroll mentioned that he was an investment banker with a special interest in the new oil industry in the Los Angeles area. "Since the recent discovery of oil, derricks are sprouting like weeds," he said with pride. "The city's population is doubling every decade."

"Then if investors were to buy the right properties," Pamela remarked, "they might make great fortunes." She was thinking of Howard Chapman. His secret files included maps of building lots and brochures describing planned hotels, railroads, and other commercial enterprises guaranteed to generate enormous profits. He might have put thousands of dollars into them. Had he been lucky?

The banker waved a disdainful hand. "And your investors might lose their shirts if they chance to buy the wrong ones."

"Is the business *that* risky?"

"Yes indeed. You really have to know what you are doing. In the 1880s, speculators bid up prices sky high, platted entire towns out of thin air, and sold them to men who had rushed out from the East, thinking they'd make quick, easy fortunes. They threw caution to the wind and didn't do their homework. In 1887 the bubble burst, property values plummeted, and the newcomers were left holding worthless deeds."

"Has oil been discovered under that 'worthless' property?"

"In some cases, yes. There's a rush underway right now just north of the city. Ed Doheny and Charles Canfield drilled into a rich pool of heavy oil, good for heating, and have made a fortune. Others have found oil but their wells quickly ran dry."

After the conversation moved on to other topics, Pamela was left wondering if Howard Chapman might be one of those unwise men from the East who were twice duped.

After lunch, Pamela mentioned that she had finished reading *Ramona.* Mary said she'd like to read it. "For a change of scenery, I'll sit in the small, quiet parlor at the end of our car."

The room was empty. Mary settled into a chair and began reading. She was soon so absorbed in the story that she didn't notice a man enter until he sat himself next to her with a heavy thump. He was the obnoxious red-haired young man who had smelled of alcohol at breakfast. He had apparently slept through the morning, eaten a nourishing lunch, and now felt frisky.

"What are you reading?" He leaned over her and peered at the page.

"You are annoying me, sir," she said sharply. "Leave me alone."

He patted her arm. "There, there, miss, I mean no harm. Besides, you look even prettier when you're annoyed. Let's get acquainted. They call me Red Rufus. What's your name?"

"That's none of your business!" A robust young man had

entered the parlor and loomed over Rufus. "Cretin! You will either leave the parlor now or I'll throw you out."

Rufus recoiled in his chair. "I was only being friendly." He tossed a glance at Mary. "Sorry, miss, if I disturbed you." He got to his feet and scampered from the room.

Mary stared at her knight errant and blinked. "Mr. Pratt! What a coincidence! So good to see you and so timely. You seem to have recovered well from your injury in the game last month at Williams."

He smiled. "Please call me Herb. Yes, I'm fine. I'd rather that we had met again under more pleasant circumstances. But I'm happy to have been helpful. Rufus is traveling in my car. A pathetic character, he drinks too much, behaves badly, and refuses to mend his ways. I asked the conductor to put him off the train in Kansas City after he kept us awake all night and then vomited his breakfast. The stench filled the car. The conductor had said, 'I'd love to put him off in Hell, sir. But his father is as rich as Croesus and is a director of the Santa Fe.' "

Mary frowned. "That's intolerable! Something must be done, or he'll ruin the trip for all of us."

"Don't worry, Mary. I've not given up. I'm organizing a petition to be signed by all the passengers in the car. I expect Rufus to be removed from the train this evening in Burrton, our next brief stop. By then, he'll probably be drunk again. Fortunately, it's a dry community of five hundred God-fearing Christians. He'll have to behave while he's there. It may do him good." He gazed at her. "May I join you and Mrs. Thompson at supper and renew our acquaintance?"

"Please do. We would both be delighted."

At supper that evening, Pamela welcomed Herb Pratt to their table and placed him across from her. Mary sat by her side. Pamela had asked the headwaiter to keep the fourth place empty to allow for a more confidential conversation. She was curious why Mr. Pratt, heir to a great oil refining business, was traveling to Southern California. Could he possibly lead her to the missing Chapman?

While waiting for their meal, Pratt said to Mary, "I recall from our visit in Williamstown's Greylock Hotel that you were interested in drawing. It's an excellent aid to traveling. Have you sketched on this trip?"

"Yes, indeed." She pulled the sketchbook from her bag and handed it to him. "Please judge kindly. It's challenging to sketch when the train bounces and rocks."

He smiled. "You are brave even to try. I doubt that I would." He browsed through the book, uttering ums and ahs, smiling with pleasure. "I see many hurried impressions that you can finish later—locomotives, railroad stations, landscapes." He showed Pamela a sketch of Charles Hart, the porter. "This is a telling image of the man. Mary has captured his commitment to service. He's submissive and deferential, but from an inner integrity."

The meal arrived and the sketchbook was put aside. Pratt turned the conversation toward Mary and her family.

"Who is your hero, your mentor?" Pratt's interest seemed genuine.

Without embarrassment Mary replied, "My mother died two years ago but is still the guiding star of my life. Though poor and sick she remained cheerful and optimistic. She seemed to draw strength from teaching English and art to children. I'll follow her example."

Pratt seemed touched. "I can only encourage you. I'm sure Edward does as well."

"He's been helpful in many ways." Her eyes began to glisten.

Pamela thought that the conversation was heading into emotionally stressful issues. So, she raised a hand and signaled the waiter for a menu. "It's time for a light dessert," she announced. They agreed on Nellis pears with dried tart cherries, poached in white wine.

While they waited, Pratt picked up Mary's sketchbook again. "Portraits that reveal a person's character fascinate me—like these two." First, he pointed to Mary's detailed, polished sketch of Chapman, drawn from the ten-year-old photograph of him. Then Pratt displayed Mary's sketch of Chapman as he might appear years later—heavier, bearded, bald, and wearing eyeglasses.

"These are of the same man, aren't they, Mary? What's the story behind them?"

Mary deferred to Pamela, who replied, "We are searching for that man. He left his wife seven years ago and probably fled to Los Angeles." She gave a brief account of Chapman's interest in Los Angeles real estate and the warm climate, a clue to where he might be found. "Unfortunately," she admitted, "we really aren't sure that he's alive. And, even if we find him, we must coax him to return to New York. That could prove difficult but worth trying."

The poached pears arrived, interrupting the conversation. Pamela was left wondering how much she should involve this young man in her investigation. Was it fair to allow him to believe that she was searching for Chapman simply because he had deserted his wife? She decided the young man didn't have to know, at least for now, that Chapman had actually fled from death at the hands of Tammany assassins and was wanted back in New York to resolve an old murder and expose Tammany's conspiracy against Harry Miller.

They lingered at the table, drinking tea, while Pratt explained that he was carrying letters of introduction to leaders in Southern California's nascent oil industry, such as Edward Doheny and his partner Charles Canfield. "I'm supposed to scout the terrain, you might say, and make useful contacts. If I can be of any help to you, please let me know."

A few minutes later, the train stopped in Burrton. A person was carried on a stretcher from one of the sleeping cars and placed on a cart, then wheeled on the platform to the small station house.

"That's Rufus," said a passing conductor to Pratt.

Pratt explained, "Shortly before supper, I learned that Rufus had drunk himself into a stupor. A doctor was found among the passengers and took charge of him. His father will be notified and will arrange to pick him up—most likely in a private Santa Fe car. I refrained from speaking of this incident during our meal because it was unpleasant and would have distracted us from what I really wanted to talk about—you and your trip."

"We appreciate your interest," said Pamela. "Before we return to our compartment, would you tell us your plans for the future?"

"In view of my family's history, you could say that my fate is preordained. After graduation from Amherst in June I'll go to work for Standard Oil."

He gallantly helped the two women from their chairs. "Good night, ladies."

When they woke up the next morning, they were in Colorado with a thousand miles still to go before reaching Los Angeles. The rest of the trip passed uneventfully. Pamela sought out the many knowledgeable passengers eager to talk about interesting persons and places in Los Angeles. Mary alternated her studies with sketching the grandeur of the Rocky Mountain scenery. Herb Pratt often joined them at meals, and he and Mary met to chat in the parlor. Though he was a gentleman and she was a sensible young woman, Pamela kept a watchful eye on their relationship.

Dan Kelly occasionally appeared in the distance. His presence wasn't threatening, but it reminded Pamela that a confrontation with him lay ahead, if Chapman was found. The uncertainty was unsettling.

CHAPTER 24

Mistaken Identity

Los Angeles
Saturday, December 15

At three o'clock in the afternoon, the California Limited pulled into Los Angeles. Since leaving New York on Monday, Pamela and Mary had jerked, rocked, and swayed for three thousand miles across the continent. In mind and body, they were eager for steadier footing.

Since the trip began, the view from the window had changed dramatically. The bleak winter landscape of most of the country had given way to a tropical paradise. In the city's outskirts, lofty exotic eucalyptus trees lined the roads, and oranges and lemons hung heavily from trees. As the travelers approached the station, they passed a small park with tall palm trees and a bed of California poppies. A warm breeze bathed them as they descended from the sleeping car. Wide-eyed, Mary exclaimed to Pamela, "I could live here."

Pamela and the Pinkerton agent had arranged by telegraph to meet covertly in the station. He would be disguised as a baggage handler. From a hiding place they would identify the Tammany man, Dan Kelly, and decide together how to cope with him.

There was ample time for this. Their porter, Charles Hart, had arranged with other porters to bring Pamela and Mary to the station quickly. The porters resented Kelly who was rude and demanding and failed to tip. He would be among the last passengers off the train and the last to find his baggage.

As Pamela and Mary entered the station's main hall, the Pinkerton in his handler's apron welcomed them and identified himself as Paul Gagnon, originally from Quebec in Canada. He had joined the Pinkerton organization in California ten years earlier. A short, sturdy man with tousled blond hair, bright blue eyes, and a ready smile, he guided Pamela and Mary deftly through the crowded station to the baggage room. A swarthy man loitering nearby gave Gagnon a hand signal.

"Ortiz is my assistant," Gagnon explained to Pamela. "You should hide now where I can see you. When the Tammany man finally arrives, point to him. I'll serve him and commit his features to memory."

Ten minutes passed before Kelly appeared, visibly irritated. Gagnon approached him officiously, nodded patiently to his complaints, fetched his baggage, and apologized on behalf of the railroad. Kelly didn't tip him.

"*Pingre,*" muttered Gagnon to Kelly's retreating back, then nodded to his assistant to follow him.

"What did you just say?" Pamela couldn't clearly hear Gagnon's expression, but she knew French and had a strong suspicion.

"Stingy bastard." Then he added with a wink of his eye, "Pardon my French, ma'am."

He collected their baggage and led them from the station by a back door to a waiting cab. "We've eluded the Tammany man, at least for now." He called to the driver. "The Nadeau Hotel."

As they drove through a run-down area of saloons and cheap hotels, Gagnon looked apologetic. "Tramps, railroad workers, and indigent men cluster between the railroad station and the downtown area where you will stay. Don't worry, your hotel is first-class and safe."

He explained that a rich fellow French Canadian, Remi Nadeau, had built it to be the finest hotel in Los Angeles. "He could afford it. Before he passed away a few years ago, he owned the largest vineyard in California and probably in the world."

"Really?" Mary looked skeptical.

Pamela whispered, "Californians tend to boast, Mary. Nonetheless, Nadeau's vineyard may be among the largest, especially since disease has destroyed so many French vineyards. The climate and the soil here is said to suit the vine."

Gagnon continued. "You will be comfortable and secure at the Nadeau. The house detective works for me. The manager and other key members of the staff know about the Tammany man. He will be unable to rent a room and will be stopped if he attempts to enter."

"When shall we see Mr. Hugh Carey?"

"Tonight. He will come to the Nadeau to dine and afterward attend a benefit concert for the local hospital. You and I and young lady Mary will observe him from a nearby table in the dining room and afterward follow him into the ballroom for the concert."

"May I ask who is playing?"

"The Los Angeles Women's Orchestra, directed by Harley Hamilton. They have been together for a year now and have become very popular. We'll find out the program at the hotel." He pointed out the cab window to a large four-story stone building on the corner of Spring and First Street. "We have arrived at the Nadeau Hotel."

Pamela and Mary exchanged glances. This was a promising start.

An hour later, Pamela and Mary met Gagnon in the lobby, impeccably groomed and dressed in a light blue suit and matching tie. Even his speech was now high-toned. His transformation from baggage handler to gentleman astonished Pamela.

He read her mind. "As a Pinkerton detective in Los Angeles, I must dress appropriately for actual or prospective clients at every level of society. Tonight at the concert, I'll be playing the gentleman. I'll also look out for tricksters in fine clothes arriving here from the East."

He drew Pamela and Mary aside. "Carey should arrive almost any minute now. He and I have met before, but I'd rather that he didn't recognize me just now. I'd have to introduce you. Instead, you should observe him unawares at first. We'll wait for him in that sheltered area." They moved to a group of chairs partially hidden by low potted palm trees.

Gagnon soon said softly, "Here he comes."

Hugh Carey's appearance was about what Pamela had expected: bearded and bald. He had also gained weight and now wore eyeglasses. She whispered to Mary. "What do you think?"

"He certainly looks like the man we imagined, but it's too early to say for sure."

Carey had come alone. In the dining room he sat down with two men his age and social rank and ordered a glass of wine with the meal. Pamela couldn't overhear anything, but their exchanges seemed lighthearted.

When the meal ended, Carey and his friends began to move toward the men's restroom. Gagnon hurried ahead of them to eavesdrop. Afterward Carey went alone to the ballroom, where members of the orchestra had begun to find their places and tune their instruments. Pamela and Mary and the Pinkerton sat a few rows behind Carey and off to one side where they could see him clearly. Pamela again asked Mary for her impressions.

"Mr. Carey is enjoying this evening and the company of others. He appears to be a harmonious, outgoing, and good-natured man. In contrast, Mr. Chapman seemed greedy, stressed, and dependent on alcohol. Of course that was his character seven years ago. Still, how much could it have changed for better or worse?"

Pamela turned to the detective. "Despite their similarities, we think that Mr. Carey might not be Howard Chapman. They appear to differ in their character." She suggested that Gagnon introduce her and Mary to Carey. "He and Chapman came to Los Angeles at nearly the same time. They had a similar background and an interest in real estate speculation. I would ask if they might have met."

Gagnon stroked his chin, reflecting. "Carey might welcome the opportunity to meet you and Mary. In the men's room he referred to you with respect, Mrs. Thompson, as a handsome woman, and to Mary as a beautiful young lady."

"That's good for a start, Mr. Gagnon. We'll look for an opportunity to speak to him during the intermission. Meanwhile, let's enjoy the music."

Barely one year old and composed entirely of some fifty amateurs, the orchestra played Franz Schubert's *Marche Militaire* in tune and with verve, followed by Johann Strauss Senior's *Radetzky March* and similar popular pieces.

Mary seemed mesmerized. "See what women can do," she murmured to Pamela, "when they are well trained and directed—like the Harvey Girls."

At the intermission Carey spoke briefly to nearby acquaintances, then walked to a buffet of refreshments in the rear of the ballroom. Gagnon approached him with Pamela and Mary in tow.

"Mr. Carey, I'd like to introduce you to two visitors from New York who arrived this afternoon on the California Limited, Mrs. Pamela Thompson and Miss Mary Clark."

"Pleased to meet you, ladies. Are you enjoying the concert?" His eyes darted with delight from one woman to the other.

"We have indeed, sir," Pamela replied. "The orchestra is worthy of your fine city."

"I thank you on behalf of the orchestra, Mrs. Thompson,

and I'll pass your comment on to Mr. Hamilton, its founder and director. He also teaches many of the musicians."

"Isn't such an orchestra unusual?" asked Mary. "I've always thought that only men could play in large ensembles."

"Hamilton thinks otherwise," Carey replied. "In the Oneida Community in upstate New York he was raised to believe that men and women were equal. When properly taught, a woman could perform music at the same level of excellence as a man. You may judge for yourself."

"From what I've heard, sir," Mary stated emphatically, "I'd say he's right."

Carey smiled politely and went on to inquire about their plans. Pamela explained that they were searching for a missing person, Howard Chapman. "We think he might have come here from New York under a different name."

"He wouldn't have been the first," Carey remarked. "If a man has had bad luck, this is a good place to start over with a clean slate. Would I have known him? I arrived from the East in 1887, together with hundreds of others seeking our fortune."

"You might have heard of him, since his background in law and his interest in real estate speculation were similar to yours. He probably came to Los Angeles in January of 1887."

Carey frowned, his eyes hooded, and said with a hint of displeasure, "You appear to know me better than I would expect of strangers."

"We had to become acquainted with Los Angeles as quickly as possible so we questioned Mr. and Mrs. Carroll, our companions on the California Limited. They gladly spoke at length of prominent residents of Los Angeles, you included."

Her explanation seemed to satisfy Carey. "You must help me, madam. Since Chapman might have changed his name, I can hardly imagine who he might be."

"For a start," said Pamela, "he would have taken a new name

similar to his old one—for example, Hugh Carey. He was also proud of his fine gold watch and enjoyed showing it off."

Carey smiled broadly. "You amaze me, Mrs. Thompson. So, I was high on your list of suspects, but not anymore, apparently. Let me try to recall anyone I've known with the initials H. C. and an expensive gold watch who arrived here in 1887. More than a few men could fit that description." With a teasing smile, he drew a gold watch from his vest and opened the case.

Pamela read the inscription aloud: "*To my son, Hugh Carey, on the occasion of his graduation from Columbia College.*" She remarked, "Howard Chapman's watch commemorates his wedding to Ellen. Your watch tells me that the concert is about to resume."

The warning bell rang. "We must return to our seats," said Carey. "Shall we meet in the dining room after the concert? Beethoven might jog my memory."

The remainder of the concert would be devoted to the first movement of Beethoven's Violin Concerto in D Major. The orchestra's principal violinist came forward and tuned her instrument. A slender, attractive young woman, she seemed mature beyond her age and confident in her ability. Mary gazed at her with rapt attention.

"The soloist is Miss Edna Foy, the conductor's best student," said Gagnon softly. "She's been playing the violin since the age of twelve. Her father is wealthy and progressive and encourages her."

Pamela was fond of the concerto and had heard professional musicians play it at Carnegie Hall. Tonight's performance did credit to the orchestra. Aside from moments of slight uncertainty in the beginning, they played as well as a regional professional orchestra anywhere. Miss Foy displayed remarkable ability and at the last note the audience rose to their feet and cheered.

Pamela glanced at Mary. She too stood up, clapping vigorously, tears streaming down her face. Pamela was touched. A new world of possibilities was opening up for her young friend beyond the low horizon of a machinist's daughter in a remote Berkshire mill town.

They waited a few minutes while the crowd left and Mary dried her tears. Then they went to the dining room, where Carey sat waiting for them. "May I offer you wine from Mr. Nadeau's vineyard?"

Pamela declined politely for herself and Mary.

Carey tapped his forehead. "I racked my brain fruitlessly during most of the Beethoven concerto, trying to think of an acquaintance seven years ago who might have been Howard Chapman in disguise." He paused for dramatic effect. "Finally, a name came to me—Herman Chabert. I met him shortly after arriving in Los Angeles. At the time, his name intrigued me. As a young man at Columbia, I had read Balzac's popular story, *Colonel Chabert*, about a French officer in Napoleon's army who was supposed to have died in battle but returned home to find that his wife had sold his entire estate and married another man. Chapman probably read the same book."

Pamela grew excited. "He was almost too clever. His new name resembles his old one." She asked, "How well did you know him?"

"I had scant opportunity. When the real estate bubble burst that year, I heard that Chabert's investments, like many others, had become worthless. Shortly afterward, he disappeared. A few years later, I saw him lying drunk in Third Street near the railroad station. His clothes were tattered, his shoes shabby. He looked pale and thin. I carried him into a cheap hotel above a saloon and left money to help him out, but haven't seen or heard from him since."

"I thank you, Mr. Carey, for this information. We'll start our search at the hotel. Someone would know if he were still there. Could you recall its name?"

"Yes, the Ramona Hotel. I must warn you, Mrs. Thompson. It's not a suitable place for a lady."

"Thank you for the warning, Mr. Carey. I'll be careful. Having lived and worked in New York slums, I've learned how to cope with desperate men and women."

Carey raised an eyebrow, quietly drained his glass, and bid the others good night.

Pamela turned to Gagnon. "Tomorrow is Sunday. What would be the best time to visit the Ramona?"

"Probably late in the morning, after the cleanup and before the lunch crowd arrives at the saloon." He paused. "Are you sure you want to do this? Couldn't I handle it?"

"Thanks for the offer, but I think we should work together. We'll dress for the occasion and meet in our hotel lobby."

Gagnon left, shaking his head.

As Pamela and Mary were walking toward the elevator, Mr. Carroll approached them. "Ladies, would you care to visit the Nadeau vineyard tomorrow together with me and my wife?"

Pamela declined for herself. "I have work to do in the morning, but Miss Mary is free to go. The visit would add to her education." Pamela glanced the question toward Mary.

"I agree gladly."

Carroll told the young woman, "Then we'll pick you up at ten, lunch at the vineyard, and return by three."

Back in their room, preparing for bed, Pamela and Mary hummed melodies from the evening's concert.

Mary remarked, "I sensed a strong bond of empathy between the musicians and their conductor, Mr. Hamilton. He believed in them, so they gave him their best effort."

"Yes, exactly. Unfortunately, men as wise and generous as

Hamilton are rare. Prescott is one such. Be grateful when you meet them."

As Pamela was about to turn out the light, she remarked, "While Mr. Gagnon and I are busy with Howard Chapman, you should pursue your educational projects. Tomorrow's visit to the Nadeau vineyard is a good start. You will experience more than the taste of grapes and the making of wine. The Carrolls are knowledgeable and will want to show you other interesting places. Learn from them what you can about California. You may want to live here one day."

"Will you be safe with Dan Kelly nearby?" Mary looked worried. "Can I help?"

"I appreciate your asking, but Mr. Gagnon will keep Kelly at bay."

CHAPTER 25

Ramona Hotel

Sunday, December 16

At ten-thirty in the morning, Pamela and Gagnon met in the hotel lobby. As they started for the door, he remarked, "Our Mr. Kelly has found lodging in the Republic Hotel, an evil gambling den on Third Street, a block away from the Ramona."

"That's too close," said Pamela. "If Chabert turns out to be Chapman, we'll have to move him to a safer place."

Gagnon nodded. "The manager has already agreed to accommodate Chapman here temporarily." As the Pinkerton helped Pamela into the carriage, he remarked, "Kelly has a contact at the Republic, a bouncer and handyman named Terry Finch. They spent most of last evening in saloons and gambling dens but drank and gambled very little. My assistant, Ortiz, thinks they were plotting mischief for us."

Pamela murmured, "I hope we find Chapman before they do."

At eleven, Pamela and Gagnon walked into the Ramona Hotel's saloon. Its floors and tables were battered but clean. The air smelled fresh. Two men in the bib overalls of railroad men stood at the bar, clasping glasses of beer. On the wall behind the bar hung a large, skillful painting of a voluptuous young Indian woman with a look of tragic longing on her face. "She's Ramona," remarked one of the railroad men.

The other man added, "The artist came from New York City and lives upstairs. He says, 'If you're going to starve, you may as well do it in a warm and beautiful place.' "

The bartender's initial frown at the sight of Pamela gradually turned into a confused stare. She had dressed in plain street clothes without jewelry or cosmetics. Yet she spoke proper English and carried herself like a lady. He approached her at the end of the bar.

"What brings you here, ma'am?" His tone was both deferential and doubtful. "No one here needs religion, if that's what you're selling."

She shook her head and showed her credentials from Prescott's office. "I'm looking for a missing man, Howard Chapman. He also might go by the name Herman Chabert. Someone resembling him was seen here a few years ago." She described him briefly.

The bartender hesitated, like a man struggling to keep a secret. Finally, he shook his head. "I'm new here, ma'am, and don't know anything."

The railroad men were now watching closely, exchanging whispered comments, and glancing toward the stairway leading to the hotel rooms on the upper floors.

"Who *would* know?" Pamela persisted.

The bartender grew flustered. "I must ask you to leave, ma'am. Women aren't allowed in here."

The railroad men snickered loudly and again glanced toward the stairs. One of them asked, "Why don't you talk to the manager, ma'am? He's up there and will set your mind at ease."

The bartender glowered at the railroad man. "Mind your own business!"

Pamela started for the stairs. Gagnon placed himself between her and the irate bartender, a big, burly man. He turned red in the face and shouted, "Leave or I'll throw you out."

She had reached the foot of the stairs when a man appeared on the landing above her. She stared at him.

"What's going on here?" he asked in a cultivated voice, his eyes shifting between Pamela and the angry bartender. Then slowly a light of recognition dawned in his eyes and he said softly, "Mrs. Thompson, what on earth are you doing here?"

"I could ask you the same question, Mr. Chapman." She went on gently. "I've come to speak to you, sir. Mr. Gagnon, my companion, is a Pinkerton detective and is assisting me. May we speak to you upstairs in private?"

Conflicting emotions of fear and anger appeared to overcome Chapman. He tried to speak but could only sputter. Finally, he beckoned them up, led them into a small office, and shut the door. He asked again, "Why have you come here?"

"Your wife, Ellen, asked me to find out if you were living or dead. The uncertainty deeply troubles her, and she feels abandoned. I believe she still loves you, so I agreed to try to find you. She showed me your papers and journals. From them I figured out that if you were alive you would likely be here."

He motioned them to chairs and again struggled to speak. "What can I say? I did abandon Ellen and have lived to regret it." His lips quivered.

Pamela calmed him with a sympathetic smile. "I've learned that you suddenly left New York seven years ago in fear of Tammany Hall. Tell us why."

He hesitated for a long moment. Then he drew a deep breath and slowly exhaled. "It's a complicated story involving my part in the notorious 'boodle' or bribery of many New York City assemblymen. I carried the cash to Tammany Hall." He pointed to a worn, black portfolio on a nearby table. Sun and rain had dulled its once shiny surface and left tiny cracks in the leather.

The letters *H C* had lost most of their gilt. "I've kept it as a reminder of my folly—and because it's still useful."

He went on to describe how a cabdriver learned of the crime and tried to extort money from the perpetrators. Chapman's voice became hoarse and dropped almost to a whisper. "They killed him—I was a witness." He paused and cleared his throat. "The man responsible for the murder feared I'd betray him to the police and arranged to have me killed. So I fled here, changed my name, and started a new life."

"What happened then?" Pamela asked.

"I arrived in Los Angeles at the peak of a real estate boom, invested heavily, and lost nearly all my money when the market collapsed."

"You were an experienced businessman. How could you invest so unwisely?"

He shook his head. "Ellen may have told you that the pressure of my work for Tammany had caused me to indulge in strong drink. It became a vicious habit and impaired my judgment. With the collapse of my investments I hardly had enough money for room and board. I felt disgusted with myself. For the next three years I drank like a fish, as they say. An alcoholic haze clouded my mind to the point that I landed literally in the gutter in front of the Ramona Hotel. A kind man picked me up, brought me into the hotel, and arranged for my lodging."

Pamela nodded. "That man was Mr. Hugh Carey, who directed us here."

"Yes, I owe him more than I can repay, but I've been too proud to thank him. I gave up alcohol, did menial jobs at the hotel for room and board, and finally became the manager."

"Did you ever think of contacting your wife and returning to her?"

He nodded. "During my recovery I often thought of her, but I decided that we would both be better off if she remained ignorant. Tammany might then be less likely to force or to trick her into revealing my whereabouts. I was also ashamed of my failures and fearful of Tammany's retribution. It eased my conscience that a large block of stock I had placed in Ellen's name now provided her with a decent income."

In a shaking voice he asked, "How is she?"

"I found her to be distressed," Pamela replied. "Due to the national economic depression, her income from stocks has fallen to next to nothing. She was selling off furniture when I first met her. Since then, St. Barnabas Mission has assisted her."

"What can I do for her?" He tugged at his patched coat and pointed to the barren, cracked plaster walls. "This job gives me food to eat and a bed to sleep on. That's about all. A few years ago, I sold my worthless land for a pittance. Shortly afterward, oil was discovered there. Were it not for that bad luck, I'd be wealthy today and could help Ellen. As things now stand, I'd be a burden to her."

Gagnon waved Chapman's objections aside. "You've overcome the main problem that brought you down, your addiction to alcohol. Now you need to come out of hiding and build up self-confidence. Then you will have a bright future here. Southern California is growing faster than any other part of the country and offers many opportunities to someone with your intelligence, education, and experience."

Chapman shrugged. "And how shall I take advantage of those opportunities? Who will hire the manager of a saloon and a cheap residential hotel? My clientele are rough men, mostly transients and railroad workers."

Pamela shook her head. "To my eye, your establishment appears clean and orderly, the marks of good management. That you serve workingmen isn't a sin. For a year, I ran a boardinghouse in a slum on New York's East Side. It was a hard but useful experience. Your situation is similar."

Gagnon raised his hand in a warning. "You can't hide forever; your past will catch up with you. Dan Kelly arrived in Los Angeles yesterday on the California Limited and is staying at the Republic Hotel a short distance from here. He has recruited a partner and they are surely hunting for you as we speak."

At the mention of Kelly's arrival Chapman began to perspire and his hands trembled.

Pamela tried to calm him. "We are prepared to protect you. But you must return with me to New York and remove the suspicion that you participated in the aldermen's 'boodle' and in the conspiracy to kill the cabdriver."

"A tall task, ma'am!" Chapman exclaimed. "If I manage to escape from Kelly's knife, will Tammany Hall welcome me with open arms?"

Pamela reassured him. "You needn't live in fear and dread of Tammany. It's in retreat. Reverend Parkhurst and the reform movement have won the mayor's office and forced Tammany's allies, Chief of Detectives Mr. Byrnes and Police Inspector Clubber Williams, to seek retirement. Several corrupt aldermen have fled the country or gone to jail. Big Tim Smith and Dan Kelly, the men who most threaten you, are under investigation. With help from the Prescott law firm you could clear your name and send the perpetrators of the cabdriver's murder to prison."

Chapman had listened to Pamela with his head cocked doubtfully. Now he gave out a deep sigh of resignation. "If I elude Kelly and go back with you, what can I give Ellen?" He waved a hand over the dingy, sparsely furnished room.

"A comfortable future in Los Angeles," replied Gagnon. "But we need to change your appearance, as well as your attitude, and move you to a safe place. I propose to lodge you today in a room at the Nadeau Hotel and put you in the hands of its tailor and barber. When you are properly outfitted, I'll recommend you to the hotel manager. He may offer you a suitable position or refer you to a reputable businessman who can."

"What must I do with the Ramona? I shouldn't just walk away."

"Give notice to its owner. Until a new manager takes your place, you'll sleep at night at the Nadeau and work here during the day. My assistant will protect you."

Chapman was silent for a long moment, then drew a deep breath. "I'll speak to the bartender now. He and the night clerk will look after the hotel for the rest of the day. I'll go with you to the Nadeau. God help me."

After Gagnon had settled Chapman in the carriage, he turned to Pamela and whispered, "Our plan is working better than I anticipated."

"Unfortunately, Kelly is a crafty devil. I'm sure he's concocting a plan of his own."

At three o'clock on the dot, Mrs. Carroll returned Mary Clark to Pamela. "Here's your girl back safe and sound. She's delightful company—so enthusiastic."

Mary danced around the room, her face flushed with pleasure. "We had a wonderful time. The vineyard was so beautiful."

Pamela reacted with a relieved smile. In fact, as the afternoon hours passed, she had grown concerned for Mary. Young and unfamiliar with the area, she was vulnerable to skilled assassins like Kelly.

While Mary entered the day's events in her journal and sketched scenes from memory, Pamela wrote a message to Prescott in New York reporting her discovery:

> *Chapman is lodged with Mary and me in the Nadeau Hotel and has agreed to wrap up his affairs*

> *here in a week and return with us to New York. He's very nervous and fearful, despite our best efforts to protect him. Unfortunately, Dan Kelly is busy scheming to kill him. I'm also concerned for his wife, Ellen. Tammany might harm her or hold her hostage.*

At the hotel's telegraph office Pamela condensed the message and sent it. Then she stopped at Chapman's room and invited him to join her and Mary at supper in the dining room. He appeared tentatively pleased with his surroundings and welcomed the invitation. Pamela crossed her fingers, hoping that he would stay with her plan.

Chapter 26

Assault

Tuesday, December 18–Wednesday, December 19

Tuesday at noon, Pamela received Prescott's heartening reply to her message telling of Howard Chapman's promise to return to New York. Larry White had reported the news to the district attorney and had suggested that he begin preparations for a grand jury. Involved in delicate pension negotiations, Inspector Williams was allowing Larry to proceed forward, step by step. He had gathered too much evidence against Judge Fawcett and Big Tim to be arbitrarily stopped.

During the past two days, Chapman had been training his replacement at the Ramona. After each day's work, he had joined Pamela and Mary for supper in the Nadeau's fine dining room. At the table tonight, Pamela became aware of Chapman's gradual transformation since moving into the hotel on Sunday. Smartly dressed in coat and tie and his beard trimmed, he now looked like he belonged in this first-class hotel.

"Mr. Chapman, would you please tell me the time?" Pamela had noticed a gold chain hanging from his vest.

He drew a gold watch from his pocket and opened the lid.

His eyes dwelled for a moment on the inscription inside, and then he read the dial. "It's five past seven o'clock, Mrs. Thompson." Without being asked, he handed the watch and chain to Pamela. "You've heard of this watch from Ellen, I assume. It's the memento of our first year together."

"Yes," Pamela remarked. "I understand what it meant to you and to her then. What is its later story?"

"It has shared my fate." Chapman explained that he had pawned the watch at the nadir of his descent into alcoholic oblivion. In his recovery he had gradually bought it back. "Today, I made the final payment and could wear it to supper."

Pamela showed the watch to Mary, then handed it back to Chapman. "I'm happy for you, Howard, and pleased that you have shared the story with us. In due time, I hope you will share it with Ellen as well."

In the conversation that followed, Pamela discovered that Chapman was proficient at chess. He had also earlier remarked that Mary was a charming, intelligent young woman. So now Pamela suggested that he give lessons to Mary. She seemed eager to learn.

"I'd be delighted." He gazed at Mary. "You have a sharp mind and should quickly catch on to the game."

Mary blushed, embarrassed by the compliment, but her eyes sparkled with delight.

After the meal, Pamela left her together with Chapman at a chessboard in a ground-floor parlor while she went on to the Pinkerton office. For the past two days, she had spoken only briefly to Gagnon. He was in the office with his assistant, Mr. Ortiz, a Spanish-speaking man, rather shy in English. Still, Pamela had come to respect him.

"Ortiz has just returned from shadowing Dan Kelly," said Gagnon to Pamela. "I've summarized his report. Here, you may read it for yourself."

* * *

Since Kelly left the railroad station Sunday afternoon, he has been searching through the gambling dens, brothels, and saloons of Los Angeles, trying to find a suitable partner or two for his "project," as he calls it. His first contact in Los Angeles, Terry Finch, the bouncer at the Republic Hotel, was Kelly's cellmate at Sing Sing. He introduces Kelly to potential partners but doesn't get personally involved. Kelly's other contacts at first seem intrigued but soon turn suspicious. They fear that he's working undercover for the police and trying to draw them into a trap. As of now, Kelly appears to be on his own but that could change. A rascal or two on Third Street might do his bidding if he were to offer enough money.

Pamela wondered aloud, "Will Kelly still try to eliminate Chapman here in Los Angeles or wait until he finds more resources back in New York?"

"He appears very eager to do something soon," Ortiz replied. "I'd say, prepare for the worst."

Gagnon looked anxiously at Pamela. "Ma'am, you may have to protect young Mary and Mr. Chapman. I'm told that Kelly is quick and sure with a knife. Can you fire a pistol?" His tone was doubtful.

"Yes," she replied. "My partner in Prescott's firm, Harry Miller, a former NYPD detective, has trained me to use a pistol. I would shoot if I had to. I anticipated that this trip could become dangerous, so I've brought along a double-barrel derringer, as well as a blackjack. A confrontation between Kelly and me could easily turn deadly."

"From his side more than from yours, I presume?"

"That's true," she replied. "Several weeks ago, when he threatened me, I tipped a tea table over on him and knocked him senseless with the blackjack."

Gagnon nodded. "He surely hates you for that." He turned to Ortiz. "Watch him as closely as you can. He'll soon act."

Early the following morning, Pamela went with Gagnon to a private firing range. Overnight he had grown anxious about the strength of her nerves and her ability to handle a gun. To reassure him she had agreed to this exercise. For her own peace of mind she had brought Mary along to see how she would react to a gunshot and to the sense of danger that it could arouse. She might faint or panic. That would be a problem in a violent confrontation.

The range was in a sandy depression on wasteland outside the city. Gagnon set up a target, a crude wooden life-size figure of a man. Pamela fired several shots at various distances. The derringer was reasonably accurate at about a dozen feet. But the low-powered bullet barely penetrated the board.

Gagnon shook his head. "If Kelly were to charge you with his knife, your derringer probably couldn't stop him. You need a standard pistol. Have you ever fired this one?" He pulled a Colt .44 revolver from his bag.

She nodded. "I'll show you." She loaded the pistol and fired several shots, again hitting the target at various distances. Gagnon said he was satisfied and gave her a small box of ammunition. "Keep the pistol. You may need it."

Throughout this exercise, Mary had stood aside, watching intently. As they were about to leave the range, Pamela asked the young woman if she wished to practice shooting. "This could be part of your education."

Mary calmly replied, "I'll try. A woman should know how to defend herself and others." Without flinching, she fired several shots at close range with the derringer and the revolver and hit the target.

Gagnon congratulated the women. "Now let's hope that Kelly won't test you for real."

When Pamela and Mary returned to the Nadeau, a message was waiting for them at the reception desk. Pamela read it to Mary. "Mr. and Mrs. Carroll are inviting us to a day trip with them on Thursday. We would leave after breakfast by train, visit the Pasadena Museum of Science and the adjacent Mission San Gabriel, and be home before dark."

"That would be lovely," exclaimed Mary.

"I'm sorry," said Pamela, "but I must remain here, close to Chapman, because Kelly might attack him today or tomorrow. But I encourage you to go. Both places would offer excellent opportunities for study and sketching."

Mary made a face. "I would enjoy the trip more if you came with me, but I understand why you need to stay. The Carrolls are decent, interesting people, and their invitation is a generous gesture. Please say yes for me."

Back in their room, Pamela replied to the Carrolls and prepared a telegraph to Prescott, while Mary wrote in her journal. At midmorning, another message arrived, addressed to both women. This time Mary received it. "Herb Pratt is inviting us to lunch at Jerry Illich's restaurant on Main Street. He gives us a telephone number. Do you think we should accept?" Her voice was eager.

"Yes, I could safely spare an hour or two for lunch. I'll call Mr. Pratt now from the telephone downstairs."

Pratt came with a carriage shortly before noon, smiling and relaxed. Mary beamed with anticipation. In contrast, Pamela struggled to appear delighted. Her anxiety about Chapman gnawed at her nerves. She had arranged with Gagnon's office to reach her at the restaurant if trouble erupted.

Under other circumstances, she would have thoroughly enjoyed the lunch. The restaurant's ambiance was Mediterranean—Jerry Illich came from Dalmatia on the Adriatic coast and had become an accomplished restaurateur. His chef's grilled salmon was fresh and delicious. Pratt and a lawyer friend royally entertained Mary with jokes and tales about fashionable gentlemen and ladies at distant tables. At two o'clock Pamela excused herself, after suggesting that Mary might benefit from visiting the city hall nearby. Pratt and his friend considered that an excellent idea and agreed to return her safely to the hotel.

Pamela was outside hailing a cab to the Nadeau Hotel when the weight of the pistol in her bag pushed her anxiety up to another level. She recalled that Chapman customarily carried a portfolio of money from the hotel to the bank at this time of day. An armed Ortiz would accompany him, so Pamela argued with herself that she really shouldn't worry. Nonetheless, Kelly would know that this was the moment when Chapman was most vulnerable.

When the cab pulled up to the sidewalk, Pamela said, "Take me to the Ramona Hotel quickly."

As her cab entered Third Street, Pamela could see past a row of pawnshops, lunchrooms, and saloons, to the simple sign for the Ramona Hotel. She was about fifty feet away when Ortiz walked out the hotel door, glanced left and right, and beckoned Chapman, who stepped out, gripping his black portfolio. Suddenly, a woman in rags, sitting on the sidewalk, leaped to her feet, drew a club from her clothes, and struck Ortiz on the head. He crumbled onto the sidewalk.

In the same moment, another woman struck Chapman and dazed him, while a third woman seized his portfolio. The three villains hustled Chapman and the portfolio into a coach and drove away at high speed.

Pamela saw Kelly's hand in the incident—an abduction disguised as a robbery. She immediately ordered the cabdriver to follow the coach at a safe distance. "There's a reward for you if we help the police catch them."

"I'll try, ma'am." He pulled a large revolver from his coat. "It's handy, when you drive on Third Street. The manager of the Ramona is a good man. We have to help him. Are you fit for a fight?"

Pamela showed him her Colt .44 revolver.

"Good. You seem to know what you're doing, ma'am."

On the outskirts of the city, the thieves turned off the highway onto a dirt road through an orchard.

"Can you figure out where they're going?" Pamela asked.

"I recognized them. They work at a storage shed a couple of hundred feet up the road. I'll drive into the orchard and hide the carriage and the horse among the trees. We'll try to take the thieves by surprise."

As they started up the road, the driver put out his hand. "I'm Johnny Card, ma'am, a sergeant in the U.S. Army, retired."

She shook his hand. "And I'm Pamela Thompson, private investigator." She hitched up her skirt and thanked God that she was wearing sensible shoes.

Dusk was providing cover. Pamela and Johnny drew their pistols and sneaked quietly toward the shed.

Johnny whispered, "The shed is full of crates. The harvest will soon begin." He scratched his head. "I can fathom these thieves pilfering fruit and stealing tools but not robbing a cheap hotel's morning receipts."

"Someone paid them well to do it," Pamela remarked. "He's

Dan Kelly, a clever, dangerous man with a criminal past who thought up the scheme and trained these men. He may soon arrive to pay them off. We must act quickly."

Pamela and Johnny walked around the shed, keeping in the shelter of the trees. The thieves had parked the coach near the door and tethered the horses at a watering trough. No one was outside the shed. With her ear to the door Pamela could hear raucous laughter. She stole a glance through a window. Three burly men were sitting around a rough plank table, drinking from wine bottles. Their female disguises were carelessly tossed aside. Chapman's black portfolio lay open on the table. Two men were counting the money into three piles on the table. The third man was twirling Chapman's watch on its chain. In a corner of the room Howard Chapman sat on an orange crate, bound and gagged.

Johnny also glanced through the window and then turned to Pamela. "Let's hope they don't have firearms." He silently tried the door. It was unlocked. He nodded to Pamela, and they burst into the room. Pistols leveled, they ordered the men to lie face down on the floor. Pamela held the pistols while Johnny searched the men, removed their knives, then bound and gagged them and dragged them into a tool room. Pamela freed Chapman, patted him on the back, and handed him a loaded shotgun from a rack on the wall.

"Thanks," he said. "Were they planning to kill me?"

"Yes," Pamela replied. "Instead, they will all go to jail. We must hide behind a wall of crates and wait quietly. Dan Kelly should soon arrive." She lowered the flame in the room's sole oil lamp.

Ten minutes later, Pamela heard a horse's hooves in the gravel outside, then a hand on the door. Dan Kelly strode in, frowning when he saw no one. Pamela called out, "Raise your hands, Dan!" Quick as lightning, a knife appeared in his right hand, the blade shining in the lamplight. But his three opponents stood apart from each other and behind their barrier of crates. Seeing they were out of reach, Kelly cursed and slowly dropped the knife.

Pamela picked it up. Chapman held the shotgun at the ready while Johnny searched Kelly and removed a derringer and another knife. Meanwhile, Pamela found rope and bound him. The anger and hate in his eyes tingled her skin.

"I should summon the police," said Johnny. "Will you two be comfortable here guarding the thieves?"

"I think so," Pamela replied, having gotten a nod from Chapman. "But hurry."

The police soon arrived—they had been alerted by Ortiz and were harnessed and ready to go. They loaded the three thieves and Kelly into a Black Maria and sped off. Chapman put the stolen money back into his portfolio and recovered his watch. Shortly before nine, Johnny drove Pamela and Chapman to the Nadeau, weary but not much the worse for the experience.

"Pamela, where have you been?" Mary embraced her, then stepped back, frowning. "You're covered with dust, and your hair is a mess. Mr. Gagnon told me that Ortiz was hurt and Chapman kidnapped, but he didn't have the details. Were you involved?"

Pamela nodded. "I'll tell you about it. But first, order food and drink for us while I wash my face and tidy my hair."

A half hour later they sat down to a late supper in their room. Pamela described the incident in front of the Ramona and the capture of Dan Kelly and the three thieves in the storage shed. "Kelly and his accomplices are now in jail. A judge will arraign all of them tomorrow. I'll be there for questioning. Later I'll speak with the judge and the prosecutor about sending Kelly to New York. He should be tried again for his part in the cabdriver's murder seven years ago, as well as for his assault on Fred Grant."

"How is Mr. Chapman?"

"He received a nasty blow to the head. A doctor treated it and recommended that he rest at the Nadeau for a day or two. His work at the Ramona is nearly finished. The owner should be pleased that we've returned the stolen money to him."

"Do you know how Chapman feels about going back to New York?"

"This episode has severely shaken him. I fear that he might refuse to confront his enemies at Tammany Hall. I'll ask him later tomorrow. You and I should leave for New York on Sunday and bring him with us. I still hope to force the authorities to acknowledge the injustice done to Harry Miller. His cause is always uppermost in my mind."

Mary pouted. "It looks like we'll spend Christmas in a Pullman Palace Car. Still, we have much to be grateful for." She paused, smiling. "Herb and his friend were perfect gentlemen this afternoon, and I properly thanked them. After lunch, we toured the city hall, where I learned how Los Angeles is governed and will note it in my journal. When I mentioned that I'd be visiting Mission San Gabriel, they urged me to see the house where the famous Ramona had lived."

Pamela looked askance.

Mary grinned. "I told the two rascals I knew full well that Ramona was the fictional heroine of Helen Hunt Jackson's novel. Did they take me for a simple schoolgirl? They laughed heartily."

"Still, take their advice and visit the house," suggested Pamela. "You should recall Ramona from your reading. Picture her at home and in the mission church where she worshipped. Sketch the sites. The livelier your impressions the better you will later write about this experience for your teachers. Now, go to bed and rest for tomorrow's trip. It may be tiring as well as interesting. I'll telegraph today's news to Prescott. He'll be pleased to hear of Kelly's arrest."

Chapter 27

Aftermath

Thursday, December 20

The next morning, in the city jail's interrogation room, Pamela and Gagnon helped a police officer question the three thieves. They had earlier admitted assaulting Ortiz and Chapman and taking the money.

"But why kidnap Mr. Chapman?" the police officer asked the oldest thief, the apparent ringleader.

"Kelly promised each of us $10, besides what we found in the portfolio."

"What was Kelly going to do with the prisoner?" Gagnon asked.

"He never told us," replied the thief. "We figured he might hold him for ransom."

"You must have known that Chapman was poor as a church mouse," Pamela said.

The thief nodded. "The Ramona's owner would have had to pay."

Pamela concluded in her own mind that the thieves suspected from the beginning that Kelly would kill Chapman. Now they feared that they might be charged with complicity in attempted murder.

When the thieves were led back to their cells, Pamela asked the police officer about Kelly.

"He's next. We've kept him separate from the three local thieves to see how their stories match."

Kelly shuffled into the room in chains, looking glum. When he noticed Pamela, his eyes seemed to narrow with hate. She glanced at his chains and felt reassured.

The police officer confronted Kelly directly. "The three men who assaulted the hotel manager and stole his portfolio claim that you hired them. What do you say?"

"I had no idea they would commit a crime. They were supposed to pick oranges for me, that's all."

The officer bristled. "In someone else's orchard? You also promised to pay them $30. The usual rate is about a dollar." The officer spoke as if questioning a naughty child.

Kelly's brow wrinkled with wounded innocence. "I'm new in the orange business and didn't know the local prices."

The officer signaled a deputy to take Kelly away. After he had shuffled out, the officer turned to Pamela and Gagnon. "Kelly refused the help of a lawyer, apparently thinking his friends in New York will save him. I'll charge him with conspiring to assault and rob the manager."

The officer gazed curiously at Pamela and Gagnon and asked, "Why had Chapman left New York and changed his name?"

Pamela replied evenly. "He feared for his life at the hands of Kelly and his Tammany associates, so he fled here. Kelly has pursued him." She showed the officer a letter from Larry White, NYPD, detective bureau, explaining that he wanted Chapman's testimony in a seven-year-old murder case involving Kelly.

The officer appeared to mull over what he had just heard. "I'll have to talk to the judge about this."

Pamela sensed a complication developing in her plans.

* * *

In the afternoon Pamela went to a hearing in the courthouse. The prosecutor presented the three thieves and the evidence against them. Without further ceremony, the county police judge declared there was sufficient evidence to convict them of armed robbery and kidnapping and promptly consigned them to the county jail to await trial.

When Kelly was brought in, he was as insolent as before. The judge was irritated but maintained a dignified calm and accepted the charges of conspiring to assault, rob, and kidnap. Kelly pleaded not guilty. The judge said, "I'll postpone your trial until I decide the question of your rendition to New York City, where you are wanted as a person of interest in an ongoing investigation."

Kelly smirked as he was led away. Did he think the judge could be bought? Pamela wondered.

The judge called her into his office. "From Detective Larry White's letter," he said, "I've learned that New York may also want to try Mr. Kelly and will need Mr. Chapman's testimony. I'll make some inquiries. Bring Chapman to my office early tomorrow morning for a hearing concerning Kelly's alleged attempt to kill him. Afterward I'll tell you whether we need to hold him for further questioning."

Pamela left the jail, disappointed. At the least, if Los Angeles were to insist on trying Kelly first and requiring Chapman to remain and give testimony, it could delay for months his return to New York and her investigation into the cabdriver's death.

When Pamela returned to the Nadeau, she found Chapman at tea in the dining room. His eyes lit up, and he gave her a welcoming smile. She reported on the police investigation and her conversation with the judge. Chapman frowned at the prospect of meeting the judge tomorrow. She asked evenly, "Will you be ready to talk to him?"

"Yes," he replied with a hint of displeasure. "I'm not going to hide anymore. With time to think this morning, I've concluded that I should return to New York with you and try to reconcile with my wife, Ellen. But I still lack the courage to testify against Big Tim. A wounded Tammany tiger may be even more dangerous now to anyone threatening him."

Pamela didn't argue his point. Chapman's bruised head was a present reminder of Tammany Hall's long, violent reach. For now, she would be content to see him soon board the California Limited for New York.

Pamela was writing in her journal when Mary returned, dusty and tired from a full day's excursion. She hung up her coat, pulled off her shoes, and dropped down into a sofa. "The trip was *most* interesting," she exclaimed. "In the Pasadena museum I learned all about fossils and sketched a few. I had no idea the earth was millions of years old."

"Did you meet Ramona in Mission San Gabriel?" Pamela asked with a teasing smile.

"Yes, ma'am, but not the fictional one you're thinking of. At the old mission church, an attractive older woman, nicknamed Ramona, was polishing brass candlesticks. Her real name was Margarita. I paid her a dollar and she posed for me."

Mary handed Pamela a crayon sketch of a lively, brown complexioned face with fine features and thick gray hair. "For fun, a priest at the church once told a group of tourists that Margarita was the true Ramona and the name stuck to her—some tourists will believe almost anything."

Pamela remarked, "This woman bears an uncanny resemblance to my image of the fictional character."

"That's perhaps because Margarita's father, like Ramona's, was Scottish and her mother Indian. Margarita acts the part of Ramona in a parish play based on Mrs. Jackson's novel."

"Really! Could your Ramona read?"

"Yes, she had gone to school and had a much happier life

than the fictional character. But she knew Indians who had suffered like Ramona and her husband at the hands of American settlers, and the government had done nothing about it."

"This evening, you must thank the Carrolls for the trip and write about it in your journal while impressions are still fresh. Now, wash up and we'll join Mr. Chapman for supper. We must build up his courage for the meeting tomorrow with the judge, and even more for the test he'll soon face in New York."

"Are you worried about how his wife will receive him after seven years?"

"Yes, Mary. With good reason, she might reject him or discourage him from becoming embroiled in the prosecution of Big Tim and his agents."

Back in the room after supper, Pamela received a telegram from Prescott. He had persuaded Ellen Chapman to move to St. Barnabas Mission. Her husband's prospective return had shocked and confused her. She also feared Tammany's retaliation.

For a minute, Pamela stared at the message, trying to put herself in Ellen Chapman's mind. Suppose she heard a knock on her door, opened it, and saw her husband standing there, hat in hand. Would she even recognize him?

He had aged in the years he had been away. His face was creased and gray, his body thin and bent from deprivation during his struggle with alcohol. His spirit had also changed. Gone was the reckless, buoyant energy and greedy ambition of the young Tammany lawyer. Chapman was now a cautious man of diminished expectations, plodding through life's daily challenges.

To his credit, he had become a kinder, gentler man. At the Ramona Hotel he was known to help men and women who were down and out. In teaching chess to Mary Clark he showed patience with a beginner's stumbling moves. Her enthusiasm for the game seemed to lift his spirit.

Following supper this evening, he had told Pamela how grateful he felt for Mary's company. After years of cheap, lonely meals in his room, this cultivated man once again enjoyed good food and conversation in a comfortable setting with delightful female companionship. "I regret that I've deprived Ellen of the joy and comfort she needed. Her life must have been lonely. I understand how she might now resent me."

Pamela showed Prescott's telegram to Mary. As she read, her brow creased with concern. "Will there be trouble ahead?" she asked.

"Yes," Pamela replied, "Tim Smith is certainly planning new measures to prevent Mr. Chapman from reaching New York or, at least, from ever testifying in a courtroom."

Mary appeared to shudder at the warning but quickly gathered courage. "Then we must watch out for assassins boarding our train in Kansas City or Chicago."

"Right. Now go to work on your journal and sketchbook, while I report to Prescott on today's arraignment of Kelly and Chapman's decision to return to New York. I'll inform him that Kelly, shackled and under guard, will board the California Limited with us on Sunday, God willing."

CHAPTER 28

Taking Leave

Friday, December 21–Sunday, December 23

At breakfast, a message arrived from Herb Pratt, inviting Pamela and Mary to visit Redondo Beach, a popular resort on the sea.

Pamela read the message aloud to Mary: "*Having traveled three thousand miles across the continent, you must go the last fifteen miles to the Pacific Ocean. I suggest a bracing walk on the beach, a lunch in the Redondo Hotel, and an interesting lecture at the Chautauqua Assembly. You will be home before dark.*"

Mary's face glowed with enthusiasm. "What a marvelous opportunity!"

"I'm sorry, Mary, but I can't go. I'm expecting an important message from Mr. Prescott. I also should help Mr. Chapman conclude his work at the Ramona Hotel, and I don't know how much of my time the judge will require."

Mary looked crestfallen. "Then I shouldn't go, either."

Pamela quickly reflected. Could Pratt be trusted with Mary alone? What would Mr. Clark, her father, think? Then Pamela chided herself. This trip would take place in broad daylight, and Pratt would be a strong, watchful guard. Furthermore, shouldn't she encourage Mary to act as an adult? She had thus far shown good sense. Pamela gazed at the eager young woman. "You may go without me, Mary. This should be an excellent learning experience."

Pamela declined Pratt's invitation to her but accepted it for Mary:

> *If you go boating on the Pacific, remember that she cannot swim.*
> *Please bring her back to the hotel by sunset.*

At midmorning, Pamela and the Pinkerton Gagnon accompanied Chapman to the judge's office. A clerk was sitting off to one side, pen in hand. The judge was at his writing table, his expression noncommittal. Gagnon greeted the judge as if they were well acquainted.

Pamela struggled with distractions, wondering how Prescott would react to her latest message. She had left it at the hotel's telegraph office after breakfast. She also still had Mary on her mind and would futilely worry all day.

"What do you plan to do in New York?" the judge asked Chapman.

"First and foremost, your honor, I intend to reunite with my wife and put our financial affairs in order. I will propose that we move to Los Angeles, where I hope to find work in the hotel business."

"I've been told that you witnessed an alleged criminal conspiracy seven years ago that resulted in the death of a cabdriver. Mrs. Thompson told me that the initial investigation of the case was flawed and might be reopened. You could be called upon to testify. What are your intentions in that regard?"

"I'll engage a competent lawyer, Mr. Jeremiah Prescott, and follow his advice. I expect to comply with any reasonable requests from the court."

"If our attorney general were to indict Mr. Daniel Kelly for conspiracy to kill you, would you make yourself available to testify?"

"With pleasure, your honor."

"I have made inquiries concerning your character and learned that you are an honest, upright man who would cooperate with this court if need be. You are free to leave Los Angeles. Good luck."

As Chapman and Pamela left the courthouse, she noticed that he carried his head higher, his smile was more confident. That boded well for the challenges they would soon face in New York.

Promptly at dusk, Mary returned to the hotel, her face lightly burned by the sun and sea breezes. "We had a wonderful time," she exclaimed. "We took off our shoes and walked barefoot in the sand and then out into the ocean—mind you, only up to the ankles. At lunch we watched the waves coming in and going out endlessly, the light shining on the water. It was lovely. I imagined China just beyond the horizon—though it's thousands of miles away."

"What was the Chautauqua lecture about?"

"The next frontier, Hawaii. The islands will soon become a territory of the United States and eventually a state. The speaker thinks that we're destined to become a great power in the world. We need a navy to match."

"What did Mr. Pratt think of that?"

"He asked the lecturer, 'What is the point of being a great power? No country threatens us.' Herb argued that a big, new navy would be an unnecessary expense. The lecturer asked for my opinion, and I added that the money for the navy could be better spent on education in this country. The lecturer seemed pleased that we spoke up. Now I'll get ready for supper."

Pamela was relieved. Pratt appeared to treat Mary with respect and supported her desire for education. She needed more of that encouragement to counter her community's expectation that she should either marry early and well or go to work in a textile mill or millinery shop.

While Pamela and Mary were eating supper in the hotel dining room, a long telegram arrived from New York. Prescott reported that Ellen Chapman at St. Barnabas Mission would like to see villains like Tim Smith and Judge Fawcett exposed and sent to prison, but she feared Tammany's reprisal if she helped send them there. She also resented her husband's long absence but was eager to see him again.

At Prescott's law firm, the financial settlement of the rich woman's divorce had come to the point that Harry Miller could again assist Pamela. Harry had compiled sufficient evidence from Fred Grant, Frank Dodd, and Catherine Fawcett to expose Judge Fawcett's corruption. Florence Mulligan and Joe Meagher, the Tiger's Den's bartender, were rallying Tammany members opposed to Tim Smith's criminal leadership of the Sixteenth Ward. By the time Pamela arrived in New York, the case for prosecuting Tim Smith, Dan Kelly, and Judge Fawcett should be nearly ready to go to the district attorney's office.

Pamela showed the telegram to Mary without comment.

"Encouraging, isn't it?" she asked tentatively.

"Yes," Pamela replied. "But our success will depend on Chapman's testimony."

Chapter 29

Reluctant Witness

New York City
Sunday, December 23–Friday, December 28

Prescott rubbed heat into his hands. He had just returned to his office from a brisk midafternoon walk in frigid Gramercy Park. A telegraph message was waiting on his desk.

> NOON. LOS ANGELES. WE BOARD THE CALIFORNIA LIMITED. CHAPMAN APPREHENSIVE AND RELUCTANT. GAGNON AND SHERIFF'S DEPUTY WILL GUARD KELLY AND PROTECT US. REACH US BY TELEGRAPH AT MAJOR STATIONS. SEE YOU ON FRIDAY EVENING. 6:30. PAMELA.

Prescott leaned back in his chair, gazing at the telegram, and indulgently imagined its author's lovely, thoughtful face. With Chapman in hand, she had brought the investigation close to a successful conclusion.

He next turned to Harry's forged extortion letter that Catherine Fawcett had written at Judge Fawcett's behest. Three weeks ago,

Prescott had engaged a well-regarded expert to examine the original copy in the courthouse archives. Yesterday, the expert had reported that Catherine's imitation of Harry's handwriting was "excellent amateur work and would pass critical scrutiny by police detectives, bank clerks, and lawyers."

The expert's eye had noticed significant differences in the handwriting. As Catherine had slowly, carefully formed the letters, she had frequently lifted her pen, causing barely detectable shaky lines and thick, dark starts and finishes. In contrast, Harry's writing was fluent and uniform.

Prescott gave himself a moment of quiet satisfaction. Then he patted the report and muttered, "That should sink the judge's ship."

Meanwhile, late Sunday afternoon, Harry Miller stroked his false beard, tugged at the old coat he seldom wore, and pulled the visor of his cap nearly to his eyes. He slipped out of his building by the back way and caught a cab to Chelsea. There he knocked on Florence Mulligan's door.

"Come in a disguise," she had said in her invitation to tea. "The Tiger has become fretful. We don't want him to know that we are talking." Florence liked to refer privately to Big Tim Smith as a wild animal.

She opened the door for Harry and urged him in. The tea table was set for three. Harry raised an eyebrow.

Florence replied to the gesture. "Joe Meagher from across the street would like to talk to you. He has heard that Kelly is arrested in Los Angeles."

As bartender at the Tiger's Den, Meagher had long intrigued Harry. For over ten years, Meagher had worked in the saloon and had lived in an apartment directly above Big Tim's office. What might he know of Big Tim's secrets? Up to now, that question seemed moot. Joe valued his life so he had sealed his lips.

Harry asked Florence, "Has the growing strength of Tammany's enemies emboldened Joe and loosened his tongue?"

Florence nodded. "Especially since Tammany Hall lost the mayor's office to a Republican last month, Joe has been gradually opening up to me. Kelly's arrest is the final straw. Joe is still cautious, but he's now willing to help bring down Big Tim."

Joe arrived just as the tea was ready. Florence filled the cups and served sweet biscuits. As Joe stirred sugar into his tea, he seemed preoccupied. Finally, he remarked, "Kelly's arrest has shaken Big Tim. I heard him say he might have to slip over the border into Canada—they don't have an extradition treaty with the U.S. He swore he'd never go back to Sing Sing."

"What's he planning in the short run?" Harry asked, surprised that Joe would speak so freely.

"He has hired McBride and Cook to kill Chapman and Mrs. Thompson any way they can."

"I'm not surprised. We'll make sure that they fail. How have you found this out?"

Joe studied his cup for a long moment, then glanced furtively toward Florence.

She spoke for him. "For the past few weeks, Joe has secretly worked with me and others who want to get rid of Big Tim. He's ruining the club."

Joe nodded. "I've made a key to his office and occasionally slip in, go through his files, and read messages on his desk. I'm careful not to disturb anything. I also listen to his conversations through an air vent."

"Have you chanced upon anything remarkable?" Harry asked.

"Yes, Big Tim's copy of your extortion letter. His comments in the margins show that the letter is a forgery and that he paid the judge $350 for it. I know where it's hidden, but I dare not remove it until you are ready to take him in."

Harry shook the bartender's hand. "Don't worry, Joe. That day is within sight. Before the week's end, Detective White will arrest Big Tim and his cronies for their assault on Fred Grant. When they are safely in jail and no threat to you, White will get a search warrant for the Tiger's Den and you can lead him to the evidence."

Harry fulfilled the prediction already on Thursday. That morning, he and Larry White brought Fred Grant to police headquarters where he formally identified his assailants, Tim Smith, Dan Kelly, and the thugs, McBride and Cook. Except for Kelly, the men were immediately put in jail. Armed with a warrant, Harry and Larry then hurried to the Tiger's Den. Guided by Joe Meagher, they seized a trove of evidence implicating the arrested men in the murder of the cabdriver Tony Palermo. The evidence also revealed Judge Fawcett's part in covering up the crime, and he was charged with fraud.

Late in the afternoon, Harry reported the arrests to Prescott at the office.

"That was a good day's work," Prescott remarked. "Congratulations, Harry. Now we must marshal this evidence for a sound prosecution and make sure that these men are convicted. In the meantime, I'll telegraph Pamela the news."

CHAPTER 30

Reconciliation

New York, Friday, December 28–Saturday, December 29

At breakfast during the stop in Buffalo, Pamela received a telegram.

> SMITH, MCBRIDE, COOK, FAWCETT ARRESTED. PRESCOTT

Pamela showed the telegram to Dan Kelly. "When we arrive in New York this evening, you will be jailed with the others. This is just the beginning of your troubles with the law."

He shrugged a shoulder, but his eyes betrayed a hint of anxiety.

In Albany after lunch, Pamela bought a New York City newspaper that described the arrests and the police search of the Tiger's Den in Chelsea. Evidence was found that implicated the four arrested men in the murder of the cabdriver Tony Palermo. Judge Noah Fawcett was also arrested and charged with fraud in covering up the crime. Charges against the suspects were also pending in the suspicious death of Michael Sullivan.

Pamela brought the newspaper to Kelly. "Here's more for

you to think about, Dan. You are the center of attention in all three cases: the attempted murder of Fred Grant and the murders of Tony Palermo and Michael Sullivan. You might consider spreading the blame."

Kelly stared quietly at the paper, gnawing on his lips. His eyes narrowed. "Are you telling me to snitch on the others?"

"It looks bad for you, Dan. The NYPD has given Detective White a free hand in these cases and he has collected a ton of evidence. Big Tim is in jail. Don't count on Tammany Hall. Judge Fawcett can't help you, either. He's likely to go to jail for forging Harry Miller's extortion letter and wrongfully convicting Harry. So you'd better think of making a deal with the prosecution."

Kelly made a nervous, dismissive gesture and stared out the window. Pamela was sure she had planted a seed.

Pamela's train entered Grand Central Station at 6:30 in the evening, predictably a busy, stressful hour. Passengers swarmed onto the platform and hurried to their connections, pushing aside porters offering assistance, and trainmen off-loading baggage and the mail.

The deafening din in the station heightened Pamela's sense of danger. Even from jail, Big Tim could insinuate Tammany's thugs into the milling crowd to attack Chapman or free Kelly. Peering out the window of her compartment, she was relieved to see Prescott, Harry Miller, and Larry White. They waved at her but would wait to remove Kelly until most passengers had left the train.

With Kelly strapped into a wheelchair, Pamela and her companions made their way to the station's waiting hall. At that point, Larry White took custody of Kelly from the Los Angeles sheriff's deputy. Guarded by Harry and Gagnon, Mary and Chapman left the hall to collect the baggage. Pamela and Prescott waited in a tearoom in the station.

"I'm happy the trip is behind me. I feel exhausted."

"Was Kelly a difficult prisoner?"

She shrugged. "He required a great deal of attention. A Tammany agent could have slipped onto the train at one of our many stops and freed him. Or, like a magician, Kelly could somehow have freed himself and caused mayhem."

"How did you manage?"

"The sheriff's deputy and the Pinkerton shackled him, chained him to his seat, and took turns watching him. He had to be fed and helped to the bathroom. I personally checked his shackles and chains day and night at odd intervals."

"So you had close contact with him. What was he like?"

"At first, he appeared calm and mostly looked out the window. When he spoke, it was with a smirk on his face. Sometimes he smiled like a cunning child, as if looking for opportunities to escape, should his guards nod off or grow bored and careless. When I checked his chains, he stared at me with a glint in his eyes. In his imagination he probably had tied me to a board and was throwing knives at me."

"Did he keep that up for six days? At some point, he must have tried to play on your sympathy."

Pamela nodded. "Near Kansas City, I mentioned that Alice Curran recalled him protecting her in Hell's Kitchen and cherished his canary. The evil look left his eyes. 'So you were friendly with Alice,' he said in a civil voice. 'I thought you were a proper *lady.*' We had our first genuine conversation, mostly about Alice and the canary."

Prescott cocked his head in a skeptical gesture. "Kelly was probably trying to get you to take off his shackles."

"Possibly. I noticed that they were cutting into his ankles, so I had the sheriff's deputy loosen them—but only a tad. Kelly's instincts are still murderous."

Prescott shrugged. "If Kelly is fond of canaries and a brothel madam, he's not all bad. Do you think we could persuade him to help us?"

"I think so. When we had left Albany and were headed for New York, he said, 'Big Tim is the guy you want. I just run errands for him.'

"I told him, 'That's what I had figured.' "

Prescott nodded. "He may be willing to negotiate a reduced sentence for Palermo's murder and other Tammany crimes. I'll pass that on to the district attorney."

"Do you have any news?" Pamela asked.

"Yes, my handwriting expert has confirmed that the extortion letter's original version in the police archives is a forgery. Since it was the prosecutor's principal evidence and the basis for Harry's conviction, a court with any integrity would now exonerate him. We'll see."

At that point, Mary and Chapman, and Harry and Gagnon, returned with the baggage. Gagnon would find hotel accommodations in the city, and Harry would escort Mary to Pamela's apartment. Chapman joined Pamela and Prescott, and they walked to the exit.

"Where are we going?" Chapman asked Prescott.

"To your wife Ellen's new apartment near Union Square. She moved there from St. Barnabas, once we put Big Tim and his thugs in jail."

As the coach crawled through city traffic, a nagging fear of Tammany Hall lingered in Pamela's mind. The dark streets were crowded with pedestrians, carts, and vehicles of every description. An ambush would be easy.

To her relief they arrived without incident at Ellen's building. Prescott led them up the stairs to her apartment, Pamela staying close to Chapman to give him moral support. Prescott knocked on the door. Long seconds passed. Prescott knocked again. This time footsteps sounded on the other side, and then the door slowly opened. Ellen stepped back, and beckoned them into the entrance hall. Arms limp at her side, she stared blankly at her husband, as if she didn't recognize him.

Chapman balked and began to tremble. Pamela gripped him at the elbow and nudged him forward. A light of recognition appeared in Ellen's eyes, then a tentative smile, and she extended a hand. He grasped it and said softly, "Ellen, it's been too long. I'm sorry."

Tears welled up in her eyes. "I've missed you, Howard. I'm so glad you're back."

After a brief conversation about the trip from California, Pamela motioned to Prescott that it was time to go. He asked Chapman, "Could we see you at the office tomorrow afternoon?"

Chapman nodded. "I should have made up my mind by then."

The next day, Chapman looked pale and fatigued as he joined Pamela, Prescott, Harry, and Larry White at the conference table in Prescott's inner office. Pamela worried that he and Ellen might have quarreled overnight and he now regretted having returned to New York.

"How are you, Howard?" she asked, studying him closely.

"I slept poorly last night, too much to think about, and I'm still recovering from the long trip. After talking things over with Ellen this morning, I've decided to clear up my situation here rather than hide again." There was resolve in the set of his jaw.

"You could begin, Howard, by telling us what happened seven years ago that caused you to flee to Los Angeles."

With a nod, Pamela directed Harry to take notes for later use in legal proceedings.

Chapman flashed an apprehensive glance at Harry but nonetheless started to speak. "In 1884 I was Tammany Hall's lawyer for financial affairs. One day, the chairman of the finance committee, Alderman Tim Smith, told me to meet with a lawyer from Mr. Jacob Sharp's Broadway Street Railway Company to arrange a donation to Tammany Hall. I wasn't surprised. Businessmen and corporations often gave money to political clubs in exchange for their good will. My predecessor in the office had negotiated many gifts to Tammany.

"After a few meetings, the company's lawyer indicated that the donation would be very large and would have to be deeply secret. That warned me to stay on the right side of the law. At the conclusion of our negotiations, the company pledged $500,000 in cash to Tammany Hall, a sum comparable to the cost of a monarch's coronation or a great mansion on Fifth Avenue. Half of the money would be paid in August of 1884 in advance of the aldermen's award of a franchise for a surface railway in Lower Broadway, the remaining half to be paid afterward. On each occasion, I would personally carry the money to Chairman Tim Smith. The agreement didn't specify a quid pro quo, but I strongly suspected that the purpose of the donation was to bribe the aldermen. When I gently probed Smith for an explanation, he replied, 'The donation is to help us do good things for the poor.' "

"That was a brazen scheme," exclaimed Harry.

"And dangerous as well for you, Mr. Chapman," added Pamela. "It's hard to imagine anyone safely carrying that much cash in a portfolio on the streets of New York."

"Nonetheless," said Chapman, "Tammany, as well as the railway company, insisted on a cash transaction, even one as large as this. Mr. Croker, Tammany's former chief, now living in exile in Britain, was known to have carried a satchel with a quarter of a million dollars in cash and even kept it under his bed overnight."

Pamela shook her head in disbelief. The others smiled sardonically—they appeared more familiar with Tammany's ways.

Chapman continued: "The company lawyer signed the agreement, to be countersigned by Smith upon receipt of the money. The first transfer proceeded without a hitch. Big Tim arranged its distribution to twelve aldermen, mostly Democrats. At a hasty meeting of the Board of Aldermen, they duly awarded the railway franchise to Sharp's company.

"After he had gained the franchise, however, Sharp refused to pay the $250,000 balance, claiming that the initial payment had nearly bankrupted him. When Big Tim threatened to vandalize his property, or worse, Sharp agreed to pay five semiannual installments of $50,000 each, beginning January first, 1885. Sharp paid regularly but continued to complain. I always had to remind him of Big Tim's threat.

"For over two years this deal strained my nerves to the breaking point. I feared constantly that I would go to prison. Sharp's competitors cried foul; the newspapers took up their cause; and the district attorney was forced to investigate. By the end of 1886, I was sure Big Tim's scheme would collapse.

"But Monday afternoon, January third, I put the final installment into my portfolio and set out for Tammany Hall, feeling immensely relieved. I had laid aside a small fortune in cash and stocks, none of it bribe money, by the way. Ellen and I would leave New York and begin a new life in California."

Pamela remarked, "We know how you left the portfolio in Tony Palermo's cab. What happened when he tried to claim a reward for returning it?"

"Someone had sent an anonymous message to Tim Smith's office in Tammany Hall, declaring he had found the portfolio and demanding $5,000 before he would hand it over. Smith called me into the office for an explanation. I had hoped to retrieve the portfolio myself before anyone at Tammany Hall knew of my folly. But now I was found out and had to tell Smith that I'd gone into a saloon and left the portfolio in a cab. 'You drunken sot!' he had screamed. 'I'd like to kill you right here with my bare hands. But first, we must find out if this nameless guy is our cabdriver.'

"In his reply Smith asked the author of the message to come to the club office in the Tiger's Den the next day at four o'clock. If he returned the portfolio and its contents intact, he would receive the reward. Smith said to me, 'I want you there, sober, to identify the cabdriver and verify the contents. Do you understand?'

"I had no choice but to agree." Chapman halted abruptly, gasping for breath, and asked for water. Pamela fetched a glass, concerned that he was about to collapse. The water and a brief rest, however, revived him.

"The next day, I was sitting with Smith in the barroom when this big Italian walked in, wearing a heavy overcoat. He recognized me and swaggered over to our table like the cock of the walk. The portfolio was under his arm. 'I'm Tony Palermo,' he announced in broken English. 'We're going to do business now.'

"I whispered to Smith, 'That's the cabdriver.'

"Under his breath Smith said, 'I've had problems with him parking in front of this place.' Smith led us into his office behind the barroom, politely thanked Palermo for finding the portfolio, and said he could expect a suitable reward when he handed it over.

"Palermo looked smug. 'I want ten percent, $5,000, and not a penny less.' He added in a threatening tone, 'Your agreement with the railway company that I found in the portfolio is worth many times that much to you.'

"Big Tim flinched, but he agreed. He had no choice. Otherwise, he wouldn't get the money back, and Palermo might sell his story to the *New York World,* which would investigate the donation and expose its true purpose. Tammany Hall would become the laughingstock of the city and the target of a serious grand jury investigation.

" 'Friend,' said Smith, 'you drive a hard bargain, but I accept. Count out the $5,000.'

"Palermo opened the portfolio, removed a ten pack of $500 U.S. Treasury notes, fanned them in Smith's face, put them in an inside coat pocket, and pushed the portfolio across the table.

"I checked the remaining packs of money and the receipt and remarked that a sealed envelope had been opened. Smith said, 'Show me the message.'

"As I removed it, I saw that it read: '*This payment of $50,000 to Timothy Smith is the final installment for the Board of Aldermen's approval of my request to operate a surface railway on Lower Broadway.*' Jacob Sharp had signed it.

"I handed the message to Smith. He gave it a quick glance and put it back in the envelope. For a few moments, he stared intensely at Palermo and was deathly quiet—I sensed the cabdriver would die for having opened that envelope. Then Smith said in a very small voice, 'Mr. Palermo, you are now a rich man. Shall we drink to your health?'

"Smith and Palermo each had a shot of whiskey—I drank water. 'You've cost Tammany enough already,' Smith said to me. He turned to Palermo. 'Have another for the road, Tony. It's cold outside.' He poured a shot into the cabdriver's glass.

" 'Thanks. Don't mind if I do. You're a good loser, Tim.' He emptied the glass in one gulp, waved good-bye, and walked into the barroom. Smith and I followed him.

"Dan Kelly stood near the door to the street. Smith nodded to him. He quickly stepped outside. As Palermo left the building, Kelly deliberately pushed him. 'You greedy Dago,' he growled. 'You cheated me on my fare.'

"Palermo grew red in the face. 'Show me respect, you little shrimp. I've never laid eyes on you.'

" 'Nobody calls me a shrimp and gets away with it.' Kelly spit on Palermo's shoe. Anger flashed in the Italian's eyes. '*Bastardo!*' he shouted, and raised his hands.

"In an instant Kelly drew a knife and slashed Palermo's throat. He fell writhing on the pavement. Smith and I rushed up to him, followed by two Tammany guards. I loosened his collar and tried to make him comfortable, but he was unconscious. Blood pulsed from his throat. Meanwhile, someone called for the police.

"While I was helping Palermo, I noticed Smith pull a knife from Palermo's belt and lay it near his hand. Then he reached into the dying man's pocket and retrieved the $5,000. Smith's eyes met mine. At that moment, I realized that this had been a cold-blooded assassination, and he knew that I knew. I glanced at my hands and my shirtsleeves, wet with blood, and I felt as guilty as if I had killed Palermo."

"You weren't aware," said Pamela to Chapman, "that Florence Mulligan had witnessed the scene from her room across the street. Her account is identical to yours."

"At the time," said Chapman, "it wouldn't have mattered if she had witnessed the crime. She would have been afraid to protest. Horror and fear took over my mind. A policeman soon arrived, and we retreated into the barroom. He questioned several of us bystanders, and then took Kelly to the station house. An ambulance came for Palermo's body."

Chapman breathed a deep sigh. "That was the most horrid incident of my life. It took place within a few minutes, seven years ago, but I remember it as clearly as if it happened yesterday. As the policeman questioned me, I could hardly speak. Tim Smith sat nearby listening, his eyes fixed on me. I knew instinctively that I shouldn't say a word about the money and our transaction with Palermo.

"As I was leaving the Tiger's Den, Smith sidled up to me and whispered, 'Never implicate Tammany Hall in what happened to the cabdriver, or you will meet the same fate. If you have any sense, you will disappear.'

"That night I took the train to Los Angeles."

* * *

While Chapman checked Harry's notes, Pamela asked Larry White what he planned to do next.

"I'll get a written deposition from Florence Mulligan. Two consistent eyewitnesses should clinch the case against Tim Smith. I already have documentary proof from Ambrose Norton, Frank Dodd, and Joe Meagher that Smith actually paid Kelly. Without that proof, Smith could argue that Kelly acted on his own."

Pamela suggested, "In that case, perhaps Kelly could be persuaded to further implicate Smith, the paymaster, in return for escaping the death sentence. Tell him how the electric chair literally fried the wife-murderer Kemmler for several minutes before he died. Some say that his body caught fire. I mentioned it once to Kelly and he turned pale."

Larry nodded. "Then he has probably concluded that cooperation is his only option."

"I'm sure the prosecutor would consider a plea bargain," said Prescott. "It's the most sure and quick way to close this case with the least damage to Tammany Hall." Then he asked Chapman: "Was Judge Fawcett involved in this incident in any way?"

"As far as I know, he had nothing directly to do with the cabdriver's death. I've been told that the judge accepted a bribe and willfully covered up the crime with forged evidence."

Larry White cautioned, "Without clear proof, the district attorney would balk at including the judge in the conspiracy to kill Palermo for fear of offending the dignity of the courts."

"Nonetheless, we have to sort out the judge's part in Sullivan's death," Prescott insisted.

Pamela pointed out, "If Kelly is charged with Sullivan's death, he will most likely claim that Smith, at Fawcett's behest, ordered him to do it."

Larry White stroked his chin thoughtfully. "Kelly's claim might be close to the truth, but I doubt that the district attorney would charge Fawcett. The judge would contradict Kelly and claim plausibly that he merely called Tammany Hall and asked for Singleton's cab. I can't prove that he was more significantly involved."

As the meeting ended, Pamela remarked, "We really don't know whether the district attorney would be willing to bargain at all."

Larry nodded. "I'll find out when I meet him early in January."

CHAPTER 31

Grand Jury and Final Verdict

Wednesday, January 9, 1895

Though wrapped in a fur coat against the winter cold, Pamela began to shiver. She and Prescott were riding in a cab downtown to the office of District Attorney John Fellows. He had reluctantly agreed to Larry White's request for this meeting.

Prescott glanced at her with concern. "Are you chilled, Pamela?" He touched her cheek with the back of his hand. "You feel warm."

"My nerves are reacting to our coming meeting with Mr. Fellows," she replied. "This investigation and much else is at stake. We must persuade him to present our evidence against Big Tim Smith and Judge Fawcett to a grand jury. That's a daunting task, considering Tammany Hall's power in this city."

"Relax, Pamela, you've built a strong case against those rascals. Otherwise Larry White wouldn't have arranged this meeting. He knows the pitfalls of the judicial process and nonetheless believes we shall prevail."

"Still," she insisted, "I'm concerned that Mr. Fellows is a

Democrat and politically aligned with Tammany Hall rather than with Reverend Parkhurst and the reformers."

"I agree on that point," Prescott admitted. "I've also seen Fellows recently and he looks tired and sick. I'm sure he'd prefer that we didn't bother him with an old, cold case of judicial wrongdoing."

When they entered the building, Larry White, Catherine Fawcett, and Howard Chapman were waiting for them. Patting his portfolio, Larry said, "The statements from Frank Dodd, Fred Grant, Florence Mulligan, and Joe Meagher are here—our reserve ammunition, so to speak."

Pamela murmured to Prescott, "Have you noticed that our chief witnesses, Catherine and Howard, look frightened and anxious?"

"Yes," he replied softly. "They now foresee more clearly the risks they face. Each of them could be accused of having taken part in the crimes we shall discuss. Moreover, if this legal process drags on, Tammany Hall's defenders could blacken their reputation, harass them in many other ways, or even kill them. Let's show confidence in our cause and encourage them."

After a short wait in an anteroom, Pamela and the others were ushered into Mr. Fellows's office. With a brave smile he rose painfully from his desk to meet them. He spoke with a Southern accent—he was raised in Arkansas and had been a colonel in the Confederate army. A popular magistrate, his manner was outgoing and gracious and his appearance friendly. Pamela felt comfortable with him but remained anxious.

Pamela and her companions gathered around a large conference table, Fellows at the head. He turned to Larry. "Please sum up the case, Detective White."

Larry put on his official manner and began in a plain, factual tone. "In the course of investigating the suspicious death of Mr. Michael Sullivan, Mrs. Thompson and I discovered that he had been murdered. Further investigation uncovered earlier, related crimes, including the murder of the cabdriver, Tony Palermo, as well as assaults, fraud, bribery, and criminal conspiracy, going back seven years and even spanning the continent. The crimes all involved the same suspects—Timothy Smith, Judge Noah Fawcett, Daniel Kelly, Patrick McBride, and William Cook—and grew out of the infamous 'Boodle' scandal of 1884."

Larry gave Pamela a sidelong glance and concluded, "Our evidence shows that Fawcett, Kelly, McBride, and Cook carried out the crimes at the behest of Smith."

Mr. Fellows appeared fully attentive, if skeptical. Several days ago, Larry White had given him a detailed written summary of Palermo's murder in 1887 and Smith and Fawcett's attempts at the time to conceal the crime, as well as Michael Sullivan's later threat to expose them and his subsequent murder. Attached to the summary were the depositions from Catherine Fawcett, Howard Chapman, Fred Grant, Frank Dodd, Florence Mulligan, and Joe Meagher that attested to the suspects' guilt.

The room grew quiet while the district attorney shuffled through his papers. Then he said solemnly, "Detective White and Mrs. Thompson, I commend your zeal and your diligence in unearthing a very serious criminal matter. I will give your evidence the attention it deserves. With the arrest of these five suspects, the newspapers are already on the hunt for other scoundrels, real and imaginary. We must deal with the case promptly, before the public is led into false accusations."

That's encouraging, thought Pamela. Mr. Fellows intended to protect Tammany Hall's reputation by quickly blaming the crimes on a few bad apples in the notorious Sixteenth Ward.

Fellows said to the others, "I'll now play the devil's advocate at a grand jury hearing." He cleared his throat and pretended to glare at Larry. "Detective White, why do you challenge the court's decision in 1887 that Mr. Kelly acted in self-defense when he killed Palermo? Two eyewitnesses swore that the cabdriver reached into his coat for a knife."

"We can prove, sir, that they lied." Larry nodded to Howard Chapman, who testified that Kelly deliberately provoked the cabdriver, and then killed him—though he had not drawn a weapon, nor was he about to. This was confirmed by Florence Mulligan's deposition.

Prompted by Fellows, Chapman told his story of losing the portfolio of "boodle" money, Smith's angry reaction, followed by his plot to kill the cabdriver. Chapman seemed to relive his story as he described Smith planting the knife by Palermo's hand and retrieving the pay-off money from the dying man, "even while blood poured from his throat."

At that graphic image, Fellows turned pale and gulped. He weakly suggested that a grand jury might nonetheless uphold the claim of self-defense on the grounds that Kelly could reasonably presume that Palermo *would* reach for a knife. In that case, Pamela retorted, Kelly could be charged with manslaughter for deliberately provoking his victim. She pointed out that Mulligan and Chapman saw Palermo merely raise his hands.

Fellows next questioned the forged extortion letter. Larry White called on Catherine Fawcett to explain how Judge Fawcett deceived her into producing it and then justified the fraud as necessary to convict a felon.

Again playing the devil's advocate, Fellows claimed Catherine had come to regard Harry Miller as a rogue cop and a danger to society. "She therefore forged the letter and sent it to Tammany Hall in order to ensure his conviction, leaving the judge ignorant of her deed."

Pamela objected. "With due respect to the devil, sir, I'd say that is groundless speculation. Documents from Smith's office show that he had proposed the scheme to Fawcett who devised the fraudulent letter and afterward gave a copy to Smith. We have Smith's comments in the margins."

At the end of an hour, Mr. Fellows said he had heard enough. For a few moments, he sat quietly, eyes cast down. Then, he drew a deep breath and announced, "I believe we can persuade the grand jury to reopen the Palermo case as well as examine Mr. Miller's extortion conviction, Michael Sullivan's death, and the other related charges. We shall argue the case from your evidence. The grand jury may or may not reach your conclusions—it is extra cautious when wrongdoing touches the judiciary's competence and integrity."

Sending the case to the grand jury encouraged Pamela. Still, she shared Fellows's concern. Courts were protective of their reputation and seldom admitted or corrected serious mistakes. Even less did they acknowledge their own criminal behavior. So, she held her hopes in check.

As the meeting was coming to a close, Fellows turned to Larry. "Detective White, why haven't you charged the police, in particular Inspector Williams, with willful negligence in investigating the cabdriver's death and willful complicity in Judge Fawcett's forgery?"

Pamela held her breath. Implicating Williams would trigger a dangerous reaction. Thus far, he had allowed Larry to proceed in the case without interfering. If Williams were to feel that his honor or his pension was threatened, he could insert himself into the grand jury's deliberations and undermine the credibility of Catherine Fawcett, Howard Chapman, and the other witnesses.

Larry appeared to recognize the danger. "Williams," he

replied, "might have been negligent or hasty in these cases, but it would be hard to prove that his faults rose to the level of a felony."

Fellows agreed, and Pamela was relieved, though she felt that Williams deserved severe punishment for his part in blackening Harry's reputation.

Three weeks later, the case went to the grand jury. To Pamela's surprise, the jury quickly found probable cause for trial on all charges and indicted Smith, Judge Fawcett, Kelly, McBride, and Cook—the press had already dubbed them the "Tammany Five."

At the beginning of March, Pamela and Prescott observed the trial before the state's highest criminal court. Pamela was disconcerted that Kelly first pleaded not guilty, despite the weight of evidence against him. District Attorney Fellows then reminded him of the strong possibility of dying in the electric chair. Sobered, Kelly changed his plea to guilty and testified against Smith and Fawcett.

When Fellows questioned Big Tim, he claimed to have paid Kelly merely to frighten Palermo. In the heat of his quarrel with the cabdriver, Kelly had gone beyond the instructions.

Kelly grew angry. "Bastard, are you trying to shift all the blame onto me? You organized the killing of Palermo and told me to do it. You recovered $5,000 from Palermo's pocket and gave me a measly two hundred. When I protested, you told me to shut up or you'd have me fried in the electric chair."

Fellows also contradicted Judge Fawcett's attempt to blame Catherine for Harry Miller's extortion letter to Big Tim Smith. The court agreed that the judge committed the fraud as part of a conspiracy to cover up Palermo's murder.

As the trial was drawing to a close, Pamela asked Prescott,

"Why has no one from Tammany Hall come forward to defend the five suspects?"

He replied, "Tammany's leaders have blamed their November electoral defeat in part on Smith's brutal method of getting out the vote and other crimes. They have therefore abandoned him and his companions and made our task easier."

Epilogue

New York, Sunday, April 14, 1895

On a mild, bright Easter morning, Pamela and Prescott went with the Sullivan family by coach to St. Stephen's Church for the eleven o'clock solemn High Mass. The congregation arrived in festive finery: the men in silk top hats, faun or gray frock coats, and matching fine wool suits; the women in colorful silk gowns and elaborate hats.

The robust music of a large choir and orchestra, the clergy's dazzling golden vestments, large banks of odoriferous Easter lilies, and pungent clouds from burning incense combined in a majestic celebration of Christ's resurrection. The spectacle mesmerized Theresa's son, James. The lilies and the incense released a flood of tears from Pamela's eyes.

Members of the Sullivan party had brought along their own reasons for celebration. Mrs. Sullivan seemed to be rejuvenating late in life. Her demented husband was securely committed in a nursing home and her daughters had restored order to the family's finances. Larry White, his wife, Trish, and their daughters reveled in his official commendation and raise in pay for work well done in the Tammany Five case. Finally, liberated from her deceased brother's tyranny, Theresa was free to marry the man she loved, Harry.

After the Mass, Mrs. Donavan served a splendid dinner at Mrs. Sullivan's new, modest apartment off Fourteenth Street to celebrate Harry's exoneration. During the meal he rose to thank Prescott and Pamela for their efforts on his behalf and announced his engagement to Theresa. She added sprightly, "We shall have a simple wedding at City Hall."

Theresa's remark didn't surprise Pamela. Harry was divorced and not a Catholic. The priest at St. Stephen's had told Theresa that he wouldn't marry them. Earlier, he had supported Michael Sullivan and Judge Fawcett's attempt to separate her from Harry. Now she was skeptical of clergy of any sort and preferred a civil ceremony.

After dinner, Pamela stood by an open window, gazing at a sky full of sunlight and breathing mild, warm air. "Would you like to walk in Central Park?" she asked Prescott.

"An excellent idea!" he replied. "We could catch up on news while enjoying the spring weather." He had been away to Washington, D.C., for the thirtieth anniversary of General Robert E. Lee's surrender, April 9, at Appomattox, Virginia. It ended the Civil War but left the country with much unfinished business. Prescott seized the opportunity to seek pensions for poor, aging, former comrades-in-arms.

As he and Pamela rode in a cab up Fifth Avenue, he remarked, "When I returned yesterday to my office, a letter from Edward was waiting for me. His studies demand a lot of time but he enjoys them. He's also practicing for the college baseball team and looking forward to playing Amherst in May."

"Then he may see Herbert Pratt again," Pamela remarked. "Are they still friends?"

"Yes, Edward is aware that Mary and Herb met on the trip to California. 'No hard feelings,' he wrote. 'I don't own her.'

Still, I think Edward is surprised and hurt that a woman he's fond of also feels attracted to another man." Prescott hesitated for a moment, then asked, "What have you heard?"

"A few weeks ago, Mary wrote to me, asking for advice. The Pratt Institute in Brooklyn had invited her to apply for a scholarship in the school's prestigious drawing program. Earlier, she had planned to attend North Adams State Normal School in order to teach mill workers' children in Berkshire County. But now she has to consider that an education at Pratt Institute would open up opportunities for much better paid commercial work in the New York City area and beyond."

Prescott frowned. "Mary would become indebted to Herbert Pratt—he surely recommended her. Even though he's a gentleman, might he expect something in return from her?"

"I've pointed that out to Mary. She's struggling with the invitation and has to decide soon. She likes both Edward and Herb but doesn't feel ready to commit to either man. Certified as a teacher, she could help the poor children of mill workers. With a Pratt diploma she'd be better equipped to help her own father and brother."

"Hard choices," Prescott remarked. "What did you advise her?"

"I told her to visit the Pratt Institute with an open mind, examine the program, and speak to students and teachers. If she wished, she could stay in my apartment and become acquainted with living in a big city. She should carefully weigh the alternatives, otherwise she might later regret that she chose badly."

"Has she taken up your offer?"

"Yes, she'll come to me after she has finished high school in June."

Prescott was thoughtfully silent for a long moment. "Mary's fortunate to have you as a mentor. You gave her good counsel."

* * *

In Central Park the wind was brisk. Still, the temperature was a comfortable fifty-five degrees and a little warmer in sheltered places. The grass was green but the trees were still bare. People had come from every corner of New York City to enjoy the park on one of its most pleasant days.

After a long walk, Pamela and Prescott sat down together on a bench looking out over the lake between Seventy-second and Seventy-ninth Street, near the great reservoir of water that slaked the city's thirst.

"I've heard from Ellen Chapman," Pamela remarked. "She and her husband, Howard, have settled in Los Angeles and are both working at the Nadeau Hotel."

"I'm happy for them," said Prescott. "I can report that our trust department is pleased with Ambrose Norton and has changed his status from temporary to permanent. He has become engaged to his girlfriend."

"Have you heard from Catherine Fawcett?" Pamela asked.

Prescott nodded. "She's grateful that I recommended her to my client, that wealthy Fifth Avenue lady involved in the financial dispute with her husband. Catherine has become the lady's indispensable private secretary."

"Has anything changed at Tammany Hall since Big Tim has gone to prison?" Pamela asked.

Prescott replied, "Frank Dodd has replaced him as boss of the Sixteenth Ward and has also taken over his position as chairman of Tammany Hall's Finance Committee. Under Dodd's enlightened leadership, the Tiger may once again represent the common people of the city. Fred Grant has recovered enough to return to his job at Tammany Hall."

"I doubt that anyone can truly reform Tammany," Pamela said. "But I wish Dodd well. What matters most to me is that we reached our chief goal, the exoneration of Harry Miller."

"Do you have any regrets?" Prescott asked.

"Yes," she replied with heat. "Justice wasn't fully served.

Granted, Judge Fawcett will spend about as much time in prison as Harry did. The other villains will be incarcerated for life. Fair enough. But I wish we could have held Inspector Williams to account for besmirching Harry's good name. In 1887, he accepted Tammany's accusation against Harry far too eagerly."

Prescott added, "He also wrongly dismissed Harry's hunch that the cabdriver's death was an assassination, regarding it as merely the result of a barroom quarrel between two lowlife characters."

Pamela wasn't satisfied. "Greed may also have misled Williams. Tammany Hall paid him for protection from reformers and political rivals. It was therefore in his financial interest to safeguard the club's reputation."

Prescott nodded. "I share your feelings about Williams. Unfortunately, he will not only retire honorably and with full pension but also continue to profit from the favors and the illegal services that he has rendered to the wealthy over many years."

"The rascal! How is that possible?"

"In his retirement, he will sell insurance, a natural, legal extension of his protection rackets in Chelsea."

"Who are his potential customers?"

"The prominent, wealthy men and women who have reasons to fear that Williams might know their hidden, unpunished crimes and scandals. If he were to offer to insure their yachts or their mansions, they would surely accept—with the unspoken understanding that he would keep their secrets. If they were to balk, they would risk being exposed to the press or to a zealous prosecutor."

"A cold, calculating, and clever man," Pamela observed.

Prescott took her hand. "The day is much too lovely to allow Inspector Williams to spoil it."

They joined a parade of young people walking arm in arm around the lake. In the distance Harry and Theresa were standing on the opposite shore in a tender embrace.

Moved by the sight, Pamela felt a rush of affection for Prescott. At the same moment, he turned to her and looked fondly into her eyes. They clasped hands, moved to a place sheltered by a thick wall of bushes, and embraced.

"Shall we have a serious conversation, my dear Pamela?" His voice was laden with feeling.

"Yes, dearest Jeremiah, I welcome it." She gestured to a bench, and they sat side by side.

"Love is apparently contagious," he began. "Observing Harry and Theresa, a few minutes ago, has given me the courage to say what I've long felt, that I love you and want you to be my wife, if you'll have me." He searched in her eyes.

She met his gaze and pressed his hand. "Working together for nearly three years, often under trying circumstances, I've come to know, trust, and love you, and gladly accept you as my husband."

They leaned toward each other in a warm, close embrace.

"Then," Prescott added, "I suggest a private wedding later this summer when Edward and our friends and your foster girls can attend." He paused thoughtfully for a moment. "The war seems to have robbed me of belief in God, but I sense that you are religious. Is there a way that our marriage could be blessed?"

"I have in fact inquired," she replied with a mischievous smile. "The chapel at St. Barnabas Mission is available for a private service. The chaplain, a kindly old priest whom I've known for years, is willing to bless our exchange of vows."

"Perfect!" Prescott exclaimed.

They rose to their feet and sealed their love with a long and tender kiss. Pamela felt euphoric, like being born again to a new, blissful life, together with Jeremiah, stretching out endlessly.

As they left the park, arm in arm, and entered the hurly-burly of the city, suddenly a tiny, familiar voice of caution spoke up in her mind, unbeckoned. *Look again before you leap,*

Pamela. Can you trust him, or any man? You are going to be a subservient partner in the marriage. He will own most of the property. Your only asset will be the boardinghouse in Lower Manhattan.

"Are you having second thoughts, Pamela?" Prescott's eyes were so full of compassion that she began to shiver.

"We'll work out the details, Jeremiah. Now let's savor the moment."

Author's Notes

The *Williams Weekly,* 1894, pp. 207–209, reported in detail the football team's victory over Amherst on November 17. The fictional Edward Prescott plays the combined role of the real Draper brothers, Phil and Fred. Herbert L. Pratt (1871–1945) was in fact the Amherst captain. He went on to become the president of Standard Oil of New York. The historical Franklin Carter (1837–1919), distinguished scholar in Latin and German, was president of Williams College, 1881–1901, and led the institution's significant expansion.

In the late nineteenth century, courts rarely acknowledged or vacated wrongful convictions in major felony cases. Hence, the police reporter and journalist Jacob Riis (1849–1914), and other advocates for judicial victims, sought redress in executive clemency. Ameer Ben Ali spent nine years in Sing Sing until his health declined to the point that he was moved to the Clinton State Prison's department for the criminally insane. In April 1901 Governor Benjamin B. Odell Jr. pardoned Ben Ali, who returned to Algeria without an apology or compensation. See Edwin M. Borchard, *Convicting the Innocent: Errors of Criminal Justice* (Garden City Pub. Co., Garden City, NY, 1932), pp. 66–72. For a recent analysis of wrongful convictions and the use of DNA to correct them, consult Brandon L. Garrett, *Convicting the Innocent: Where Criminal Prosecutions Go Wrong* (Harvard University Press, Cambridge, MA, 2011).

For a century and a half, Tammany Hall dominated politics in New York City. In 1894 the Hall itself was located in Manhattan on East Fourteenth Street between Irving Place and Third Avenue. See Oliver E. Allen, *The Tiger: The Rise and Fall of Tammany Hall* (Addison-Wesley, Reading, MA, 1993), for an overview of the organization. Tammany's remarkable success was due primarily to the services it offered to millions of poor immigrants and their impoverished descendants in the city. At its best, as in the fictional characters Florence Mulligan and Frank Dodd, Tammany found food, clothing, heat, and jobs for its clients, helped them navigate the judicial system, and represented their interests in the political arena—all of this, of course, in return for their votes. At its worst, Tammany's leaders siphoned off large sums of money for themselves, sometimes shamelessly, like Boss Tweed (1823–1877); sometimes more discreetly, like Richard Croker (1843–1922). Tammany's allies and agents, such as the fictional Judge Fawcett and Tim Smith, also resorted to fraud and bribery as well as violence. In 1871 at the height of Tweed's corruption, the cartoonist Thomas Nash created the iconic image of Tammany as a tiger mauling a prostrate figure of democracy.

New York City's nineteenth-century legislature, the Board of Aldermen, was notoriously corrupt, earning itself the nickname "The Forty Thieves." In the 1880s the Aldermen also gained the title "Boodle Board," from the Dutch word meaning "bribe money." The "Boodle" of 1884, an historical fact, lacks a comprehensive history. Businessman Jacob Sharp (d. 1888) bribed the aldermen to gain a Broadway railway franchise. Legal pursuit of the thieves went on for several years. In 1938 the Board of Aldermen was replaced by the City Council.

Mr. William Kemmler, convicted of his wife's murder, was electrocuted at Auburn Prison in upstate New York, August 6, 1890, the first use of the electric chair. The next day, the *New*

York Times reported that the powerful eight-minute electric shock filled the death chamber with a dreadful stench of burning flesh, sickening many observers. It was widely but wrongly reported that his body caught fire.

The novel's fictional Pullman porter, Charles Hart, illustrates the situation of blacks in late nineteenth-century America: separate and unequal, experiencing systematic discrimination in Northern as well as Southern states. For George Pullman's views see Larry Tye, *Rising from the Rails: Pullman Porters and the Making of the Black Middle Class* (Henry Holt, New York, 2005).

By 1894 transcontinental travel by rail had become relatively rapid, comfortable, and inexpensive. See John H. White, Jr., *Wet Britches and Muddy Boots: A History of Travel in Victorian America* (Indiana University Press, Bloomington, IN, 2012) as well as his authoritative *The American Railroad Passenger Car* (Johns Hopkins University Press, Baltimore, 1985). Prices for a ticket from Chicago to Los Angeles ranged from $59 for a drawing room in a Pullman Palace Car to $4 for a double berth in a Tourist Car. By 1894 telephones could be found in business and professional offices. See Claude S. Fischer, *America Calling: A Social History of the Telephone to 1940* (University of California Press, Berkeley, 1992). For telegraph service consult David Hochfelder, *The Telegraph in America, 1832–1920* (Johns Hopkins University Press, Baltimore, 2012). In 1890 the average price of a ten-word message from New York to Chicago was forty cents.

Los Angeles in 1894 is described in B. R. Baumgardt, *Tourists' Guide Book to South California* (B. R. Baumgardt & Co., Los

Angeles, 1895). Remi A. Nadeau's *Los Angeles: From Mission to Modern City* (Longmans, Green, New York, 1960) captures the boom and bust character of the city in the late nineteenth century and the entrepreneurial role of Edward Doheny (1856–1935) and Charles Canfield (1848–1913) in the city's oil industry.